The Abduction

The Abduction

Gerd Christian Seeber

SECKER & WARBURG
LONDON

First published in England 1982 by
Martin Secker & Warburg Limited
54 Poland Street, London W1V 3DF

British Library Cataloguing in Publication Data

Seeber, Gerd Christian
  The abduction.
  I. Title
  823'.914[F]   PR6069.E/

  ISBN 0–436–44460–7

Photoset and printed in Great Britain by
Redwood Burn Limited, Trowbridge, Wiltshire

For the Great Zwag and Tiggy
with equal love and affection
and a little bit
or as the case may be
also for Lizzie

Author's note

I had completed the second draft of my story when news reached me of the Kronzucker case. I would like to assure its unfortunate victims that none of the disturbing parallels between what happened to them and what I invented are anything but pure coincidence.

The geographical references in my story are based on the general geography of the land. In many cases, I have switched place names deliberately in order to avoid precise identification of certain locations.

One

'I SAY, JAMES!' Glyn Burford shouted over the hubbub of the crowd which, under the balcony, impatiently thronged the sides of the vicious, dipping Curva di San Martino. 'You know this guy?' Pink with heat, the cameraman looked up from the viewfinder. Blinking into the still bright light, he swivelled round with his seat. He focused on the director.

'Who?' Puzzled, James Grey flicked his sun-bleached hair from his face.

'Take a look! I've gone right in on him.'

Over the cameraman's shoulder, James peered through the viewfinder. From the embrasured top of a grey stone *palazzo*, on the far side of the square, a pair of powerful binoculars were trained on the balcony. They moved. Head on, they stared into the camera. The hands, which gripped the twin black tubes, and a head of dark hair were all that James could see of the observer.

'I noticed him this morning, during practice. He was doing the same thing.' Uncomfortable, young Francesca Ceccarelli clutched a clipboard to her breasts.

James stood up, unbending his boyish frame. 'Maybe he's fallen in love with you.' He winked at his assistant, brushing back his unruly hair yet again. 'Don't let him worry you. He's curious. Maybe,' he chuckled, 'he hopes you'll offer him a part.'

'I'll not waste any film on him,' Glyn growled. 'He's ugly as hell. Like something out of a bloody war movie. But he's sure got a good view up there.' Shrugging, he turned, to aim the camera at the start again.

Francesca shot a last uneasy glance in the direction of the stranger. From a pocket in her wide, loosely hanging dungarees, she produced an old-fashioned stopwatch. On tiptoe, she reached to hang its ribbon round James' neck. Then she turned to the

1

soundman, who knelt in the door of the balcony, busy relacing the tape in the recording machine.

The mood of the crowd, increasingly intense and excited as the day's most important event approached, had risen from buzzing anticipation to shrill impatience. Shoulder to shoulder, an immense and infinitely colourful multitude of chattering, shouting, arguing and laughing Sienese, *contadini* from the surrounding country, students and tourists packed the fan-shaped centre of the Piazza del Campo to the last square inch of its old brick floor. Restive, they shoved and pushed at the inside rails. Any moment, they threatened to spill onto the encircling race track. Across that, those more privileged or simply luckier on the day, stood, sat or perched on ludicrously overloaded stands, filled the balconies or hung from the windows of the ancient houses and *palazzi* which overlook the great square.

Wiping his brow with the freckled back of his hand, the cameraman turned to James again. 'After the race – are you going back to Terrarossa?'

'I can't. Pasquale's taking me to meet a friend. He may have a couple of donkeys. For my children.'

'That'd be nice. When are they coming?'

'Friday week. You can take the Chevy if you want to go on home. Anna will feed you. Pasquale's brought the van. I can go back with him.'

Undecided, Glyn faced the start again. The last of the ten horses and their bareback jockeys, in flapping Renaissance colours and each armed with a heavy whip, were about to be enclosed inside two ropes. Rough and thick, they spanned the track. Nervously, the animals wheeled and danced, stamping on the sanded surface.

James looked over the Campo and the positions he had chosen for the others. He could see the tall figure of the Italian, who, with a handheld camera, had already begun to film from behind the post. The other two cameramen, each in a window over one of the far corners, had not moved since the pageant had begun.

The last horse, drawn by the Contrada della Selva, the parish of the forest, still resisted the pushing and pulling lads. The crowd fell silent. A solitary, raucous shout, nervous and unintelligible, broke the hush. Sparse laughter acknowledged it. James looked up, a last check on the light. Pale, hazy, disturbed only by the rapid swoops of feeding swifts and martins, pierced by their thin cries, the early

2

evening sky hung over the ancient city and the radiant heat of its worn brick walls and clay-tiled roofs. The man with the binoculars had disappeared. James focused on the start. Selva's bay was nearly in.

'Roll sound!' James directed.

'Sound running,' the soundman replied at the Nagra while Francesca picked up the clapperboard.

'Turn over!' James said.

'Speed,' Glyn replied, confirming that he had begun to film.

Leaning over the balustrade, in front of the camera, Francesca brought down the clapper with a brisk snap. Picture and sound were synchronised. The race of the year's *Palio*, traditionally run on the second of July, was about to begin.

Two

AT THE FAR end of the village, James left the old Siena road. With a fast and smooth turn, he steered his big four-wheel drive Chevrolet onto the difficult dirt track which leads up to Terrarossa. Suddenly, sand and grit flew behind the growling wagon. Zigzagging across steep and partly open slopes, a fast trailing plume of dust announced the white car's rapid progress from the foot of the hills.

By his side, Caroline Martin, the children's nanny and herself not yet twenty, had fallen asleep. The hairpin turns made her head roll to the sides and back. With a jerk she awoke, blinking through unprotected, painful eyes.

'We're almost there! I'm sorry I fell asleep.'

James smiled, pointing over his shoulder. 'I'm glad you did. You'll all be able to stay up longer.'

She undid her safety belt and looked over the back of her seat. Sucking his thumb, Thomas was curled up on his knees in the corner of the seat behind her. Below, navy shorts, white socks were down to his ankles. His urchin cut, light brown hair was ruffled. Emma lay stretched out across the bench, her bare feet touching his back. Fanned out on the seat, her long blond hair shone softly on the biscuit material of its cover. A contented smile played on her pale face. A thin arm dangled into the foot well, swinging with the pitching and rolling of the car.

'They were so excited on the plane.' Caroline fastened her seat belt again. 'They're ever so fond of you. When are their friends coming?'

'They're here. It's a surprise.' He braked, then accelerated out of a steeply rising turn. 'David joined up with Suzanne and the girls yesterday. They hired a car in Florence.'

'How old are they?'

'The girls?' He looked across for a moment. 'The same as these two. Sarah's six. Rachel – two months younger than Emma, nearly nine.'

'I hadn't realised they were so close. Emma says they go to a French school – '

James turned down the air conditioner. 'They're about to. David, their father, recently transferred from New York. He's a banker. They started in a school where both languages are spoken.'

'I'd like to go to Paris one day. I've never been to France.'

Brilliant against the deep blue sky, a whitewashed shrine, little more than man high under a red tiled roof, blocked the view above the next bend. James eased his foot on the accelerator, blew the air horns twice and turned his head to see through the gaps between the cypresses by the road side. 'Maybe they'll ask you. When they're settled in.' He steered the car out of the hairpin and into a rising, stone walled straight, which narrowly divided a grey and airy grove of olives from the lush greens of an overgrown vineyard.

'I'd like that.' She folded down the visor in front of her. Sitting up very straight, she peered into the mirror on its back. Quickly, she removed her hairgrips. Taking them in her teeth, she began to fix her auburn curls behind her ears. 'This year I'll be more careful not to get so burnt,' she said when she had finished and turned the visor up. With her palms, she flattened the skirt of her blue and white seersucker dress. Raising her slim body, she pulled it straight. Then she sat quite still.

Bumping, juddering over the rough road, the car gained height. Gradually, the panorama of the hills of the Chianti Classico opened up before them. Woods and fields, vineyards, soldierly rows and tight clusters of cypresses, villages, houses, castles and ruins surrounded the travelling car. Dense forests of black parasol pines, layered cedars and lighter, billowing chestnuts and oaks covered the hills. Deep valleys cut between sun drenched slopes. All shades of ochre, striped by their rows of plants, the vineyards lay in the landscape. Olives, small and silvery, curiously twisted with double trunks, stood about almost everywhere. A vast and infinite motley of silent greens and old yellows, the land displayed the seasoned colours of the Italian midsummer. Undulating and seemingly endless, it rolled into the heat-hazed distance.

'They got awfully lost yesterday,' he said. 'Despite my map. And so hot! I felt quite guilty.'

'It is difficult to find. The first time – '

'I'll never forget. Claire and I, we had some vague instructions. In the most ridiculous English. We drove around for hours! There was no one to ask! How is she?'

'She's very well. She gave me a book for Max. I can't say his name. She said you'd remember the book.'

'Max Kleinschmied. Kline – sch – like Schweppes – and mead. Max Kleinschmied.'

She laughed. 'It's about an artist. Piero – I forget.'

'Piero della Francesca. I gave the book to Claire, after we had first been to Arezzo. Before even Emma was born.' He shook his head. 'I dropped Max in Siena. On my way to the airport.'

She looked at the children again. 'I can't wait to see what you have done. Emma read me your letters. The house sounds bigger.'

He laughed. 'It's big enough! We made more rooms – downstairs.'

'I remember you mentioning a staircase?'

'I agonised over that! Traditionally, the old farmhouses here don't have them. I didn't want to break with that. In the end, I did. Anna and Pasquale thought I was quite mad to get so worried.'

Caroline giggled. 'Why's that?'

'What? Thinking I'd gone mad?'

'No! No staircases.'

'I don't know. Downstairs was always used for stables, storage, things like that. Quite separate from the living rooms.'

In front of a group of cypresses the road forked. An old milestone, half on its side, had sunk into the ground. They turned right. A bright green snake, four, maybe five feet long, lay on the white track, only a few feet from the next bend.

James braked. Locking its wheels on the loose surface, the car slid to a halt.

A horn blared. A grey saloon came careering round the corner. Its sliding rear wheels threw up a wall of dust. Nose to nose with the Chevrolet, the car stopped.

Rattled, James shook his head. 'So much for the snake,' he said quietly. 'Serpe bella.'

Furiously spinning wheels pulled the Fiat back over the mangled snake. Its shredded body flew to the roadside. Grey, no longer green, dripping with bright red blood, it hit the dust.

Sickened, James wanted to shout at the careless driver. The thought of his children in the back stopped him. He kept his

6

window shut. Slowly, he advanced to the point where he could pass. An insolent stare from the driver's darkly bearded face parried his own hostile glare. The man was young, not a local. No local drove like that. Except for the thighs, which bulged in faded denims, he could not see the passenger from his elevated seat. Pretending to take no notice of the men, he edged past the Fiat. He forced himself to look ahead only.

'I don't like snakes,' Caroline said when they had rounded the corner. 'But I am sorry they killed it. You tried to save it. I realised this morning: it's the thirteenth.'

He gave a dry laugh. 'Friday the thirteenth. You aren't superstitious?'

Vigorously, she shook her head. 'I'm not. Are you?'

'No. We didn't crash – '

At the end of a short ridge, which projected from the open slopes ahead, Terrarossa came into view. Still half a mile away, maybe a little more, its shallow gable roof, expansive with weatherbeaten clay tiles, rested on squat walls of pale stone. Welcoming, they shone in the warm light.

Caroline turned to the children. 'Emma! Thomas! Wake up! We're here!'

Thomas, his thumb still in his mouth, sat up.

'We're here,' Caroline repeated. 'Did you have a good sleep?'

The little boy nodded. Yawning, he took the thumb from his mouth. Through half-closed eyes, he looked out from between the front seats.

'Emma? Are you awake?' James asked.

'Awake, Daddy.' She sat up. 'I had a lovely dream.'

'Where's Pasquale?' Thomas asked.

'I imagine he's in the vineyard,' James replied. 'What was your dream about, darling?'

'I could fly, without wings. I flew over the hills. There was a big, big field. With millions and millions of poppies!'

'That's not nice!' Thomas objected. 'I'd be scared if I could fly high up in the air.'

James laughed. 'I wouldn't mind. I could make a lovely film. Just think!'

A determined, final turn brought the car through the stone gate and onto the gravelled drive, which led down to the house. Slowly, the Chevrolet came to a halt next to a small, white Fiat. James opened his door. Hot, arid with the scent of baking soil, the air flooded into the wagon.

'This isn't Pasquale's car,' Thomas said. 'Whose is it?'

'Ah! There are two surprises!' James turned to his children. 'This car belongs to one of them.'

'What are they?' Emma was a split second faster than her brother.

'One's here. The other one is at Anna and Pasquale's house.'

'I know: rabbits.' Emma sounded very definite.

'Wrong!'

'Pasquale's new tractor!' Thomas cried.

'That's no surprise, dummy! Daddy's told us about it,' Emma said scornfully. 'Something Max brought. When did he get here?'

James shook his head. 'Max arrived two days ago.'

'Where is he?' Thomas wanted to know but James had already jumped from the car and was about to open its tail gate.

'We can't guess, Daddy. And neither can Caroline!' Impatiently, Emma turned on the rear seat. 'Why did you buy such a ginormous car?'

'For my work,' James explained. 'You know, I can even put a cameraman on the roof.'

Two little girls, all spindly legs and arms, the smaller in a red, the taller in a yellow bikini, tiptoed gingerly over the gravel from behind a high hedge by the side of the house.

Emma's eyes opened wide and blue. 'Sarah! Rachel! Daddy didn't tell us you were already here!' Excitedly, she clambered over the driver's seat and jumped from the high door. Pushing, Thomas followed right behind.

A sturdy woman, wiping a pair of big, worn hands on a faded, blue apron, appeared in the front door, at the head of a short, stone staircase. Behind her back, she undid the belt and left the apron on the wall which surrounded the landing outside the entrance. Steadying herself with one hand, she descended.

'Emma! Thomas! Say hello to Anna!' James called.

Thomas turned from the girls. On his toes, he kissed Anna on both cheeks. Suddenly shy, Emma held out her hand. The woman laughed. The little girl's shoulders disappeared under her hands as she embraced her and kissed her on the forehead. 'How much you have grown!' she exclaimed in Italian. 'Soon you'll be taller than me!'

8

David and Suzanne Wright-Garrison emerged from behind the hedge.

James took Caroline by the hand. 'This is Caroline Martin. She's been with my children since she was seventeen.'

'I'm David. This is Suzanne. Those wild girls over there are Rachel and Sarah. Don't let them give you any trouble, Caroline.' The voice was low and friendly. He was a youngish man, in his mid-thirties. He held out his hand.

'We didn't tell Emma and Thomas you were already here.' Caroline shook the couple's hands.

'I see!' Suzanne flicked up her green sunshade. 'That accounts for the excitement.'

'Come and help take in your things, children!' James called Emma and Thomas who, with their friends, had disappeared behind the hedge.

'Ah don't wanna come! Ah wanna swim!' Thomas tried to imitate an American accent.

'You're a clown!' James called. 'Come on now! Help!'

They began to take the bags from the car. David, taller even than James and considerably bigger in build, took most of the soft bags under his arms. 'If there's no money left in banking, I could always become a porter,' he said. Sideways, he climbed the stair.

'I wouldn't like to be a porter!' Thomas followed empty handed. 'It's too heavy.'

'You got it! Absolutely!' David confirmed. 'And it's dull.'

Anna waited by the open door. It led directly into the cavernous kitchen, traditionally the main living room of the house. Unglazed brick, thin after centuries of use, covered the floor. The walls, several feet thick, were whitewashed. The sloping ceiling was the gable roof itself – red clay tiles rested on long timbers and rough rafters. A smoky scent hung in the still room. Welcoming and warm, it evoked the memory of countless fires under the huge chimney, which dominated the kitchen. The fragrance of fresh basil and tarragon and wild garlic drifted through the soft light.

'Ravioli, bread, salt, *polenta*, vegetables, fruit and all the other things you wanted me to get.' With some effort, James heaved a couple of capacious wicker baskets onto the clothless table.

'Will you eat at eight?' Anna asked, reaching for the first basket.

'I think so,' James replied. 'Shall we eat at eight?'

'Yees!' Emma cried. 'What is there?'

'Prosciutto and figs, ravioli from the baker and lots of other lovely things,' James answered.

'Green or white ravioli?'

'Green ones.'

'Yummy!' Emma turned to Rachel. 'They're my favourites!'

'What's for pudding?' Thomas wanted to know.

'You'll see. Provided you eat the main course,' James said. 'Right! Let's go!' He picked up two of the bags and made for the narrow stairway in the far corner of the room. 'Mind your step, children!' he called and began his descent. One by one, the others followed. Anna brought up the rear.

On the ground floor a long hall, with a grey stone floor, gave on to a deep loggia which spanned the south side of the house.

'This doesn't look different, Daddy.' Emma sounded disappointed.

'Wait!' James opened a pine door. Shuttered against the heat of the afternoon, the room lay in the half-light. Anna lifted and turned the iron latch, which held the shutters in place, and pushed them out. White, the sunlight fell into the room and over its brick floor. Warm, it reflected from whitewashed walls.

A brass bed, with painted metal head and toe boards, stood in one of the corners, near the window. Boats sailed on a lake, surrounded by green hills. White clouds drifted in the blue sky. Opposite the bed, a scrubbed old table, with a single drawer, served as a desk. A brown wardrobe, decorated with pink roses and green leaves in the Tuscan style, stood next to it. A stack of books and a yellow terracotta vase, filled with wild flowers, sat on the bedside table.

'Books! Oh, Daddy! And a new bed! And a cupboard! Is this my room?' Emma hoped he would say yes.

He nodded.

'Oh, Daddy! It's lovely! Thank you so much!'

They went to Thomas' room next, which was similar in style to that of his sister. A blunderbuss James had found in a Perugia junk shop immediately took the boy's fancy. 'Bang!' he cried, swaying under the weight of the heavy gun, pretending to shoot Caroline.

'Bang to you!' she replied. 'Can we have a swim? It's ever so hot!'

'What about our surprise?' Emma protested.

'Let's swim first,' James agreed with the nanny. 'We'll go to Anna and Pasquale's house afterwards.'

Emma looked unhappy.

10

'It won't be so hot then,' James tried to appease her. 'I'd like to walk. I'll see you in the pool.'

He returned upstairs and went to his bedroom, which, together with his study, occupied the south west corner of the house, giving on to a balcony, above the loggia. Quickly, he stripped and put on his trunks. He went outside. Suzanne sat by the pool, reading under a white parasol. David lay on a day bed, protected by an olive tree. A book lay in the grass, next to him.

James dived from the spring board. He let himself glide, until he touched the bottom at the shallow end. The sensation of the cooling water, rushing over his skin, made him wish he could have repeated the first dive over and over again.

'Ouch! Hot!' Emma had stepped out of the loggia and on to the terrace. She began to run. Holding her nose, feet first, she jumped over the side. She hit the water with a splash. Eyes shut, she surfaced. Puffing up round cheeks, she pushed her hair from her face and over her shoulders.

'Where's Max?' She dog-paddled towards her father, who was floating on his back in the middle of the pool.

'I left him in Siena, on my way to pick you up. He's coming back on the bus. Is Mummy well?'

'Very! And Tony. Mummy says she hopes Thomas is going to swim, now he's six.'

Hand in hand, Caroline and Thomas appeared in the loggia.

'I'm sure he will,' James said quickly. 'But you mustn't tease him! Promise?'

'Promise.' She swam to the other side.

Splashing and screaming, the children played with James and Caroline in the pool. At first kept back by their mother, Rachel and Sarah eventually joined in the games. Time and again, James was pushed from the diving board, chased round the pool, pulled over the sides. With two children on either arm, he resisted at the edge, crying for mercy in pitiful tones. It was to no avail. Splashing, he went in. Gurgling, he re-emerged. Then, holding up his right hand, he waved good bye and let himself sink to the bottom of the pool.

'He's drowning! He's drowning!' Sarah cried, looking very alarmed.

Emma giggled, holding her mouth. 'He always does that. Don't worry! He likes to sit on the bottom.'

11

Three

THE SUN WAS going down over the vineyard above the house when, except for Anna, they all set out to see the promised surprise. Chattering, the children and Caroline led the way through the stone gate and up to the road, which, past Terrarossa, rounds the top of a deep ravine. The direct heat of the sun had gone. But the long stone wall, built to pin the road to the steep slope, was radiating strongly enough to make them quite hot.

'Where does this track end?' David asked, unbuttoning the top of his loosely hanging shirt.

'In the valley again. You'll see, when we get to the other side,' James explained. 'It goes down past Valcortese, an abandoned farm.'

A light breeze greeted them at the point where the road, viewed from Terrarossa, disappears from sight. Wide open and green, filled with the long and blue shadows of the early evening, the valley of the Arbia lay at their feet, more than a thousand feet below.

James pointed at the far end of the flat hilltop they were now on, directly opposite the house. 'There was a castle over there. Under the cedars. The Florentines sacked it in one of the many wars with the Sienese.'

'Is there anything to see?' Suzanne wanted to know. 'I'd like to take some pictures.'

'Rubble,' Emma said. 'And scorpions, Daddy says, and vipers if you're not careful.'

They looked back at Terrarossa. Anna was turning on the sprinkler on the lawn, by the pool. It had taken them some ten minutes to walk to where they were but, across the ravine, she seemed very close. She moved to the terrace. She picked up one of the garden chairs. Clearly, they heard it scrape on the stone floor.

'Let's go, Daddy!' Thomas waved to Anna and pulled his father by the hand. 'I want to see what it is!'

A steep track led down to Anna and Pasquale Neri's house. Pines, oaks and thick bushes overhung it. The light under the trees was soft. Faintly, the scent of the pines hung in the warm air. They heard a tractor, going up and down some vineyard in the distance.

'Pasquale's spraying,' James explained. 'We restocked the vineyard a couple of years ago. Next year, I hope we'll start again, properly.'

'I thought you once brought a bottle of Terrarossa wine to New York,' Suzanne said. 'Four or five years ago.'

'Six,' James corrected her. 'I remember. We had just bought the place. But it wasn't very good. Pasquale made wine for the man we rented it from too.'

Ahead, Emma and Rachel had stopped where the track came out from under the trees and, abruptly, flattened.

'Will you give us a clue, Daddy, please?' Emma begged.

James sucked in his cheeks. Baring his gums, he made his upper lip quiver. With his hands, he imitated long, upright ears.

'But that's your rabbit face, Daddy!' Emma protested. 'You said it wasn't rabbits!'

'Bigger. Keep your ears open!'

'A horse! It must be a horse!' Rachel cried.

James grinned. 'Not bad. But wrong!'

'I know,' Emma stretched the last word. 'And I'm going to find out first!' On the spot, she turned. With flying hair, she ran towards the small house which, with a pair of sheds and a large barn, all of them built of stone, stood on a nearly flat natural terrace in the hillside.

'Wait!' Thomas cried running after her. 'Emma! Wait for me!'

Catching up with him, Rachel and Sarah followed. The children disappeared behind the first shed. They reappeared on its far side. Still led by Emma, they ran into the barn.

They came out of the barn. 'Nothing!' Emma stamped her foot. 'Only rabbits and stupid chickens! Where are you hiding it?'

James gave in. Turning, he pointed to where the hill rose, behind the house. The grass was long and green there. Olive trees stood about in a small grove.

Two little donkeys, light grey and each on a long leather leash tied to a tree, were grazing in the grove.

Thomas' eyes popped, grey and round. 'Donkeys!' he cried and

13

started to run, Emma, Sarah and Rachel on his heels.

Stroking and patting the furry animals, the children did not stop them from grazing. Seemingly taking no notice of the visitors, they tore and munched the lush grass. Then one of them stopped and stood quite still. Only its tail moved, fanning from side to side.

'May we ride them?' Rachel asked.

'I think so,' James replied. 'But we'd better ask Pasquale to help. They are very young.'

'What are their names, Daddy?' Emma asked.

'You must name them! One is for you, the other for Thomas.'

'Oh, Daddy!' Emma hugged him round his waist. 'What a wonderful daddy you are!'

The siblings almost began to squabble over the division. The donkeys were too alike.

'Why don't you take this one, Thomas?' James suggested. 'He's a male. And Emma can take the girl.' He was glad Pasquale had chosen one of either sex.

'Then I shall call my donkey,' Emma paused, to make sure everybody would hear her announcement: 'Pasta!'

Applause and laughter greeted the name.

Tickling his ears until they twitched, Thomas could not decide on a name for his donkey. Emma offered to help. Instantly, she came up with a string of names. But he insisted on finding his own. Unwilling to even consider her suggestions, he asked her to be quiet.

'You can think about it overnight,' Suzanne said.

Thomas nodded.

'Maybe he'll dream a name!' Emma was scornful. It upset her to think that he might choose a name which would not match Pasta.

The noise of the tractor grew louder. Clanging on its metal tracks, it came into sight, bright red, a little below the house. A big man sat on top. He looked up and turned the machine towards the visitors. A heavy hand pushed his limp straw hat to the back of his head. Under an open brown waistcoat, he wore a white collarless shirt. Its sleeves were rolled up over powerful dark forearms.

Thomas ran towards the approaching tractor. It stopped by one of the sheds. With a jump, the driver got off. In a single move, he picked up the squealing little boy and swung him into the driving seat.

'Pasquale Neri,' James said and introduced the Wright-Garrisons.

Pasquale gave a nod and lifted his hat. His hair was cut very short and was nearly white. A smile ran over the weather-beaten face. For an instant, it lit up a pair of deep, dark eyes as they rested on the children.

'Can the children come tomorrow? To ride the donkeys?' James asked in Italian.

'I'll be here in the morning. I'll make reins for them tonight.'

'We want to go to Siena in the morning.'

'In the afternoon then. Tomorrow it'll make no difference to me.'

Pasquale lifted Thomas off the tractor and drove it into the shed. The sun was about to sink below the hills in the west. Slowly, the party began its way back up the steep track. They reached the top of the hill and looked across to Terrarossa. Silent and grey, the old farmhouse stood on the hillside, its lawn and pool terraced into the slope. Above the house, on the very top of the vineyard, which belonged to a farmer in the village, the neat rows of trained vines caught the last of the sun's long rays. A golden green, they shone in the paling, limpid sky.

'I was intrigued to meet Pasquale,' Suzanne said as they rounded the ravine. 'I imagined him a much smaller man.'

'Maax!' Thomas' voice echoed in the ravine.

On the balcony, a man in blue shirt sleeves stood at the iron balustrade. Raising his arms overhead, he waved.

'He's back,' David said. 'I meant to ask: where does the bus stop?'

'At the milestone.' James pointed in the direction of the road. 'Before it reaches Terrarossa. Have you heard its horn? It comes twice, mornings and afternoons.'

'Can we run ahead, Daddy?' Thomas asked. 'Say hello to Max?'

James let go of his children's hands. 'Be careful! Don't fall!' he called after them.

They overtook Caroline, who was holding hands with Sarah and Rachel. The nanny looked back.

'It's alright!' James called. 'I said they could run ahead.'

'I wonder what he saw today?' David came back to Max again. 'I enjoyed his account of San Marco. It was almost as if we hadn't seen the paintings before.'

'It must be wonderful to have an artist here to explain,' Suzanne said. 'There's so much to see!'

'What if you don't agree?' James objected. 'He went to see the Duccios, in the Cathedral Museum. You ought to go and see them too.'

At the gate, they encountered Anna. She was on her way home. Heavy, battered outdoor shoes were now on her feet. From her arm hung one of the baskets James had taken to the market in Siena. A flat, yellow loaf of corn bread and a bag each of *polenta* and salt lay inside. She stopped, to tell James about dinner. The others went on and into the house.

'The children look very well,' she said at the end. 'I hope they will come more often now.'

'So do I.' He smiled. 'Emma named her donkey Pasta.'

'Pasta.' For a moment, her small but lucid eyes expressed amusement. 'My sons, when they were little, never gave names to the animals.' Carefully, she bent down to lift the basket. She refused his help.

'I shall see you tomorrow then.'

'Tomorrow. I wish you a pleasant evening. You look happy. I hope the *signorina* Kazue will join you soon.' Her much lined face smiled. Then she was gone.

Four

UNDER CAROLINE'S SUPERVISION, the children had gone for a quick, last swim and changed for dinner. By half past seven, hunger had driven everyone to the kitchen. Waiting for the water in a deep, copper cauldron to come to the boil, James offered olives, slices of a coarse, *casalinga* salame and fresh, ruby-red Chianti from a terracotta pitcher. Emma took some olives to the sitting room. Appetisingly, they glistened in their white, earthenware bowl. Her tongue between her lips, Rachel followed, eyes fixed on a tray of glasses of apricot juice for the children and wine for Caroline.

'Did you know new Chianti was so fragrant? Some people say it smells of violets.' Max helped himself to a second glass.

'I can't believe this is your first visit to Italy!' Suzanne ignored the question. 'What kept you away?'

The painter put down his glass. From his tanned, open face, he looked at her with luminous, searching eyes. 'When I was young, the war. After it, poverty.' A short, nodding smile softened the directness of his reply. He picked up his glass. In a loose white shirt now, over faded jeans and bare, well-worn, open sandals on his feet, he sat down on the edge of the old hearth stone.

Uncomfortable, Suzanne glanced at her husband. 'I'm sorry! I didn't mean to be personal!'

'Why not?' Max exclaimed, intending to put her at ease. 'True answers are likely to be personal when we talk about ourselves. I see nothing wrong – '

'Did you like what you saw today?' David interrupted. 'How does it compare with the Fra Angelicos at San Marco?'

Puzzled, Max looked at the much younger man. 'I knew I'd like what I went to see. As for the comparison, I don't think that can be a question.'

David sat up straight, on his kitchen chair.

17

'You mean, you were certain you'd like the Duccios?' James intervened. 'Before you actually got to the museum?'

'Of course!' Max was emphatic. 'I'd seen reproductions. And I know other Duccios in the original. What's surprising about that?'

'Point taken,' James conceded. 'Children! We can eat!'

Carefully, he slid the soft ravioli from the paper trays they had been put on at the baker's. He adjusted the flame. 'It's difficult enough to get so much water to the boil on this cooker. But to keep it simmering is something else! Some kind of high wire act.'

The children entered from the sitting room. Caroline came last and switched off the light. 'Leave the door open, please!' James asked. 'We shan't be cold.'

The temperature had dropped several degrees with the setting of the sun. The windows, no longer shuttered, stood wide open. The light evening air carried the scent of wild herbs and dry earth. Softly, the blues and greys of nightfall pervaded the house. The candles, which Anna had lined up on the long kitchen table, flickered gently in the warm draught. Open, the heavy timbered front door was fastened back. Outside, all was still. Only the frogs croaked in the well pool, not far from the gate.

Max, with Caroline and Rachel at his side, took the far end of the table. James sat down last, at the head and nearest the cooker. Suzanne was on his right, Emma on the left. For the first time, the young girl wore a white summer dress which her mother had given her on her recent, ninth birthday. Caroline had washed Emma's hair after the swim. Two bright blue butterfly grips fastened it over her ears. To James, she looked so beautiful, he found it difficult to take his eyes off her.

The meal was simple. Salt-cured ham and fresh, purple figs were an easily prepared starter. The ravioli, which were filled with ricotta, spinach and herbs, came next, as the main course. A salad of green beans and raw mushrooms, dressed with virgin oil, lemon, much basil and wild garlic, helped to refresh the palates. Local *pecorino* cheeses, both dry and a little more fat, peaches, nectarines and pieces of sweet panforte from Siena brought the meal to a leisurely end.

The Chianti soon showed its effect on the adults in the dinner party. The conversation relaxed. Louder, faster, it caused increasing laughter. The children joined in, teaching each other rhymes, which they recited to everyone's great amusement.

18

Thomas raised his left arm. His right hand indicated something about to climb it. His eyes glittered in the candlelight. The party fell silent.

He began to recite: 'Little Mousy Brown climbed up a candlestick.' His hand stopped. 'But he couldn't get down. He cried for his – grandma!' Light and clear, the voice rang out. 'But grandma was in town.' His hand formed a small fist. 'So he curled himself up in a little brown ball and rolled all the way down.'

Applause greeted the perfect performance. Outside, the last light had long gone. The night was black in the windows. A slight breeze made the candles flicker more than before. James got up to shut the front door.

He froze in the frame.

'What is it?' Max was quick to ask.

James motioned him to be quiet. Listening, he turned his head.

A hush had fallen over the room. The children's eyes were wide with expectation.

'Footsteps. I thought I heard footsteps in the drive.' At last, James broke the silence.

Thomas shook himself. 'I hope it's not a ghost! Look! I've gone all goose pimply!'

Caroline put a hand on his arm. 'Don't be frightened! Maybe it's somebody going to see Pasquale, up on the road.'

With a shrug, James shut the door. Nobody, he thought, visited Pasquale so late, he was up before dawn every day. However, the incident, whether imagined or real, had caused enough alarm already. He returned to the table.

'Can we have a fire, Daddy, please?' Emma asked.

'Oh yes! Let's have a fire!' Thomas cried.

Anna had laid tinder and logs at the back of the old hearth stone. Some ten feet square – except for a semicircular incision at the front, so that the cook would have had better access – it still formed the centre piece of the old kitchen. The stone platform was more than two feet high. A cavernous hood, plastered and whitewashed, overhung it from the roof. The irons, which in the past had served to hang kettles and pots over the fire, were still intact.

Glad of the diversion, James struck a match and held it to the kindling. Instantly, it caught fire, burning fiercely up the high chimney. White light fell into the room. Soft shadows began to dance on the walls.

'This afternoon who would have thought we'd end the day with a fire?' David asked, accepting half a black *toscano* cigar, which James had cut at its thickest, central point.

'We're high here – more than fifteen hundred feet,' Max explained. 'I love the air at night. Have you heard from Kazue, James?'

'Not yet. She likes to phone, at the last moment. Of course, she can't do that here. I expect the postman will have a cable from her. Maybe on Monday.'

'Cables are delivered with the regular mail?' David sounded doubtful. 'Who's Kazui?'

'Kazue,' James emphasised the 'e'. 'Siena phones cables to the village. The postman brings them with his next delivery. Kazue is my Japanese friend. I met her when I made the art series for the Germans. She's a dealer – in Kyoto.'

'An art dealer?'

'Yes.' He drew on his cigar. Deep red, then white, its end lit up.

The smell of burning olive logs filled the room. Thomas and Emma had begun to show how tired they were. It was well after ten, time for all of the children to go to bed. Together, they circled the table, to say good night. Then Caroline took them downstairs.

'How is your new series, James?' Suzanne asked.

'I'm having a super time! Some of the pageants are so spectacular! Quite unspoilt by modern times. The Festa of the Ceri, at Gubbio, came out well. You should have seen the masons and the farmers and the shopkeepers race up Monte Ingino, each team shouldering one of the *ceri*, a massive, twenty foot timber column. They weigh tons! And I bet they used to be phallic. Now a tiny figure of a saint sits on top! The first Palio came out well, too. The race was superb! I'd never have guessed the winner!'

'Who's taking it?' David wanted to know.

'So far, CBS and Fuji. There may be one or two others. At least, I hope so. I should know in a couple of weeks or so.'

'So you're really settling here? All on your own? For ever?' Suzanne sounded quite concerned.

James laughed. 'Who knows? If I could stop things as they are I'd love to. I wouldn't mind.'

They ended their evening on the balcony, outside the sitting room. The long grass under the olive trees, below the house, was black and alive with fireflies. Nightingales sang in the cedars on the other side of the ravine.

'They're loud tonight.' Max looked up at the brilliant, starlit sky.

'Too loud,' James seemed to object. 'I still can't make up my mind whether I like them or not. I think blackbirds have a sweeter song.'

The thin white headlights of a car felt their way along the valley below. A bird suddenly screeched from the roof. Suzanne started.

'Don't be frightened!' James patted her hand. 'It's our little owl. You'll hear it cry in the dead of night. That's all it is, a tiny owl.'

Five

NEXT MORNING, SATURDAY, Caroline woke Thomas and Emma at nine, then gave them breakfast in the kitchen. 'Have you thought of a name for your donkey, Thomas?' she asked. The little boy nodded. 'Yes,' he said seriously, 'Eeyore.'

At half past nine, everybody squeezed into the Chevrolet, four children, five adults. Through the hills, avoiding the old main road, they drove to Siena. Emma and Thomas taught their friends their game of spotting wild animals from the travelling car. Marks were awarded to the participant who pointed out an interesting animal first. A pheasant, for example, counted one point, rabbits and hedgehogs two, snakes and hoopoes three. A porcupine – they hardly dared to even hope they would ever see one – had been fixed at a fantastic six points.

Max was the winner, scoring twice with rare golden orioles, much to Emma's annoyance for, both times, he had preempted her by fractions of a second, putting her into third place.

They entered Siena through Porta Pispini. James left his car with a friendly parking attendant, who remembered him well for his tips, in the market square. There they split up. Max took Emma to look at the old frescoes in the thirteenth-century hospital. Caroline and the other children climbed the Torre del Mangia, which soars over the Piazza del Campo. David and Suzanne accompanied James on his round through the market and on to the baker and other shops, where he usually bought whatever was needed at Terrarossa.

They had agreed to meet again at Nannini's, an old-established café and confectioner's shop, in Banchi di Sopra. James lived through some increasingly tense moments when Emma and Max were more than half an hour late. At last they appeared, singing and laughing, both of them sporting new straw hats. Max apologised. 'With my bald head, I had to get a hat. My brain sizzles when I'm

22

out drawing in the hills.' Then they returned to Terrarossa, where they stayed for the rest of the weekend.

The following week at first brought increasing heat and long, lazy days, spent mainly by the pool. One evening, they went to Montalcino, another to the Badia a Coltibuono, once a monastery hidden deep in the woods, now a restaurant.

On Monday morning the postman, who on most days came up from the village in a tiny Fiat, brought James a telegram from Kazue, saying that she would arrive next Sunday.

Francesca arrived on Tuesday to help James prepare some material she was going to take to Rome for him on Wednesday. After that, she intended to take a short holiday, to coincide with his.

Max spent most days out in the hills, drawing.

Pasquale helped to break in the donkeys. Every morning, soon after their first swim, Caroline walked with the children along the road to the cedars and down the track to the Neris' house.

On Thursday, after lunch, heavy clouds appeared over the vineyard above the house. Thunder rolled in the distance. Soon it closed in.

Gusts of wind shook the parasols by the pool. Quickly, James shut them and took them into the loggia.

The birds changed their song and the swallows and martins darted low over the ground, diving in and out between the olives in the ravine. For a short while, there was silence.

A strong smell of impending rain blew up. The storm was overhead.

The rain fell suddenly, hitting the dry and dusty soil with thick thuds. The wind drove the drops fiercely, so that they fell in long, swaying strings through the air. Waves of light grey swept across the slopes, as gust after gust hit the vines and turned up the bright undersides of their leaves.

James hoped the storm would not last. He knew what damage it could do to the vines, ripping off leaves and fruit within minutes.

Hail fell from the clouds. The stones were small. Madly, they danced on the roof, bounced and rolled into the gutters. The lawn by the pool turned white.

Lightning struck. James was not sure it had hit the pool. A blinding flash, it suddenly stood before the house. Fiery roots reached deep down into the ravine. A splintering, cracking sound and the instant, accompanying clap of thunder hurt the children's ears. Intense, a sour smell hung in the air.

The centre of the storm passed over Terrarossa within minutes. The rain stopped two hours later. When the sun set, the sky was a deep, flaming red, the air crisp over the steaming earth.

On Friday, early in the morning, the view from Terrarossa was clearer than James could remember it. Max borrowed a tripod from him, to take photographs on the balcony. For some time, he worked on the panorama. The castle of Montenano, too, the most important in the distant view, had caught his eye.

The afternoon brought another storm, less violent than Thursday's. It rained well into the night, long after lightning and thunder had travelled to the south and on. 'The farmers should be content,' James said. 'You'll see, tomorrow we'll have dry weather again.'

Six

BANKS OF MIST lay in the steaming valley early on Saturday morning. They dissolved gradually in the increasing heat of the sun.

James left for Siena at nine o'clock. Only Suzanne accompanied him. Max set off at the same time, to draw by an old chapel he had discovered near the road from the village.

David put up the parasols. James' prediction proved right: the sky was clear, already it was warm.

A few minutes after eleven, Caroline, Emma, Thomas and Rachel began their daily walk to the Neri's house, to ride Pasta and Eeyore. Sarah had complained of tummy ache and had stayed in her room, with a new book she had borrowed from Thomas.

David sat by the pool, reading. Anna was inside the house, sweeping the brick floors, which she had first sprinkled with water. The heat loss, caused by the evaporating water, and closing the shutters during the day kept the rooms cool.

David looked up and saw the children walking along the road on the other side of the ravine. Caroline held Thomas by the hand. Emma and Rachel were behind. David waved to them. In the still morning air, he heard their voices clearly, even some of the words when only one of them spoke at a time. They reached the cedars. Waving to him one last time, they walked from his view.

The postman arrived from the village. For a moment David heard him talk to Anna at the front door, then his little car was off again, in the direction it had come from.

Anna was on the lawn, halfway to David. The mail was in her hand.

A scream pierced the air, across the ravine. On the road, Rachel ran with flying pigtails. 'Mummy! Daddy! Help! Help me!'

A dark figure caught her, grabbing at her shoulder.

She stumbled. Falling by the edge of the road, she tumbled over its

25

supporting stone wall and rolled down the steep slope. She came to rest in deep grass, almost out of sight. She was quiet now.

The man shook a fist at David and Anna, turned and disappeared behind the bend. They heard a car. Too stunned even to shout, they had been pressing against the railing round the pool terrace.

David ran inside for his car keys. Anna met him at the car. Sarah appeared at the front door. David shouted at her to go back inside.

The Fiat's wheels spun madly until it reached the gate. David almost lost control in the one bend he had to take to round the ravine. He was still in second gear when he brought the car to a skidding halt. He jumped out and down the wall, stumbling towards his daughter.

Rachel lay curled up in the grass. Her face was hidden.

'Darling! Rachel! Are your hurt?' He bent over her.

She did not move.

'You must tell me! Are you hurt?' he shouted, stopping himself from picking her up.

She began to sob.

Gently, he lifted her, pressing her small body lightly against his own. Her face was grazed. Her eyes were shut.

'What happened?'

Shaking, she would not reply.

'Where are the others?'

'It – I – Mummy – '

'You must tell me! What happened?'

She shook so much, she could not speak. She was incoherent. He gathered Emma and Thomas had been kidnapped. He guessed Caroline was hurt.

Quickly, he carried Rachel up the slope and lifted her over the wall. Anna had gone, running down the track to her house. He remembered looking down into the valley from behind the bend. James had pointed out a small bridge where the roads joined.

He put Rachel on the back seat and drove to the point from where they had looked down. It was no more than a hundred yards away.

He saw the bridge instantly. A flock of sheep was on and around the narrow road, just in front of it.

A light coloured car, possibly pale green, was among the sheep. Slowly, it progressed towards the bridge. Some sheep were on the bridge. Someone by its near end was trying, so it seemed, to stop

26

more sheep running on to it.

David backed his car to where the track to the Neris' house branched off. He was about to turn when he saw the van come up the track. Pasquale was at the wheel, Anna next to him.

'*La signorina Caroline sembra morta!*' Anna pointed down the track.

David did not understand. '*Io,*' he touched his chest, then pointed to the other side of the hill. 'Darling, Anna'll look after you. I won't be long.'

Rachel clung fiercely to her father as he lifted her from the car and put her in the van. He told her her mother would be back very soon. She cried loudly when he set off down the hill. It hurt him to leave her. He forced himself to go.

He drove as fast as he dared. He did not know the road. He remembered James saying that it was narrow and steep. Instantly, he found out that it was also extremely bumpy and twisted. Time and again, he locked all four wheels, skidding on the loose surface when he braked for corners. Once, twice, he went into long, snaking slides but each time he managed to correct before the car spun.

His confidence increased. He went faster still. Was there a chance of catching up? If he did, what then?

He came to a fork in the road. Both branches appeared to go downhill. For a moment, he hesitated. He turned right.

A long, open curve encouraged him to accelerate. Next, a blind corner forced him to brake hard. Emerging from it, he saw a farmhouse. It was deserted. He remembered James mentioning the name of an abandoned farm. He had gone wrong.

Furiously spinning the steering wheel, he turned. He reckoned that he had lost at least half a minute.

He caught a glimpse of the bridge. The sheep had gone. So had the car he had seen. In the next bend, he went into a drift. He controlled it with opposite lock. But he had not allowed for the next turn. Without time to set his car up for it, he braked. He ran out of road. Rolling many times, the Fiat came to a halt, its wheels in the air.

Seven

ANNA HAD FOUND Caroline by the side of the track, face down under a bush of Spanish broom. The back of her shirt was torn. Marks on the ground indicated that she had been dragged. Blood showed on one side of her head. Finding Caroline's eyes open but without response of any kind, Anna had left the nanny for dead and had run to find her husband.

On his knees, Pasquale bent over Caroline. He had seen people in the war who had suffered shock. The colour of her face told him she was alive. He tried to find her pulse.

'*Signorina Carolina, sono Pasquale. Ritorniamo a casa,*' he spoke softly. Carefully, he took her hand and repeated what he had said.

Anna helped from the other side. Together, they got her to her knees. Pasquale looked for blood, from nose or mouth. There was none.

Rachel had come out of the van. Crying, she looked on.

Pasquale lifted Caroline and laid her down, in the back of the van. Anna got in with Rachel and held the nanny's head. Slowly, Pasquale drove them back to the house.

They put Caroline on the bed in her room, while Sarah tried to find out from her sister what had happened. But Rachel only cried and would not say anything she could understand. Sarah, too, began to cry.

Pasquale rushed off, anxious to follow David. He knew that, from the bridge, he could take the main road back to the village to get help. First, he had to find out if the American had had any success in his pursuit.

Eight

'Signor James! Signor James! Emma, Tommaso, sono stati rapinati!' Anna came rushing down the stair, towards the Chevrolet.

For a moment, James was incredulous. Looking down at her from the car, he could not grasp what she was saying. Never had he seen her so agitated. She seemed strange, someone he had never met. Then he began to understand. His face drained. Helplessly, he looked at the gesticulating woman, then at Suzanne, who was still on the passenger seat beside him. Nausea gripped his chest and stomach. He could not breathe. Tightly, he held on to the steering wheel.

'What is it?' Suzanne was alarmed.

'The children. Taken!' he whispered.

'Rachel? Sarah?' Her voice was shrill.

'No. Mine.'

Suzanne scrambled from the car. Jumping, she fell on her hands and knees. Picking herself up, she rushed to the steps and inside the house.

Tears sprang from Anna's tormented eyes. 'It happened on the other side. Pasquale and the *signor* Americano have gone to the bridge. What are we going to do? What are you going to do, *signor* James?'

He shook his head. His eyes stared. Desperately, he tried to order his thoughts. How often he had felt, even said, that the only thing he really feared was that something terrible should happen to his children. He had not dared to imagine any detail. Was this it?

The Chevrolet's engine barked as he started it up again. Its big wheels bit into the gravel with a vicious sound.

He rounded the ravine. Then, helped by its four-wheel drive, he hurled the white wagon down the tricky road. He knew it well. He

29

remembered every bump and corner. Out of a flying cloud of dust, the car burst downhill. Sideways, it slid through the turns. He shouted to himself that he must go fast but not crash. If he was to get the children back, now was not the time to have an accident.

After less than four minutes, he had passed the road to Valcortese. He saw David's Fiat on its roof in the long grass of the flattening slope, below the road. The driver's door hung open. Nobody was inside the car. He pressed on.

Pasquale's van was parked in front of the bridge, where the single track widened, to let oncoming traffic pass. Skidding, he pulled up behind it.

Pasquale and David were with a man, some three hundred yards downstream, in a field. A dog was with them. A second dog circled a flock of sheep in the background.

James blew his horn. Urgently, Pasquale beckoned him to come.

'Didn't you stop them? Where are they?' James shouted, running towards the men.

The shepherd acknowledged him with a nod. He looked old. David, in shorts and tee-shirt, barefoot, seemed unhurt.

Rapidly, Pasquale told what he had found out so far. The shepherd had seen a pale green car. He was angry because its driver had run straight into the flock and would not wait for the sheep to finish crossing from one field to the one they were now in. The driver had been the only person in the car. The shepherd did not know the make of the car, maybe it was a Fiat. He had never seen the driver before.

'Did you see the car go up the hill? Before it came down?' James asked the shepherd.

The old man seemed startled by the direct address. '*Nossignore*, I did not see it.' His answer came slowly.

'David, did you see the car pass Terrarossa? Round the ravine?'

'I didn't. Are there any other places up there? Aside from the farm?'

James shook his head.

The shepherd and Pasquale, unable to understand, watched in silence.

'I saw another car go up,' the shepherd suddenly volunteered.

'When?' Pasquale and James asked together.

The shepherd looked at the sun. 'Maybe two hours ago. A little more.'

30

'Did you see it again?'

The shepherd shook his head.

'David, did you see a second car?'

'A second car? I saw the postman's – '

'Then – that car's still up there!' Surprised by his own conclusion, James pointed uphill, rigidly holding out his arm.

David blinked. He was not sure he understood.

James turned to the shepherd. 'Do you remember how many people there were in the car? What colour was it?'

'It was grey, bigger than the one which came down. Two people were in it.'

'Did you see them? Did one of them have a beard?'

'I was on the hill, over there. Too far away.' The shepherd pointed to a hillock, maybe half a mile upstream.

'Pasquale, that car is up there! Go to the village! Get the *carabinieri*! We're going to Valcortese!'

James started to run back to his car. Pasquale was with him. David, still not sure what was going on, limped behind them. The shepherd shook his head in bewilderment. Then he began to walk in the other direction, to join his flock.

Pasquale started the van and set off across the bridge. At the junction with the main road he turned right, towards the village.

James leaped into the Chevrolet and started to turn it round. David arrived and climbed in. James floored the accelerator. With spinning wheels the car shot off, back up the hill.

'How's your leg?' James shouted over the thrashing engine.

'I pulled a muscle getting out. James, I'm sorry! There was nothing I could do!'

They passed the Fiat.

'I rolled a few times. The seat belt held me.'

James gave a curt nod. 'The other car must be at Valcortese.'

'The farm?'

'Where the road forks.'

'I went there by mistake – '

'You see anything?' James was quick to ask.

'I didn't go up to it. I guessed I'd gone wrong.'

They reached the junction and turned left.

'What if they're there? We have no weapons,' David said.

James did not reply. The farm came into view. The main building, of good proportions, bigger than Terrarossa, stood on the left. A barn and other, smaller outhouses surrounded the dusty farmyard, which was also the end of the road. A small wood began not far behind.

They stopped about a hundred yards away, blocking the single track road.

Deserted, Valcortese's doors and windows were empty holes in old stone walls. Sparrows hopped in and out of dust baths they were remaking in the middle of the farmyard. The rain had washed away their old ones.

'Hadn't we better wait for help?' David asked. 'We may be walking straight into a trap.'

'I'm afraid they've slipped through the back already. On foot. It'll take Pasquale ten minutes just to get to the village. Let's go! Lock your door!'

James jumped from the car. He locked his door while David, in pain, lowered himself on the other side. As fast as his limp would allow they advanced. The sparrows were the only form of life they could see.

They separated when they entered the farmyard. James took the side of the house, which was built in the traditional style. Slowly, step by step, he moved forward; along the arched stables of the ground floor. They seemed empty. Between the arches, where the wall was solid, the heat was intense. The sparrows chirped busily, seemingly undisturbed by the two intruders.

Under the last arch was a grey Alfa Romeo.

James stopped. David came hobbling across the yard. He too had seen the car.

'Emma! Thomas! Are you here?' James' voice echoed in the building.

He moved, towards the car.

'*Stop! Non girare! Mani sulla testa! Anche l'americano!*' The voice was close behind. It was male, muffled.

David saw James put his hands on his head. He did the same.

'*Avanti! A destra!*'

'Walk!' James translated. 'To the right!'

They reached the flat stone wall of a shed. The voice ordered them to stop and put their hands on the wall.

'Are the keys in your car?' the voice demanded.

'Yes – in the car,' James replied.

In the background, footsteps faded. They sounded light.

'The other one's a woman,' James whispered.

'Quiet! And don't move! Not until we have left!'

At a fast pace, the footsteps returned.

'It's locked!' a woman called out of breath.

'Are you trying to play games with us?' Angry, the male voice closed in on James. 'The keys! Quickly!'

James sensed the man right behind him. A stunning blow to the side of his head knocked him to the ground.

'The keys! Throw them behind you!'

With fumbling fingers, James unhooked the key ring from his belt loop and threw it behind him. Ringing, it hit the ground. He felt faint. Dust was in his nostrils. His right eyebrow was cut. Blood dripped from his cheek.

The footsteps faded again. The engine of the Chevrolet burst into life. The car came nearer. Its motor stopped.

'Stay where you are! Another trick and you pay!'

The Alfa Romeo started.

James was on his feet again. His hands were back on the wall. Out of the corner of his eye, he saw the car roll forward. Dry, yellow mud was on its tyres. The car stopped. Its engine continued to tick over. A door slammed.

'Where are my children?' James shouted and turned.

Emma was halfway between the house and the Alfa Romeo, some thirty yards away. She was gagged. Her hands were tied behind her back. The man was pushing her towards the car. He carried a light machine gun. He wore brown cords and an olive-green anorak. His face looked grotesque under a hood made from a stocking, his features squashed flat.

'Emma! Where's Thomas?'

The little girl tried to break loose. Easily, the man held her back by her tied wrists. She strained towards her father. Her eyes were black with fear. Her hair was dishevelled. Under the gag, she tried to speak.

Roughly, her captor pulled her round. He slapped her face, right and left, pushing her towards the car.

The woman, smaller, otherwise similar in appearance to her companion, aimed her gun at James.

'We've no chance,' David, who had also turned, warned.

The man opened the boot of the Alfa Romeo. From the distance, it appeared empty. He picked Emma up.

James dashed forward.

A burst from the woman's gun hit the ground before him.

He fell to his knees. 'Please! Let me have my children back! I beg you! Where is my son?'

The man dropped Emma in the boot. He slammed the lid shut. He turned. He walked up to James.

'You're lucky we don't kill the boy. We could! You'd still pay for the girl! You get the children when you have paid. You'll hear from us. There!'

A kick to the side of the chest, below the heart, knocked James out. Face down, he sprawled in the dust.

'You! American!' The man motioned with his gun. 'You come with us!'

Instinctively, David let himself fall round the corner of the shed and out of the kidnappers' line of fire. Before they could aim their guns at him again, he was back on his feet and behind the barn.

The woman stopped her companion in his pursuit.

'*Carabinieri!*' she shouted. 'Let's go!'

He listened.

Faintly, a siren sounded in the distance.

Running, he came back. They both jumped into the Alfa Romeo. On spinning wheels, the car raced out of the farmyard.

Nine

PUSHING HIS SMALL van to the limit, Pasquale had reached the village in barely five minutes. An open, navy blue jeep was parked outside the *carabinieri* station. Two young men, one of them a sergeant, were on duty.

Pasquale knew the sergeant. Rapidly, he reported what had happened. He urged the men to be quick.

Stunned, they grabbed their submachine guns and dashed to the jeep. 'We'll call headquarters on the way!' the sergeant shouted. Then they were off, their siren blaring and lights flashing, racing towards Valcortese.

Pasquale had no chance of keeping up with them. For a short while, he heard the siren in the distance. Then the noise of his hard revving engine drowned the fading sound.

The kidnappers heard the siren when their Alfa Romeo was less than half a mile from the bridge. Quickly, the sound grew louder. They were trapped: had they tried to cross the bridge, they would have met the *carabinieri* head on, before they could have reached the main road. Had they decided to turn back up the hill, they would have been visible for most of the way.

They pulled their car off the road, not far from the bridge, behind some dense bushes which grew along the banks of the Arbia. The woman took up position behind a low stone wall, to the east of the track, some seventy-five yards from the bridge. The man hid under it.

The *carabinieri* switched off the siren and turned into the side road. The jeep skidded wildly as it left the asphalt surface and hit the loose dirt. They slowed down on the approach to the narrow bridge. They rolled on to it, rumbling across the planks. They scanned the slopes before them. Their radio was on. So far, headquarters had not come back to them with instructions.

They reached the far side. The driver accelerated. A hooded figure rushed up the bank from under the bridge. From behind he lobbed a grenade towards the open jeep. Falling in a smooth curve, it hit the driver's left shoulder and dropped behind his seat. Instantly, it detonated. The woman opened fire from the front.

The explosion blasted the two *carabinieri* out of the jeep and blew the vehicle off the road. The remains of the men's bodies and limbs hit the ground, broken, mangled, torn, with barely a shred of their uniforms left.

A mass of twisted metal, the jeep lay nose down. It burst into flames. The blaze was fierce. A pall of black smoke rose from it. The pungent smell of burning rubber tainted the air.

Pasquale heard the blast when he was less than a mile from the bridge. He saw the smoke. Instantly he guessed what had happened.

He stopped the van and climbed up the slope on the south side of the road. He could not see the bridge because of some trees along the river. Seconds later, he saw the Alfa Romeo approach the junction and drive out of his sight.

He waited, in case the car came his way. He climbed down the slope and drove to the bridge.

The jeep was still burning, its tyres ablaze. There was no sign of James or David. The shepherd and his flock were nowhere to be seen.

Pasquale arrived at Valcortese as James was making his first attempts to walk again, leaning on David's arm. He told what he had seen. Dazed, James tried to take it in.

There was nothing for them to do at the bridge. Nor was there any point in pursuing Emma's captors now. Too much time had elapsed since they had crossed the bridge. The keys to the Chevrolet had gone. Its steering was locked. The van was slow. Both David and James were hurt.

They decided to go back to Terrarossa.

Ten

THE NEXT HOURS saw a stream of cars, jeeps, vans and trucks arrive at Terrarossa. They brought ordinary policemen, *carabinieri*, reporters, television crews, nurses and a doctor. Never before, even in Pasquale's memory which included a multitude of local weddings and funerals, had so many people came to the house on the same occasion.

An ambulance rushed Caroline to Siena hospital. Rachel was well enough to stay at Terrarossa. She needed her parents and their comfort more than anything else.

The doctor examined James and attended to his split eyebrow. Four stitches neatly closed the cut. As for David's leg, only time would heal the pulled muscle.

The great number of people milling about the house and over its grounds bewildered James, especially when he found himself confronted by both police and *carabinieri*. Frantically, he rushed about. Dazed, he was anxious to make himself as useful as possible to the countless officers and other officials who had come, so he assumed, to help, to take action. His background and the little he had witnessed of the crime he told quickly, urgently, as accurately as his recollection would allow. He tried to describe the man with the binoculars, the incident with the snake, the footsteps at night – all of which, he had convinced himself, connected. When no one seemed to suggest any kind of pursuit, and he was asked to repeat over and over again the same points and facts, which he did until the words sounded less and less meaningful to him, he grew all the more desperate. Angry, finally, he shut himself away in his study. Somehow he needed to think, to get hold of himself.

Who was in charge of the investigation? Who, if anyone, would stop the chaos outside from becoming, he feared, totally unproductive? The crime affected Emma and Thomas, Caroline, the two *carabinieri*, the children's mother, even himself. They were all victims. But, first of all, the children had to be found! They had to be returned safely! Action was needed, not statements typed badly in quadruplicate, on official paper, which seemed yellow with age even before it was used.

He realised suddenly that he must send a message to Claire, the children's mother, his former wife. Already, there was the possibility that the news would reach her before he could get in touch. Caroline's father, too, had to be contacted.

He went outside. A high ranking officer of the *carabinieri* was being briefed by two of the men who had been taking statements from him, David, Anna and Pasquale.

James had not seen the officer before. He approached him. Would it be possible to send a message to the children's mother in London?

The officer, an imposing man, maybe in his early fifties, introduced himself: Colonel Enzo Amorini. His men would try to establish a telephone link via headquarters. James gave the telephone number. Then he requested a private interview with the Colonel.

In his study, James quickly came to the point. 'I am sorry for the death of your men but I am confused by what is going on! No one seems to be doing anything practical!'

The Colonel eyed the agitated Englishman in silence. For a moment, he reflected on what he had heard from his men. 'Mr Grey, I understand your impatience. It will not help you but I, too, get a little confused at times, in situations like this.' The voice was careful, stilted in its correctness. A sympathetic smile faintly lifted the officer's thick and greying moustache. 'Most of the men who are helping to cause the confusion will soon be gone, I can assure you!'

'But – who's in charge?'

'I will be taking charge, Mr Grey. Unfortunately, I was unable to be here from the beginning. I was in Volterra when I was first informed.'

'What's been done so far?'

'Our stations, within a radius of one hundred kilometres and further, along the motorway to Rome, are on urgent alert. There are roadblocks. We have begun to evaluate the information contained in your statements. A long and laborious process! We have informed the ministry in Rome.'

James sat down. Tears came to his eyes. The extent of the

operation seemed only to confirm the seriousness – the reality, even – of the crime.

The Colonel sighed. 'I know – believe me, I understand very well how you feel. I too would like to run after the abductors. But where to? And – even if we knew – I am bound to point out, perversely, although several serious crimes have been committed, this is also a very private matter.'

Dejected, James did not respond.

'You see, Mr Grey, we may not always be able to help you as much as we would like. They have your children. We must not increase the risk to their lives!' Squarely, the Colonel faced James. 'I assume you have never before been the victim of a serious crime. That in itself is an experience you will have to learn to live with. Not accept! But to face! To survive! In this case, you will need to be patient. You may have to wait for a long time. And you must not assume that the criminals' demands will necessarily appear to be rational.'

'I'm not sure I understand.' James' voice was low, hoarse.

'Their motivation may not be clear. It may be purely commercial, if we can call it that. Or political. Or both. Quite possibly both. Also, I must not conceal it from you, often in these people there is a degree of violence which is – difficult – to understand.'

'What – what are the chances?' James forced himself to ask.

'I don't know, Mr Grey.' The Colonel shook his head. 'None of us can make you any promises. Except, of course, that we will work hard. You must not assume that the chances are better than even. It may depend on you! On how you negotiate.'

The man at Valcortese said, 'you get your children when you have paid. That is commercial, as you say?'

'I hope so, Mr Grey.'

'What about the journalists? So far I have avoided them.'

'I suggest you say no more than they know already. Surely they have the story. If you like – if it helps you – I can speak to them. Later, we may need their help. But we don't want them to say anything detrimental.'

There was a knock on the door. James opened it to a junior officer. Contact with London was expected any moment now.

They went outside. A jeep, with an unusually tall aerial, had been parked at the top of the drive. The radio operator was speaking to Siena. He turned and held the handset out to James. Tony Rudd,

Claire's husband, was on the crackling line.

'It's James. Is Claire there?'

'She's right here. What's going on? Has something happened?'

'James?' Claire's voice was full of alarm.

'Claire! The children have been taken! I'm speaking from a car of the *carabinieri*, they're here, from Terrarossa – '

'Thomas! Emma! Kidnapped?'

'Yes.'

He waited for her to speak. 'Claire? Are you there?'

'I – I – can I still fly today?'

'There were no flights today. Nor tomorrow either. There's a strike at the airport. Take the first plane on Monday! I'm told it will be some time before we hear. Bring Tony!'

'I – I come – Monday.' She was barely audible.

'Caroline's in hospital. In Siena. She was hit over the head. The doctor thinks it's mainly shock. Please tell her father she's in good hands. I'll meet you at the airport.'

'Yes – Monday.'

The line went dead.

'James! What happened?'

He gave the handset back to the operator. He turned.

Max stood before him, a large pad of drawing paper stuck under his arm. He had just returned from the chapel, where he had gone in the morning. Shielded by the straw hat, his dark face was rigid with foreboding.

'Emma – Thomas – they've been kidnapped. I had,' James choked, 'I just had to tell Claire.'

Speechless, Max stared at his friend. Swaying, he shut his eyes.

'Let's go inside.' Gently, James touched Max on the elbow, suggesting he turned.

'Poor children!' the painter whispered. 'When? When did it happen?'

'Eleven. Just after. David will tell you. I must speak to the Colonel.'

In silence, side by side, they returned to the house.

The Colonel called off most of his men. He ordered four of them to remain on guard, to be relieved every eight hours. He promised to stay in touch through their radio. He would call in person as often as possible.

He made his statement to the remaining journalists. He repeated quickly what had happened. He stated the children's names, gave their ages and showed recent photographs. Copies would be available from his office. He described James as an independent television producer who, over the years, had rebuilt Terrarossa, now his principal home. Without overstating it, he was careful to make the point that James was not a rich man.

'Where's the children's mother?' one of the journalists called out. 'Has she been told?'

'She is in England. She has been informed.'

'Will she be coming here?'

'Probably. In due course. Ladies and gentlemen, would you please leave now! I promise we will keep you informed. But may I impress on you to use your best judgement so as not to endanger the children's lives more than they are endangered already. I cannot say anything else now.'

The Colonel took his leave from James. He had to go and see the families of the two dead *carabinieri*.

'Please offer them my condolences. Please tell them – I am deeply sorry they had to die when they were trying to help us.'

'I will. Thank you.' The Colonel bowed, shaking James' hand. 'At least, you can hope. You must hope!'

The sun hung low in the west when silence fell over Terrarossa. There was no noise of playing children. No one was in the pool or on the terrace. In the kitchen, there was only Anna.

The guards parked their jeep outside the gate. Two men controlled access from that side. The other two positioned themselves separately on the slope below the house, where they could call to and see each other.

At eight, Anna called the household to supper in the kitchen. Dejected, despite their comparative good luck, only David and Suzanne answered her call. The girls had been fed and put to bed before seven. Max did not want to eat.

James stayed in the study. Before Anna returned to her house, she brought him some plain bread, a piece of cheese and a glass of wine. 'You must eat!' she said. 'You must not make yourself more ill than you are already.'

Max entered soon after she had gone. Softly, he put his hands on James' shoulder. 'Is there anything I can do?'

James shook his head.

'May I sit with you?'

James motioned him to a chair.

'I have been thinking. Of the day they took my friend.'

'What was his name?'

'Günter,' Max gave a nervous snort. 'A good German name, I thought.'

'Was he a Jew?'

'Yes. They took him to one of the camps. After the war I found out that they killed him.'

'You never told me.'

'I tried to forget.'

James shook his head. 'Better to be silent – '

'It does not always help. Sometimes it's better to talk.'

'Maybe.'

James had not touched the food nor the wine Anna had brought him. Motionless he stared through the window, out over the darkening hills, until the night was black in the open frame. He did not want a light in the room.

Max got to his feet. 'You should try to rest, take a sleeping pill. Have you got any?'

'Yes. I have.'

At midnight James sat on his bed, long after Max had gone to his room. Alone, he began to realise all the more that he could do only one thing: wait. Hesitant at first to follow Max's advice – because he felt that he should be alert, ready at all times – he had nevertheless taken some Mogadon.

Dared he hope? From his interrogators he had gathered that there was usually a good deal of similarity between cases, especially the way they developed after the hostages had been taken. The fact that the children were foreign did not make their abduction as unusual as, at first, he had believed it to be. He had become a resident, somebody whose wealth the kidnappers could have assessed before their strike.

Yet why had they chosen *him*? Apart from Terrarossa, he owned little: the lease of a small flat in Covent Garden in London, an old Bentley, his equipment, a little cash – which he had invested in a modest portfolio of British shares. He earned his living from project to project. He knew he had been watched at his work, filming in the Campo. Had the kidnappers been misled by the superficial glamour which attached to some aspects of making films or television features?

Were the chances of getting the children back alive really no better than even? He knew now that many hostages had never been seen again, that many had been found dead after their ransom had been paid. Children especially belonged to this category of the disposable.

It usually took a long time to negotiate a release. But, from what he had heard, he feared that time was not on the children's side. The more difficult they were to conceal, to look after, the more likely they were to be killed.

He forced himself to imagine slowly, in slow motion, the events David had described to him. He tried to relive what had happened when he himself had been present. Maybe there were clues which would prove useful.

Why was the car with Emma's captors at Valcortese? Why had the shepherd seen their car go up the hill but not the other, which, clearly, must have had Thomas in it? Were there more than three kidnappers involved? Were they locals? If not, how well did they know the surrounding country? The mud on the Alfa Romeo's wheels probably meant that the car had come from a place in the country. Did it return there?

Countless questions came to his mind. Time and again, he forced himself to return to what had happened.

The process was painful. It led to increasing despair. Lying on his face, on his unopened bed, he buried his hands in his hair. His tension, both of body and mind, eased when he began to cry. He began to feel where he had been kicked. A dull ache accompanied every sobbing breath he took. The tears ran down his nose and fell from his eyes. Cold, they soaked the bedspread under his cheek bones.

How could he hope to find the children in a country, which, although he had always felt welcome and at home there, was nevertheless strange, impossible to penetrate, hopeless to search? Even if, by some miraculous chance, the children's whereabouts were to become known, how could they be freed without their abductors' consent? They held the children's lives in their hands. For them, he would have to wait.

He would have to wait. He fell asleep.

Eleven

A TERRIBLE DREAM made Thomas whimper. Caroline struggled with a man, a man who had jumped suddenly from the bushes. From behind, a hand roughly held his own mouth and nose. Painfully, it twisted his head. He struggled. He could not breathe. The man swung a cosh. With a thud, it struck the side of Caroline's head. Her eyes turned white as she sank to the gound.

'Thomas? Thomas? Are you here?'

With a jolt, the little boy awoke. He tried to see from eyes sticky with sleep. It was dark. A blanket, smelly with petrol and damp, covered his face. He was hot. He was not sure he had heard a voice. He had been alone when he had cried himself to sleep. The dream, he knew, was true. It was better to lie still.

'Thomas? Is it you, Tommy?'

'Emma!'

'Here! In the corner! I can't move,' she whispered. 'I didn't know you were here. It was all dark when they brought me. They've gone to sleep now.'

Overjoyed not to be alone any longer, he tried to sit up. His tied wrists and ankles hurt.

'You're making a noise! You'll wake them up!'

Terrified that the woman who had tied him up for the night might come back, he sank back to the floor. He lay quite still.

'You can whisper. I don't think they can hear us. They're downstairs. They stopped talking.'

'Who are they? Robbers?'

'Kidnappers.'

'What's that?'

'People who steal children and ask for money before they give them back to their parents.'

'How much money?'

'Lots!'

'What? Hundreds?'

'Thousands! They don't take poor children. That's the point!'

Thomas tried to understand. 'Are there kidnappers in London?'

'No! But there's lots of them in Italy. That's why Daddy always watches when we go out.'

He had never noticed his father's concern. The fact that the danger had been concealed from him now frightened him all the more.

'I'm boiling!' Emma rolled to the side, trying to rid herself of her blanket. 'Did Caroline escape?'

'The man hit her on the head. I think she's dead!'

'Dead? She can't be!'

'I saw her fall to the ground. Her eyes were horrible! They rolled! They went all white!'

'He knocked her out! Maybe they didn't want her. Her daddy's poor. He isn't even nice to her!' She sniffed. She had convinced herself that the nanny could not be dead. 'Rachel was lucky!'

'Did she get away?'

'She did. She ran back to the house. The man didn't catch her.'

'Gosh! She must have run fast!'

'She did. She ducked. Then she ran, like a weasel.'

Silent, Thomas imagined what he had just heard.

'Ssh!' Emma warned. She thought she had heard a murmur from downstairs.

Petrified, they held their breath. They could hear only the pounding of their own hearts.

'I'm frightened, Emma! It's so dark! Where are we?'

'I don't know. They put something over my eyes. This must be an old house. I thought this room was empty.'

'It looks like an old house in here. It wasn't dark when I came.'

'Who brought you?' Emma asked.

'A man. Only one at first. Then there was another man. And a woman. She's horrible! She hit me! She hurt me when she tied me up for the night!'

'What does she look like?'

'She's got black hair. A bit like Francesca – '

'Francesca's gone to Rome for Daddy.'

'I know. She's not very old either. But she can't speak English.'

'I came with a man and a woman too. She shot at Daddy!'

'Is he dead?'

'No! Daddy and David came to free me. They found the hiding place. But they didn't have any guns.'

'Is Daddy hurt?'

'No! He shouted "Where's Thomas? Give my children back!" The man said something in Italian. I heard him say "Pay". I was in the boot.'

'So was I. I was sick.'

'Me too! It was terrible! Some people put their dogs in the boot.'

'Maybe they don't mind?'

'Of course they do! Especially when it smells of petrol. Dogs have much better noses than we do. But we didn't drive very far. The man and I got out. We walked through a forest. He said he'd kill me if I tried to run away. We walked for a long time. Then we sat and waited. The car came again and another man.'

'Gosh! There must be hundreds of them!'

'Not hundreds, dummy! They're a gang. Gangs are small.'

'How many?'

Steps sounded from the bottom of the stairs outside the room. Quickly, the children rolled to their sides, away from each other. Tightly, they pulled the blankets around themselves.

The door creaked open. A torch beam shone through the gap, falling on Thomas. A grey bundle, shapeless and curled, he lay in one of the far corners.

Over the bare brick floor and through the empty room, the light travelled to the other side. Emma's hair stuck out from under the end of a dirty blanket similar to her brother's. A flick to the window, which was covered by another, hanging rug, and the door shut. It was dark again. The steps faded downstairs.

'Thomas?'

'I'm frightened, Emma!' he sobbed.

'So am I! But we mustn't show them. Don't cry, Tommy! You'l see: Daddy'll get us out.'

'And Mummy!'

'Of course! And Mummy. I'm sure she'll come! Try to sleep now Tommy.'

Twelve

THE SOUND OF cars woke James soon after eight. His eyes were still shut when the previous day's events reimposed themselves on his mind. At random, it flicked through the scenes it had stored. All of them had happened. The children were not at Terrarossa.

He sat up. A stabbing pain, deep into his chest, reminded him of the kick he had received. He was about to rub his eyes when he touched the stitched eyebrow. He dropped his hands and got off the bed.

The cars were from Avis. A man and a young woman had brought a substitute for David. The Chevrolet was parked in its usual place. Pasquale and Max had retrieved it, using the spare set of keys.

He stripped and shaved. Under the shower, he washed his hair. He wondered why? He had not had his swim yet. He was not going to swim. Massaging the scalp helped to dissipate his drowsiness. He thought the sleeping pills must have caused it. He was not used to them.

He thought of Kazue's impending arrival. Her cable had not said where she was coming from or when on Sunday she would be arriving. She had not asked to be met. He had checked: no airline flew direct from Tokyo to arrive in Rome or Milan on a Sunday. Later, he had been given conflicting information. No one had seemed sure whether intercontinental flights would be allowed into Italian airports.

Perhaps the strike had caused her to change plans altogether?

Kazue had been to Terrarossa before, three or four times. An art historian by training, she read and spoke Italian fluently. She knew Tuscany and Umbria well, some parts of them better than he did. Unlike him, she loved to travel by local trains and buses. Maybe, it occurred to him, she had arrived in Italy early and had decided to come cross-country? She had done so before.

Anna gave him a shy glance when he arrived in the kitchen. Anchored, as it seemed, to her washing hands in the sink, she tried to find out how he was. Yes, he had slept. No, he did not want to eat. A cup of coffee would do. Helping himself from the hot *napolitana* on the stove, he asked if she had seen the evening news on television. Pasquale had but she had been too late by the time she had returned to her home. 'You would not have recognised yourself!' he had protested. 'Nor little else here. Incredible! Lies!'

'What about Caroline?' James asked. 'Did they say?'

'She seems all right, thank God! Nothing is broken. She is badly concussed. Of course, there is the shock!'

James nodded. He was relieved her injuries were no worse than the doctor, who had stitched him up, had suspected. He could well imagine what Pasquale had complained of. Prevented from interviewing those directly involved, the journalists had used speculation to flesh out the story.

'I hope we don't get too many sightseers and other gawkers,' he said.

'Pasquale says there are *carabinieri* all over the hills. They'll keep them away. When do you expect the *signorina* Kazue to arrive?'

'I have no idea. We'll just have to wait. Where's Pasquale?'

'In the vineyard.' She pulled her hands from the sink and began to dry them on her apron. 'He's doing what he meant to do yesterday.'

'Are the others still asleep?'

'I haven't heard the Americans yet. The painter went for a walk, a good hour ago.'

He finished his coffee and took the car keys from their usual hook by the coat stand. 'I'm going to talk to Pasquale. I'll be back later.'

The guards at the gate looked at him with unconcealed interest. They did not know him from the previous day. They had come on duty only an hour or so earlier. But they gathered who he was.

'I'm going to the vineyard,' he explained, pointing in that direction.

Slowly, he rounded the ravine. He looked back at the house. From this distance, all seemed normal, tranquil even, as it had been less than a day ago. Indifferent, the early sun reflected from the walls. He had no eyes for the beauty of the picture. For him, a greying chill had fallen over the land.

He stopped at the top of the track, where the children had been ambushed. Searching for clues, the *carabinieri* had spread over the sides. In many places, the thicket lay flattened or pulled apart. For some time, he rummaged through the bushes and trees. Disconsolate, his feet stamped on the sandy ground, taking him here, then there, without system or plan. He had little hope of finding anything. He needed to satisfy himself that he had been to the place again, had experienced its feel, that nothing was to be seen.

He climbed back into the wagon and descended to the house. His chest tightened even more when he saw the donkeys grazing in the olive grove. Nauseated, he stopped. His head dropped to the steering wheel. When the worst was over, he dragged himself from the car.

He found Pasquale near the top of the vineyard, trimming some unwanted shoots the rain had helped to bring out. Silent, he watched James approach. Massive fingers crumpled the straw hat he had taken off his sweaty brow.

'Pasquale, you grew up in this country. You must know many places where the children could be hidden.'

'I do.' The straw hat described a shallow arc around the hills they could see. 'Too many, I'm afraid!'

'Do you think they were locals?'

Pasquale shook his head. 'I can't believe that. Though I heard, down at the saw mill they sometimes employ some strange folk.'

'What do you mean?'

'Sardinians.'

'You mean – exiles? Bandits?'

'That's what I hear.'

James was alarmed. The thought that men who had been exiled from Sardinia because they were suspected of serious crimes – kidnapping was said to be a speciality of theirs! – might be working in the nearby woods shook him. Presumably, the *carabinieri* kept a close eye on them. He knew that the idea behind the *soggiorno obligato*, the enforced stay abroad, was indeed to keep the exiles better under control than would have been possible in their own much wilder country.

'I don't think they were Sardinians,' James said after some thought. 'There was nothing – nothing rustic about them. In a way, they seemed out of place. They wouldn't have had a woman with them.'

'Town folk! I was thinking – I should go to see my friends. They may hear of something.'

'Will you? Can you go today?'

'This job – '

'I can do it. I'd like to if you'd let me. It'd help, take my mind off things!'

The thought that Pasquale's old comrades might help electrified James. Here was hope! One long evening in the winter, when they had shared some *grappa* by the fire, Pasquale had begun to talk about his years immediately before and during the war. Very young, he had been recruited by the Communists. Organised in small cells, they had resisted Mussolini's Fascists. Later, as partisans, they had fought the Germans. 'Those were cruel times! Many innocent people lost their lives. Even women! Children!'

Not a boastful man, Pasquale had offered little detail. But it was clear, from other remarks, that he had indeed been in the thick of it all. Some of his comrades survived. Occasionally, on their rare travels, they paid visits to each other.

'Will you show me what to do?' James begged.

With few words, Pasquale explained. Carefully, he showed what he wanted him to trim, what needed to be left alone. 'You have enough work here for a couple of days. I'll be some time making the rounds.'

James wished him a good journey. They shook hands. Then Pasquale climbed to the top of the vineyard and was gone.

Methodically, James began to work from vine to vine, down and up the steep rows. The dusty slope was ablaze with the whitening sunlight. The air glittered with heat wherever he looked when, every now and then, he paused to straighten his back.

After the first hour – he estimated the time for he had not brought his watch – he realised that he had been working too fast, throwing up too much dust. He was tiring quickly.

He slowed, to a plodding, more purposeful rhythm.

He became thirsty. Unprepared, he had not brought any water. He wondered whether Anna would have a spare flask he could bring the next day. Then he remembered that he would have to go to Pisa to collect Claire from the airport.

Doggedly, he worked on. He was determined not to stop. He was thirsty but not hungry. His back ached. He would have plenty of time – too much! – to rest in the evening. But at least the day would have passed.

The sun stood high overhead and he was almost at the bottom of the third row when he heard his name called. He knew it was Kazue's voice. He looked up. At the end of the row, high above him, he saw her slight figure against the deep blue sky.

Immobile, he watched her approach.

She held out her hand, her arm stretched rigidly straight. Searching, she looked into his eyes as they shook hands. Suddenly, she flung her arms up and round his neck, pressing her light body against his chest.

'Oh, James! I am so sorry!'

He picked up his tools. Silent, she followed him to the top of the vineyard.

A basket of bread and cheese, some fruit, bottles of water and wine, were on the table outside the Neris' house. Anna had given it to Kazue.

They sat down.

'Where did you come from?' he asked, taking a glass of watered wine. 'I was afraid the strike might hold you up.'

'I was warned in New York. So I flew a day earlier. I thought I would spend the day seeing some dealers in Rome. I heard late last night. I took the first train this morning, to Chiusi. I got a taxi in Siena.'

He shook his head. He knew how tired she must be. He had made the journey from New York himself.

'How long can you stay?'

'I have a whole week. I must be back in Kyoto on the first of August.'

'I am glad.' He recalled her last visit when she had had only two days.

'There are road blocks on the way. At one of them they suspected me of being a journalist.'

'Did you see the papers? Do they say anything about the kidnappers? Who they are?'

'They say they're terrorists. Are they right?'

'I suppose so.' He shut his eyes for a moment. 'Many criminals cause terror. I imagine – out there – in places like Chiusi and Siena everything is as it always is? Normal?'

She seemed disconcerted. The thought embarrassed her. 'Yes,' she admitted. 'Except I saw people reading about it on the train. They talked. They were concerned. Of course, when you come closer, the *carabinieri* are very visible.'

'It's too late! Isn't it?'

'I don't think so! I saw Pasquale go off. Anna almost pushed him from the house!'

'Did she know he had meant to go?'

'I think so.'

'She didn't tell me when I saw her in the morning.'

'Maybe she thought it wasn't for her to tell you. They really care! I know this country only a little. But I feel – in my heart – Pasquale and his comrades have a chance. Their eyes and ears may be older now. But they're still sharp. And they are out there!'

Thirteen

SIDE BY SIDE, Kazue and James worked in the vineyard for the rest of the afternoon. They stopped at six o'clock. They climbed back to the top of the vineyard, picked up the food basket and drove back to the house.

They were still in the kitchen, talking to Anna, when the Colonel called on the radio. Startled, James ran to the gate.

'I hear you have been working in the vineyard,' the Colonel opened the conversation. 'You must be very tired – '

'It's something to do – '

The Colonel explained there were no new developments. Caroline's progress was satisfactory. She would be allowed a short visit in the morning. James was surprised to hear she had been taken to the old rather than the new hospital.

'I'll go and see her on my way to Pisa,' he said.

'Do you want an escort? At the airport?'

'Wouldn't that attract even more attention?'

'How are you going to cope with the press when your wife – forgive me! – I mean the children's mother arrives?'

'Do you think they'll be there?'

'I'm sure of it! It's obvious she'll be on the first flight in! She may be grateful for a little protection.'

The Colonel went on to say that it would be no problem to have some of his men standing by. They would stay in the background unless needed.

James thanked him and asked if he could put some questions.

'Please. Go ahead.'

'I've been wondering, Colonel: the Alfa Romeo at Valcortese had mud on its wheels. Do you believe the kidnappers are hiding in the hills?'

'It's possible. Especially if we don't find they changed cars.

53

Yesterday, I was rather afraid they might have got onto the *autostrada* at Montevarchi. But that seems less likely now.'

'Because – by now – you would have found the car?'

'That's right. And there's no trace of the Fiat either – '

'How do you know it was a Fiat?' James was quick to ask. 'I thought the shepherd didn't know the makes of cars?'

'Ah! Simple! We showed him photographs, of course. We believe it was a 128, stolen in Arezzo last Thursday.'

'I heard there are some exiled Sardinians in the area. Is that true?'

For an instant, James thought, he heard the Colonel chuckle. 'True. But it's not their usual way to blow up our men with grenades. However, we are checking.'

James had wanted to ask about terrorists. Now he felt it was better to leave the question for their next conversation. 'Will I hear from you tomorrow?' he asked instead.

'I will visit you if I can free myself here. Otherwise, I'll call.'

From the jeep, James went straight to his room. He showered and changed. Kazue had brought some of the Sunday papers: *La Stampa, Il Messaggero, Il Giornale,* the *Corriere della Sera.* In the study he spread them out over his writing table.

All of the newspapers had front-paged the story, with more inside. Everywhere the children's photographs had reproduced badly, which was not surprising, considering the originals had been only snapshots.

He wondered whether anyone would be able to recognise Emma from the pictures. She looked posed, unattractive – unpleasant, even.

Thomas appeared more natural. He had been photographed while playing.

The rest of the pictures were of the house, the bridge, the two *carabinieri,* their burned-out jeep. There were long-distance shots of himself and the others at Terrarossa. The Colonel, too, was shown.

He began to read one of the papers: 'Terrorists strike in Chianti', followed by a racy breakdown of the day's events. Several paragraphs about the background completed the story: Terrarossa, himself, his guests. He stopped reading. He had experienced the same feeling before, when he had been written about in the trade press. He hardly recognised himself. Many of the facts were wrong.

Suzanne, who had taken over from Anna in the kitchen, called them to dinner. Slowly, quietly, the party came together. They sat down. Told by their parents to be as still as mice, Rachel and Sarah hardly dared lift their eyes from the plates which were put before them.

James made no effort to talk. He forced himself to eat a little of what Suzanne dished out for him.

Max broke the silence. He had met Kazue before. Seated next to her, he began to explain how difficult he found the Tuscan landscape to draw. 'It may be what some people mean by a classical landscape. I suppose because we see it in the backgrounds of paintings by the great masters. But it is so complex! Nowhere else have I seen such detail. So many layers and levels. Such depth when the day is clear. I wonder whether anyone could count the number of hills and woods?'

Hesitant, the conversation spread. Words, phrases crossed the room in front of James. He did not take in what was being said.

Suddenly Sarah asked him to light the fire.

Disconcerted for a moment, he got up. As he passed her, he put his hand on her shoulder. Lightly, for a second only.

The fire and the wine drew the party together. The girls, fascinated by her kimono, came up to Kazue. 'What is your dress called? Does it have a special name?'

'It's a kimono, a summer one.'

'But in your language, what's the name?' Rachel insisted.

'Ah!' Kazue realised the little girl thought 'kimono' was an English word. 'I'll say it slowly: *Asa-No-Kimono*. A kimono made of *asa*.'

Together, the girls repeated the name.

'Now say it faster! Each of you, alone!'

Sarah, less self-conscious than her elder sister, repeated it first.

'That's very good! Both of you! Your accents are very nice!'

Suzanne thought it time for the girls to go to bed. In opposite directions, they circled the table to say good night. They reached James. He held out his arms. Gently he pulled the girls to his sides. They kissed him on the cheeks. Tears sprang to his eyes as he felt how light, how fragile they were in his hands.

The children's departure and James' obvious distress brought silence again. Soon, David followed his daughters and Suzanne, who had not yet returned from putting them to bed. Max stayed a little longer. Then he, too, excused himself.

For a long time, Kazue sat with James in front of the fire.

'I wonder how the children are?' he said at last, taking his eyes off the dying flames. 'I just hope – I pray – they are not too frightened. Not hurt!'

'They must be asleep now,' she tried to reassure him. 'Children adapt quickly. They are stronger than we think.'

'But this! It will leave them scarred! Damaged for life!'

'They will forget. So will you. Or not forget but, at least, accept.'

It was after midnight when they went to bed. James clung to Kazue as if he had nothing left in the world to hold on to. In the dark, his composure broke. His body shook violently. In her arms, he cried himself to sleep.

Fourteen

MONDAY MORNING. At half past eight, James set off for Siena.

Two reporters were waiting at the gate. They were English. Would he see them? Had there been any new developments?

He stopped for a moment only. He had nothing to say. In the rear mirror, he caught a glimpse of the men, looking rather forlorn with the two *carabinieri* guards.

'Try again tomorrow!' he called back to them.

On the road, he wondered whether he should try to drive all the way to the old hospital which, on the highest point of the old town, faces the cathedral. Only once had he tried to get further than the market place: he had got lost in the one-way system and finally found himself heading for the country again, circling the old walls. He decided to leave the car in the usual place.

The market square seemed unusually busy, especially for a Monday. At first he could not find a space big enough for the wagon. Eventually, his friendly parking attendant directed him to squeeze in between two of the market trucks.

He saw some beautiful nectarines at his favourite fruit and vegetable stand. Its owner and his wife, who had often given strawberries and cherries to the children, said how sorry they were about what had happened. They refused to take money for the nectarines when he said he was about to visit Caroline. Embarrassed, he thanked them and went on quickly.

He bought a small bunch of red roses at a florist in Via di Città and continued to the hospital.

He entered by the main door and approached the porter, who sat in a glass box under the painted vaults of the thirteenth-century hall. He said his name and asked to see Caroline. The porter picked up the handset of his telephone and dialled a number. James saw that he had been reading a newspaper. He saw that football scores were making the main headlines on the front page again.

A policeman appeared from inside the building. He asked James to come with him and led the way through the continuation of the hall, up some narrow, side stairs, finally down a long and painted corridor. A young houseman, in white coat and trousers, met them there.

'Only a few minutes,' the doctor said. 'And, please, very gently! She is still very frightened.'

Softly, James slipped into the room.

Staring at the ceiling, Caroline huddled deep in her bed. An extensive bruise on her right temple showed where she had been hit. Bandages covered her head where the hair had been shaved before the split scalp had been stitched up.

'How are you?' He showed her the roses and the nectarines and put them on the bedside table.

'My head hurts. Have you heard anything?' Her voice was thin.

He shook his head. 'Not yet.'

'I don't understand.' Tears filled her eyes. 'I can't remember – '

'Nothing?'

'Nothing. A policeman came earlier. He spoke English. I tried – '

'Did the doctor say when you will be allowed out?'

'No.' She tried to turn her head to the side. 'Have you told Claire?'

'She's on her way. I'm going to pick her up now.'

The cathedral bells struck a quarter to ten. He had to go soon if he was to be on time.

'I'll bring Claire to see you.' He took a tissue from the bedside table. Leaning over her, he mopped up her brimming eyes. He dried her cheeks and wiped her nose.

'Blow!'

'It hurts!' She tried to smile.

'You'll see: we'll get the children back soon! I know we will! And you'll be better – '

In the corridor, he realised what he had just said. He stopped. Had he said it for her or for himself? He kept thinking about the question on his way back to the market square, until a noisy group of young tourists distracted him.

Fifteen

THE PLANE WHICH brought Claire was almost an hour late by the time it taxied to a halt at Pisa airport.

From the terminal, James looked out for the woman who had been his wife for more than eleven years. He wondered whether Tony Rudd, for whom she had divorced him, had come with her.

The first passenger, she emerged from the front door, a small face under dark glasses. Disregarding the handrail, she descended the steps. She was alone, without her husband. She began to cross the airfield towards the customs hall. Her usual softly colourful looks – fair complexion, blonde hair, which she liked to match with a limited range of blue and beige pastels – had faded to near transparency. The self-assured bearing, horsey at times, was gone. A headscarf covered most of her fastened-back hair, above a matching pale coloured light coat. A carpetbag hung limply from one hand, her passport stuck in the other.

For a minute only, she disappeared from his sight in the customs hall. Then she was through, looking for him.

Too late, he realised they were not alone.

A barrage of flashlights hit them as they shook hands.

They were surrounded.

'Mrs Rudd! Will you be staying at Terrarossa? How long is it since you last stayed there?'

'Mr Grey, can you tell us if there have been any new developments today?'

'Mrs Rudd, how much do you expect to have to pay?'

'Are you prepared to meet the kidnappers' demands – whatever they are?'

The intensity of the blazing lights increased. Two television crews moved in front of them. All at once, the small hall was packed, milling with people shouting in English and Italian.

Dazed, James glanced at Claire. She was white with shock.

'Please! Get me out of here!' Her grip tightened in his hand.

'I'm sorry, Claire! I should have realised – '

The number of reporters in the hall increased as they came off the plane. Most of them were men. The latecomers, anxious to get closer, pushed from behind, cameras overhead. Shouting, they tried to get attention.

'Mrs Rudd, look this way, please!'

'Would you mind shaking hands again, please?'

'How long will you be staying, Mrs Rudd?'

The men and the only woman in the front line, themselves pushed from behind, came closer.

James raised his arms. 'Gentlemen! Ladies! Will you at least give us some room! This is senseless if you want to talk!'

The reporters tried to hear what he had been saying. Quickly, he used the silence: 'If you step back, I'd like to make a statement!'

The pressure eased a little. Still jostling for good positions, the reporters moved back some five or six feet. The flashlights ceased.

Expectantly, microphones and note pads ready, the crowd looked at the couple. The television cameras were on.

'I'm afraid,' James began, 'there have been no developments since Saturday. We're waiting. We have heard nothing.

'The only positive thing I'd like to mention is that Caroline Martin, who was with the children, is on the way to recovery. We are relieved her injuries are less serious than they could have been.'

He paused. Still holding Claire by the hand, he looked around.

'Before I finish, may I impress on you – no, may I beg you! – not to write or to allow to be published anything that could prejudice the safe release of our children. I fear already there has been a certain amount of speculation which can only be harmful. I am not sure – I can't believe – it can be helpful to speculate too much about the kidnappers' motivation or indeed their identity in political terms.'

A flashlight made him blink.

'It can only do harm if there is totally unfounded and misleading speculation regarding our wealth. We are not rich!

'Finally, may I plead with you: the less you say – I know that's tough to ask of you – the less you say, the sooner we will be able to negotiate the children's release. I'm sure of that. Now, we'd be grateful if you'd let us go.'

For a moment, there was silence. Some of the reporters were still writing. Then all hell broke loose again.

James headed for the exit, afraid they would be trapped. Holding Claire's arm with one hand, her bag in the other, he pushed forward. He answered a question here, replied to another there, disregarding most of what was asked. Claire said nothing at all.

They squeezed through the front door. On tiptoe, he looked for the Colonel's men. He saw a couple of navy blue Alfa Romeos. Between them, their crews stood watching.

He waved.

The *carabinieri* sprang into action. At a fast pace they advanced. Spreading out, they formed a ring round the couple and cleared the way to the Chevrolet.

'Please wait in your car, *signor* Grey! We will escort you,' their lieutenant called.

James unlocked the passenger door. With his free hand, he helped Claire up to the front seat. He walked round the bonnet and let himself in, putting her bag on the rear bench.

'Don't you want to take off your coat?' He adjusted his window. 'It'll be warm, even with the air conditioner.'

She shook her head.

He pulled out the seat belt for her. Reaching, he caught the faint perfume of the shampoo she had used to wash her hair in the morning. He did not know the scent. For an instant, while his fingers were busy finding the lock, he reflected how unused to each other they had grown. To touch only the top of her coat felt stranger, less permissible than it would have been to put his hand on someone he had never met before.

He realised she was crying. Silent, her body shook on the seat.

'I'm sorry, Claire! I should have known better.'

He locked her seat belt.

'It's their questions! They're so heartless! Don't they understand?' She pulled a bunch of white tissues from a pocket in her coat. 'I don't know how to get through this! I realised I can't even speak the language any more! I forgot most of what I knew. How can I help?'

Lights flashing, the *carabinieri* pulled up alongside.

'Are you ready?' The lieutenant looked up at the wagon.

'Ready.'

Only a few of the reporters stood still about. The others scrambled madly for whatever transport they had or could get to go in pursuit: taxis, hire cars, when there were none of those left, even private cars if their owners were willing to accept the large amounts of money proffered.

The *carabinieri*, one car in front, the other behind the Chevrolet, switched on their sirens. The lead car accelerated and the convoy was on its way, speeding towards the *autostrada* to Florence.

At the first toll gate, the sirens fell silent. One after the other, through the same lane, they collected their ticket and were off again. They settled down to a steady one hundred and forty kilometres per hour. Needing to concentrate on his driving less than before, James glanced across to Claire. Shielded by the new, black glasses, she stared at the road ahead. She seemed more composed than before.

'Did they pester you on the plane?'

'They tried. I was in first class. Tony couldn't get anything else. At first they said even that was full.'

'It's the holiday season. Of course, there must have been quite a few people stuck – with the strike. I suppose being in first class you were away from the press – '

'Two of them were there. They said they wanted to buy the story. Exclusively. I nearly hit one of them. Then I said I'd talk to you about it if they left me alone. The steward kept out the others. I never thought I'd need an Italian to defend me from a horde of Englishmen.'

'Did they cause the delay?'

'I don't think so. Tony warned me I'd arrive late. He never takes off on time when he flies from Heathrow. He said I'd have to be patient.'

'I suppose – he didn't want to come?'

'It wasn't that.' She sat up straight. 'He thinks it's wiser if someone stays behind. We may need someone on the ground.'

They slowed down and stopped at the second toll gate. James pulled a bank note from his shirt pocket and passed it through the window. He held out his open palm for the change. The gatekeeper counted some coins and notes into it. James closed his hand and let the car roll forward.

'*Signore!*'

He stopped. He looked back.

'Another five thousand!' The gatekeeper came out of his cabin, to hand him another, larger note. 'You will need your money, *signore!*'

Disconcerted, James thanked the young man and they went on.

'What was that he said?' Claire asked.

'He said we'd be needing the money.'

For some miles they continued in silence.

'Do you have an idea? How much they'll ask?' At last she had found the courage to ask.

'No – at least not in terms of a number.' He shook his head. 'Only – it's going to be far more than we have. We'll have to negotiate.'

In a low voice – barely audible at times over the noise of the rushing car – he recounted what he had learned since Saturday. He spoke methodically, seemingly without emotion. They were about to start skirting Florence when he told her of Pasquale's offer to ask his old comrades for help. 'Kazue agrees with me, they may come up with something.'

'But – she's Japanese!'

'She knows the country better than I do.'

'I always felt Pasquale didn't like us. Not me, at least – '

'You never told me!' He protested. 'What makes you say that? He's very fond of the children!'

'And you really believe they're hidden in the hills? I thought terrorists operated in cities. That politician they kept for so long and then shot – they hid him in Rome. Didn't they?'

'Aldo Moro. I think so – though I didn't really follow the case in detail. The Colonel seems inclined to think they're still in the hills. They put up roadblocks very quickly. And they never found the two cars.'

'You didn't tell me: is the Colonel a local man?'

The question surprised James, especially since he had not thought of asking it himself. 'I assume so. It never occurred to me to ask. I'm impressed by him.'

'Do you think they'd let me join the children? If I give myself up as a hostage? I'm sure they wouldn't exchange me for them.'

Startled, he looked at her. 'It'd only increase their risk. How would they take you? They'd suspect a trap – '

'But,' her voice broke, 'somebody's got to look after them! Who's looking after them?'

Although right behind the lead car, James almost took the wrong turn. At the last moment, he corrected his mistake. Crossing the double white line, he got back on course. 'We can ask the Colonel – if you want to. We're going to Montevarchi. Not through Siena.'

'Isn't that where that wine came from?'

'You mean Montepulciano, further south.'

They fell silent again.

'I must try to be with them,' she suddenly said. 'I should have put the question in front of the journalists.'

'Let's ask the Colonel first, please. We mustn't do anything that could upset his plans. You'll probably meet him tonight. He said he'd try to come. Or tomorrow. Ask him then.'

They left the *autostrada* near Montevarchi and turned west, towards Siena. The road was narrow here, climbing steadily towards Coltibuono. Then it dropped again, more steeply, to Gaiole.

The many corners and hairpins, one after the other, with hardly a straight stretch in between, made Claire car sick.

'Do they have to go so fast?'

James slowed down and turned up the air conditioner. The *carabinieri* guessed why James was falling back. They, too, reduced their speed.

'Do you remember?' he asked, negotiating a long and continuous curve.

'No – what?'

'Up there.' He pointed over his shoulder, to the top of the densely wooded hill they were circling. 'The ruin you liked so much. The one you thought might have made a better house than Terrarossa.'

'It's desolate.'

They passed Gaiole in Chianti. Soon after the small market town, they entered the valley of the Arbia. They turned off the main road at the bridge. The burned-out jeep had been taken away.

'Is this where they ambushed the *carabinieri*?'

'Over there.' He pointed to the field on their right. 'The grass is growing already. I must write to their wives. Tomorrow.'

They arrived at Terrarossa a few minutes after three. Without a word or look even for their escort, Claire got from the car. Anna stood waiting for her in the door.

James thanked the *carabinieri* and invited them in for some coffee.

The lieutenant declined. 'I hope the *signora* recovers a little,' he said as the drivers began to turn the cars. 'We had better get back.'

Sixteen

CLAIRE CHOSE TO stay in her son's room. James put the carpetbag on the bed and left her while she unpacked. She had brought little: two summer dresses, a pair of cords, some shirts. She needed a pair of sandals. In the past, she had bought sandals in Siena when she had come to Terrarossa at the beginning of the warm season.

She opened the wardrobe doors. Thomas' clothes lay neatly folded on the side shelves. His summer jacket – chunky, blue and white stripes on cotton – hung from the brass rail.

Through burning eyes, she looked around. A white paint box and a flower press, neither of which she had seen before, sat on an old pine table by the window. A stack of books was piled next to his Donald Duck watch on the bedside table. His best shoes and a pair of plimsoles were lined up on the floor, by a chest of drawers. The blunderbuss leaned in the corner, on the other side of the room.

Anna knocked on the half-open door. She brought an armful of towels. Fighting to hold back her tears, Claire took the top one, picked up her sponge bag, and rushed to the bathroom.

The shower and a change of clothes did little to refresh her. She went to find James. He was talking to the Japanese woman – she had difficulty with the name – and Anna, in the kitchen. A piece of maize bread, some *grana* – a dry cheese, similar to fresh Parmesan – and a glass of red wine were on the table before him. It was wrong, she felt, that he should even touch food or drink.

'Will you have something to eat?' he asked. 'This is Kazue, I told you about her in the car. She arrived yesterday.'

Standing by the fireplace, Kazue bowed. She seemed much younger than Claire had imagined her. 'I hope you will forgive my presence, Mrs Rudd.'

Claire cast a disconcerted glance at the woman her children had also mentioned, not without affection. 'Claire. Call me Claire!'

A cup of tea was all she would accept.

Kazue excused herself.

Speaking very clearly in her pure Tuscan, Anna asked Claire whether there was anything else she needed for her room.

'No, grazie,' she thanked the woman. 'When is Pasquale coming back?'

James translated.

Maybe tomorrow or the day after was the answer.

James took Claire outside. He introduced her to David and Suzanne who were sitting under the parasols by the pool. Rachel and Sarah were in their room, having a sleep. Suzanne tried to engage Claire in conversation.

David pulled James aside. 'I think – we decided – it's better to leave. If you don't mind, we'd like to leave in the morning.'

'I understand.' James comforted his embarrassed friend. 'This isn't the place it – '

'If there's anything we can do you must let me know!'

'I may need your help when it comes to raising the ransom. As a banker, of course!' James was quick to add the qualification. He realised that Claire had left the pool side. He saw her re-enter the house through the loggia.

Max returned soon afterwards, earlier than on previous days. As usual, he clutched his pad of drawing paper under one arm. With his other hand, he carried a battered tin of pencils, brushes and some water colours. The straw hat sat low on his forehead. He looked drawn, grim.

'Where's Claire?' he asked James, who, restless, had gone back to the kitchen. 'Hasn't she come?'

'She's in Thomas' room. Why don't you knock on her door?'

'She may be resting – '

'I wish she'd rest! I don't think she can! She got a terrible reception at the airport! It'll do her good to see a friendly face.'

Max nodded. He hung his hat on the coat stand. Then he went downstairs.

The Colonel called on the radio at six. Work at his office kept him from coming in person.

James thanked him for the escort.

'Don't mention it! I gather you found your friends from the press a little – overbearing? I hope you don't mind me saying so: I was interested to hear the English are no better than our own journalists.

66

My colleagues from the *polizia stradale* stopped quite a few of them,' he chuckled. 'Speeding after you! I will call, of course, if there's anything new. I am looking forward to meeting Mrs Rudd tomorrow.'

Max persuaded Claire to join the others for dinner. Rachel and Sarah were introduced to her. But she was unable to respond to their simple questions. She could not bring herself to eat. Her silence, far tenser – and unlike James – seemingly indisposed to admit hope at all, compounded with his brooding presence at the table.

Afterwards, she came out on the balcony. 'I remember listening to the nightingales. In the cedars. They were peaceful. If I had known that there – '

Overcome, she could not finish the sentence. James offered to take her downstairs. Max – more welcome as it seemed – took his place.

David sat up with Kazue and James a little longer.

'Where are you going?' Kazue asked.

'We'll head straight north, along the coast. If we can find a place, we'll rest for a day in the south of France.'

'I'm sorry your introduction to Tuscany has been so unhappy.' James got to his feet, to find yet another cigar. 'I meant to say – you mustn't feel guilty because Rachel – you – were lucky. If they'd taken all of the children, it would have been more difficult still. For all of us.'

Later, when they were on their own, Kazue asked James whether Claire had objected to her presence.

'You mustn't think that! She has no right! She asked for the divorce – not I!' For an instant, he sounded bitter. He paused, drawing on his *toscano*. 'She's so hurt – a different person. I thought we'd help each other. Her pain torments me even more. I feel guilty when I look at her. We can't even share our loss!'

Seventeen

'*Ecco, ci siamo!*'

A dismissive grunt was all the second man would utter.

Emma knew the speaker was the man who had taken her from Valcortese. From his position, she had guessed that he was driving. She had never seen his laconic companion. Nor had she heard his voice before their departure from the house, where they had been hiding since Saturday.

Pitching, bumping, the car shook to a halt. A gear grated. The car reversed. It stopped. The motor died. For a second or two, all was quiet.

The front doors opened. The men got out. They spoke rapidly, busily, keeping their voices down.

The rear door, by her head, opened. A tug on the blanket and it slipped off, brushing along her legs and arms. Chill – yet rich with the humid scent of the forest – the dawn air fell on her gagged and blindfolded face.

The door by her feet opened. Fingers tickled the sore skin of her ankles. The string which bound them loosened. She winced, moaning under the gag, when the last burning pull ripped off the bond.

Big hands grabbed the sides of her chest. Roughly, they lifted her to a sitting position. Dizzy suddenly, she slouched against the cold plastic of the backrest. Her bound wrists fell into her lap. Her dress, a pale blue shift of light cotton, was torn on one side and dirty.

The man moved away. She was sure he was the one she had not met before. The boot lid opened behind her. The two voices murmured under its cover.

The dizziness passed. Determined not to provoke her captors' wrath again – as she had done, screaming and shouting, when she had realised that Thomas was not to come with her – she kept quite still. Her cheeks still burnt from the woman's slaps. Disoriented, she pressed her feet firmly on the floor of the car. It felt hard, without carpet. She guessed the drive had taken less than an hour. For most of the way, they had travelled very slowly over bumpy roads. She knew it was Tuesday, early in the morning. She had told herself she must not lose count of the days. She expected she would have to walk soon. She had walked through a forest on Saturday, after she had been kidnapped.

The man – instantly, she sensed the heat and recognised the sour odour of his body – came back to untie her wrists. His hair – the smell of stale tobacco smoke hung in it – fell onto her forehead. The string came off. He pulled her by her freed hands.

'Out!' he ordered.

She stumbled from the car. The hands let go. Freer than she had been for some time, she tried to stand on her own. The blindfold both unsteadied and paralysed her, rooting her to the spot. Swaying, she gasped for air. Her tears had almost blocked her nose. The gag, made from sticking plaster, nearly sealed her mouth.

The car doors slammed shut. The motor started.

'*Ciao!*' the driver called.

'*Ciao,*' the new man replied, taking Emma by the hand.

Quickly, the noise of the car faded. They began to walk.

Stumbling along on the flat and slightly oversize soles of her sandals, Emma fell in step with her captor's slow and purposeful rhythm. The scuffing of material – a jacket rubbing against some other piece of clothing, she thought – accompanied their steady progress. The path felt level and smooth. In the trees, the birds' dawn chorus was in full cry.

They veered right. The path narrowed. Twigs and branches scratched and whipped her left side. Leaves and ferns – cool, some of them damp – brushed over her legs and bare arms. Often the man's hand tightened, pulling her away from the edge of the path. Otherwise his grip was firm but light. Nevertheless, his hand was hot. It became sticky. It felt unclean.

The path began to climb. The light she perceived through the blindfold brightened. She needed more air. Short of breath, she moaned. Her free hand pointed at her mouth and nose.

Her captor's hand held her back as he stopped suddenly. It let go of hers. Fingertips came to the sides of her mouth. Clumsily, they began to peel the sticking plaster from around her lips.

A rapid rip jerked her head and neck forward.

She cried out, instantly afraid he would put the gag back again. She took a deep breath. 'Thank you!' she whispered. Panting, she breathed in and out. 'Where is my brother?'

'*Non parlare!*' the voice said quietly. 'No talk!'

'Is he all right?' she whispered. 'Please!'

'*Si.* Is okay.'

Relieved, happy to believe what he had said, she fell in step with him again.

Of course! Suddenly, it occurred to her. They had also been taken separately to the house. That way, the kidnappers were much safer. If they got stopped with one of their hostages, they still held the other. She would see Thomas at the end of the journey, before long! Already her imagination ran ahead, trying to picture the next hiding place.

The path continued to climb for the better part of an hour. Then it fell steeply, only to regain the height lost. Occasionally, the faint warmth of an early sunray found its way to her face or arms. The birds' song had lost its concerted stridency. Scattered, sweeter, it called to her sharpening ears.

A root abruptly stopped her in mid-stride. Bare and sticking from under the front strap of her sandals, her right toes had hit the obstacle hard. The pain buckled her legs at the knees. The man's hand tightened its grip. Tears welled up in her eyes. The blindfold soaked them up.

'I'm hurt! Please, stop!'

To her surprise, the grip relaxed. He let go of her hand. He turned to her. A ragged edge, the zip of his open jacket, she guessed, rubbed her cheek. He undid the double knot of the blindfold on the back of her head.

The light stung her eyes. She shut them. She was not sure but she thought she heard him chuckle. Blinking, she reopened her eyes.

A bearded face loomed over her. The man was very tall for an Italian. Like the beard, his hair was shaggy and black. The eyes were dark brown. Maybe amused, they looked down at her. He was much younger than the beard had made him appear at first.

She dropped her gaze. The man's feet were shod in maroon lace-up boots. They were huge and quite new. Faded jeans were rolled up over their tops. An olive green anorak and a bulging rucksack of similar colour would have made him look like a hiker had he not carried a gun. Short-barreled, all black, it hung from his right hand.

The unexpected removal of the blindfold had made her forget the pain. Stinging, it came back. She looked at her foot. It looked quite normal. She could not see any blood.

A wave of the gun motioned her to go on. Gritting her teeth, she looked ahead. The path was about to narrow. They would have to walk one behind the other. She realised it was not kindness that had made him relieve her of the blindfold.

Thirsty, tiring, she led the way.

The forest was denser than she had imagined it. The trees, though, were lower. A mixture of pines and many others, which she did not know by name, they admitted no direct sunlight from above. Here and there she saw the sky – patches of pale blue, without clouds. She wondered what the time was. Ahead and to her right, the sun still stood low.

Another hour and she slowed. Plodding, hotter as the sun rose, she dragged her feet over the path. Her soles were on fire. The back straps of her sandals bit into her heels with every step.

'I have blisters!' She did not dare to stop. 'I can't go on!'

'*Bister?*'

'On my heels!' She stopped and turned. She pointed at her feet. 'Blisters. They hurt.'

'*Siediti!*' He motioned her to sit on the path.

He put down the gun. He swung the rucksack from his back. He took off his anorak. Then he knelt to examine her feet.

With clumsy, big fingers, he undid the buckles of her sandals and pulled them off.

He shook his head when he saw her raw soles and heels.

Frowning, he turned to the rucksack. He unstrapped one of its outer pockets.

'*Ecco!*' He produced a flat tin of sticking plasters.

She supported herself on her palms while he lifted one of her feet to his lap and set about covering the blisters with the biggest plasters he could find in the tin.

'What is your name?' Emma asked.

Obviously quite unaccustomed to what he was doing – and all the more absorbed by it for that – he ignored her question. The size and shape of the blisters were difficult to reconcile with those of the plasters.

'Can't you tell me your name?'

'No name,' he said, putting down her foot and picking up the other. 'No name.'

'But – what shall I call you?' she insisted while the second lot of plasters went on her foot.

'*Barba*,' he suddenly said and set down her foot.

'Barba?'

'*Si, Barba*.' He pointed at his beard.

'Is that what it means? *Barba* means beard?'

'*Si, la barba*.' He touched his beard. '*Andiamo!*' He handed her the sandals.

'*Barba*,' she repeated, doing up the buckles. 'Tell me, please, have you written to my daddy?'

'*Non capisco*,' he said and got to his feet.

'Have you asked for money?'

For a moment – from the sudden change of his expression – she thought he had understood.

'Have you?'

His face darkened. '*Andiamo! Non parlare!*' He strapped the anorak to the top of the rucksack.

'I only meant to say my daddy isn't very rich. You must not ask for too much money.' Pleading, she looked at him.

Picking up the gun – the rucksack was already on his back – he avoided her eyes.

'*Andiamo!*' The gun motioned her to go on.

From behind, he suddenly pulled her from the track. In the undergrowth, he forced her to her knees, next to him. He held his breath. His head tilted.

A faint, slow, knocking noise further up the hill made Emma's heart pound.

'Help! Help!'

On all fours, she scrambled back onto the path.

'Help me! Help! I've been kidnapped!' Shouting at the top of her shrill voice, she ran up the path, faster than she had run ever before.

Almost instantly, Barba caught up with her. Roughly, he swiped her off the path and back into the undergrowth. His hands grabbed her round the neck. Terrified, she stared into his angry face.

'Don't kill me! Please!' she whispered.

Grim, he averted his eyes. He listened. The noise had not changed. Monotonously, it continued in the distance.

Her hand gripped tightly in his, she followed him to the place where he had hurriedly dumped the rucksack.

'I can't breathe!' she tried to object when he put a new gag over her mouth.

He ignored her tears. A prod of the gun barrel moved her on again.

A little further up the track, they reached the source of the increasingly clearer noise. A couple of beeches stood closely together. Indifferent to what was going on below them, two of their branches tapped together in the freshening breeze, near the top of the hill.

Eighteen

TUESDAY. At seven-thirty, the Wright-Garrisons had finished breakfast in the kitchen and were ready to leave. David was anxious to start driving before the day grew too hot. They had a long journey before them.

James picked up Rachel and Sarah and kissed them goodbye. He embraced Suzanne. Tears were in her eyes. 'Good luck!' she whispered. 'To all of you!'

'If you need me, we'll be back in Paris by Saturday at the latest.' Firmly, David shook his friend's hand. 'I'll expect your call.'

They got into their car. Sitting low on its springs, it climbed to the top of the drive. Arms waved from the windows. They were gone.

Voices sounded from the other side of the ravine. Side by side, Max and Claire were coming back from a walk. His straw hat in his hand, he waited for her to enter the house first. The fresh morning air had brought a little colour to her face, despite her obvious tiredness. She had slept hardly at all.

Max had picked some wild flowers for Caroline. Carefully, he arranged the blues and pinks, the whites and yellows on the kitchen table. Anna tore up an old newspaper and dampened some of its sheets. Together, they wrapped the flowers in them.

Except for Anna, they all set off for Siena soon after eight. Claire and Max were to visit Caroline. James needed to telephone his lawyer in London. Kazue was going to help buy food for the next few days.

Avoiding the valley where they might have run into journalists on their way to Terrarossa, they took the back road, through the hills. Over them, the air was still. Soon it would begin to simmer. A pale, hazy blue, the sky rose out of the landscape, without horizon.

'Earth and sky inseparable,' Max broke the silence. 'Nowhere have I seen the old elements so close.'

They parted in the market square. Max suggested they all met at Nannini's at half past ten. It would be easier to wait there if James' call were to be delayed.

Quickly, Kazue made the round of the market stands to buy what was on her list. Meanwhile James completed his part of the shopping.

They left what they had bought in the car and went to the telephone office in Via dei Termini. James placed his call with one of the operators, who asked him to take a seat. The waiting time could be more than half an hour, maybe a little less.

'That wouldn't be so bad,' he said to Kazue. 'I've waited here two hours and more.'

The call came through after twenty minutes. 'Cabin four for London!' the operator called out.

Over the years, James' lawyer had also become a friend who knew most of his affairs intimately. Richard Hall expressed his horror. Deeply upset, he offered his condolences. 'I hoped you'd call. What can I do for you?'

Directly, James came to the point: 'We must prepare to raise the ransom. We mustn't waste any time!'

'Any idea how much it'll be?'

James gave a bitter laugh. 'Multiples of what I can pay.'

'So?'

'It's brutally simple. How much can we raise if I sell everything I can sell, borrow to the hilt? The absolute maximum.'

'Are you prepared to repay for the rest of your life?'

'What else can I do? Yes!'

Richard said he would start work immediately. He would be standing by over the weekend. James thanked him and rang off.

He paid for the call and looked at the clock on the wall behind the operator. It was time to go and meet the others. 'Let's go through the Piazza Salimbeni,' he suggested.

The narrow streets were crowded now, the shops and cafés full. Everywhere voices buzzed in the old town.

At the entrance to the piazza, a group of young men hung about. James did not notice them.

'Grey! You'll never see the children again!'

James was not sure he had heard right. He looked up. He saw the men. He stepped forward. Hate clenched his fists.

'What did you say?'

75

Insolently, a slight figure pushed himself off the wall he had been leaning against. Suddenly, he ran. He disappeared at once into the milling crowd, heading towards Banchi di Sopra.

Stung, James started in pursuit. In front, a mop of black hair bobbed over the countless heads and shoulders which moved in the narrow pedestrian road. In flashes, he saw the energetic swing of the young man's arms as he ran easily, leaping downhill with powerful bounds.

Once, twice, James ran into oncoming men. Stumbling, he knocked over an elderly woman. Angry voices shouted after him. He took no notice of them. His eyes fixed on the man in front, he continued the pursuit.

The fugitive darted to the left, down a steep passage of steps. For an instant, James feared that he had lost him.

He caught him there.

Misjudging the steep stair, the man had slipped. Hurt, he lay at the bottom.

Furious, out of breath, James pulled him up by his shirt. He forced him to turn.

'What did you say? What do you know about the children? You must tell me!'

The man struggled. James pushed him against the wall, shaking the slightly built figure so that his shirt tore.

People surrounded them. The captive remained silent. Impassive, he stared to the ground. The crowd grew, the murmur increased.

Two policemen arrived. They pushed sideways through the spectators.

'What's going on?' one of them demanded of James who was still holding the man tightly.

'I am James Grey, from Terrarossa. This man said that I shall never see my children again. Then he ran. I must know why! I must know what he knows!'

Astonished, the policemen looked at each other.

'Can you walk?' one of them asked the man.

He gave a nod.

'Then let's go!'

At once, the officers forced the man's arms up behind his back. Handcuffs clicked shut on his wrists.

Pushing him along between them, the policemen marched the arrested man towards their station. James and Kazue, who had quickly caught up, kept right with them.

'You had better go and tell the others,' James said to Kazue. 'Take the keys. We'll meet at the car.'

The walk to the Questura took only a few minutes. By the time they arrived, a veritable procession had built up behind the officers, their captive and James. The rumour that one of the Terrarossa kidnappers had been arrested was spreading fast.

James repeated his simple statement to the officer in charge. He asked for Colonel Amorini to be informed.

'This has nothing to do with him,' the police officer objected. 'He's *carabinieri*. He'll be informed in time.'

'I don't understand how you split your departments. I'd be grateful if you let him know nevertheless. He has been very kind to us – taking a personal interest.'

The officer smiled. He dialled the number of the *carabinieri* and asked for the duty officer. He told him what had happened. '*Signor* Grey is anxious your Colonel Amorini should be told.' He hung up.

Meanwhile the arrested man was being interviewed in another room.

James waited.

After more than half an hour, the examining officer came to speak to him. 'We're not getting anywhere. At least, nowhere useful. He's a student. He recognised you from seeing you on television. He said what he said because he is against foreigners buying land here. His parents were peasants in Chianti.'

'Is that all? I can't believe it!'

The officer shrugged. 'For the time being – '

'Is he really a local? You won't just let him go?'

'Don't worry!' The officer raised his hands. 'Of course not! He has no papers – '

'No papers?'

'No. For that alone we wouldn't let him go. And we want to make sure – quite sure – he really doesn't know anything.' An unpleasant smile was on the officer's smooth face.

'What's his name?'

'Sachetti, Carlo.'

'Sachetti?' James had never heard the name. 'Where from?'

'A small place – Carpignalle. Quite far from here.'

'I don't know it.' Disappointed, James got up. 'You will let me know if you find out anything?'

'Of course, *signor* Grey! Naturally! Rest assured!'

The procession to the Questura had also been noticed by some of the British reporters who had been sitting outside one of the cafés in the Campo. Now they waited for James to come out. Most of the crowd had drifted away.

'Mr Grey! What happened?'

'Mr Grey, who is the man?'

'Why don't you go in and find out for yourselves?' he snapped, pushing a photographer out of his way.

On his way back to the market square, James thought about the little he had been told. Sachetti's explanation sounded implausible, lame. Traditionally, the Tuscans were hospitable, quite used to foreigners coming to live in their country.

Was there a connection at the university?

The papers had called the kidnappers terrorists. Many terrorists – both of the extreme right and left – were students. Although – students of what? Sachetti claimed to be a student. Siena was a university town. But so were many cities in central Italy: Bologna, Florence, Perugia, to name but a few. There was nothing useful in superficial speculation of this kind. It led everywhere, only to end in deeper and deeper despair. Something tangible had to be found. If Sachetti was no more than a mixed up young man, even Pasquale would be able to verify his local background. Pasquale had been gone for nearly two days. When would he be back?

Claire, Kazue and Max were waiting in the shade of the market hall. Some of the stalls were already empty, sold out. A man with a broom was sweeping the floor. He put the refuse in a bin on wheels.

Claire came running towards him. 'James? Did he say anything?'

He shook his head. 'Nothing, Claire. Some mixed up kid. A nut. That's all.'

Dejected, she climbed into the hot Chevrolet. She wanted to sit in the back. Max joined her, trying to comfort her.

'How was Caroline?' Kazue asked.

'She sends her love,' Max replied. 'She's very thin.'

'Did you ask when she'll be allowed out?' James wanted to know.

'I didn't want to ask. I thought she'd tell us if she knew.'

Out in the country, James recounted what he had learnt at the Questura. 'It's difficult to believe there's nothing behind it. I thought – I hoped – we had something.'

'Maybe it'll help put things in a new perspective?' Max suggested.

'I don't understand – '

'If he really is no more than a silly student, there could still be some kind of connection – at the university.'

'I've been through that already.' James was dismissive. 'The police should soon find out. Although – there's one thing – it just occurred to me.'

'What's that?'

'The kidnappers were young. The same age – I'm sure. The way they moved. Their bodies. And their hands. They were young. Clean. They didn't look like the hands of people who have to work with them.'

At Terrarossa, they found that Anna had been awaiting them anxiously. From the *carabinieri* she had heard that something had happened to James in Siena. James wished he did not have to recount the events again. When he had finished he felt tired, drained. His voice was hoarse.

Nineteen

FROM THE KITCHEN, James went to the study, to write the notes he meant to send to the dead *carabinieri*'s wives. He intended to write simply, saying how sorry he felt that their husbands had died when they had been trying to save his children.

He found the task difficult. It was rare that he had to write in Italian. He was afraid both of being either too colloquial or too impersonal, thus showing no compassion. The two letters had to be different. Not – so he felt – because the families might show them to each other. It would have been undignified – cheap even – to attempt a short cut of that kind.

He recalled the pictures of the two men and under them the captions, giving their names – surnames first, Christian names second – as they had been published in the newspapers. Pictures of men he had never met – and yet whose lives, now over, had touched on those of his children for a short, fatal span of only minutes.

Both men had been young, married, had had children. He wondered whether their wives and mothers were blaming him for what had happened? If he had never come to Terrarossa?

He wrote several drafts, consulting his dictionaries many times.

He was about to write out his final clean copies when Claire knocked on the door.

'Can I make you some tea?' she asked.

'Thank you.' He was glad to see her active. 'I'll come and help you.' He replaced the cap on his fountain pen. He got up and pushed the chair under the writing table. They went to the kitchen. He filled the electric kettle and switched it on. 'It's still the same house,' she said. 'But you've done a lot of work on it.'

'Do you like it?'

'I think so. What were you writing?'

'The notes – to the *carabinieri*'s wives.'

She gave a feeble nod. 'I remember you saying something – '

The water began to boil. He could not find the tea pot.

'I think – Kazui may have taken it, out to the pool,' she said.

'Kazue,' he corrected her. 'There's one downstairs. I'll get it.'

He made the tea and they sat down by the kitchen table.

'That's something we used to do.' She pointed at some pink and blue viper's bugloss Max had arranged around some tall stems of fennel, in a painted *maiolica* vase. 'Have you taught the children?'

'Emma's been trying. I'm not sure she's got an eye for it. Not yet. Like Thomas she's much more interested in pressing flowers.'

James poured the tea. Silent for a while, they began to sip it, each of them alone in their memories of the house when they had still been married. When Claire had spotted it – advertised for rent – in the Personal Columns of *The Times*. Later, when they had bought it, with a little money James had inherited from his uncle.

Claire got up and walked to the single window facing east. 'I've been looking out over the hills. All the time, I want to look for them, out there. It's a strange thought – somewhere – as my eyes travel over the landscape – they also look at the place where they are hidden.' She came back to the centre of the room. 'If only I knew where to stop!'

'I have been thinking much the same.' Suddenly, he wanted to touch her hands. Out of his reach, thin, with nothing to do, they hung by her hips.

'I feel they're near. Maybe it's only because of what you told me. James, I want to be with them! Do you understand? I must look after them!'

'*Permesso?*' One of the guards stood in the door.

'What is it?' James jumped to his feet.

'A message from Colonel Amorini, sir. He will be here in half an hour, sir.'

'Is that the whole message?'

'*Sissignore*, that is all!' The *carabiniere* saluted, turned, was gone.

White, Claire stared at James. 'Do you think – '

'I don't know! He did say he'd come,' he cut her short. 'I had better go and finish my letters. I was hoping he'd take them.'

He forced himself to sit down in the study. With trembling fingers, he completed the notes and sealed them in two envelopes. From the newspapers, he had noted the wives' names. Suddenly he realised that he did not know which letter each envelope contained. He addressed two fresh envelopes. He tore open the first envelopes, took out the letters and reinserted them in the freshly addressed ones. He thought the Colonel would not mind passing them on for him. He went outside. The half hour was almost over.

Pacing up and down by the pool, he listened for the first sound of the Colonel's approaching car.

A flapping, beating noise came from the far side of the hill. It grew harder, deafening. Out of the sun appeared the black silhouette of a helicopter. Slowly, it regained its colouring – navy and white – as it dropped to the darker background of the vineyeard, above the house.

On a cloud of spreading dust, the aircraft hovered over the gate. Its body swung round and it set down. The Colonel sat next to the pilot. The rear seats were empty. The engine cut. The rotor blades slowed.

James glanced over his shoulder. Claire had come out of the house. Behind her, Kazue and Anna stood in the door. Only Max was missing – he had gone out, to draw.

'A *surprise!*' James shook the Colonel's hand. 'I expected you to come by car.'

The Colonel looked back, as though he wanted to be sure the pilot would not hear him. 'I much prefer cars. They tell me this machine is more convenient. Occasionally it saves time. This is chiefly a social visit.'

James took a deep breath. He felt relief yet – at the same time – also disappointment. Confusingly, he experienced both feelings together.

'I wish we could have met under less distressing circumstances, *signora!*' The Colonel bowed deeply to kiss Claire's hand.

James invited the officer to the sitting room. He thought he had better offer drinks. Claire declined. After a moment's hesitation, the Colonel asked for some Scotch.

'How do you take it?'

'With soda – and ice, please. I know!' Defensively, he raised his hands. 'I went to Scotland a few years ago, on holiday. Here it's too warm to drink it the way they do there – '

'Don't worry. You're safe here – whatever you do to it! I don't even like the stuff. Despite my mixed ancestry.' James left the room to get some ice.

82

The Colonel turned to Claire. 'My English is terrible, nonexistent.' He pronounced the English words carefully, pausing between them. 'Do you speak Italian, Mrs Rudd?'

'I used to be able to follow what was being said. I found that to speak Italian well is much more difficult than most people believe. Colonel: do you think the kidnappers would let me join my children? If I gave myself up, as an additional hostage? To look after the children?'

Surprised, the Colonel sat up. He considered. 'I don't think so, *signora*. I cannot believe they would accept such a proposal. I'm afraid they already have all they need. They would only have to hide and guard you as well.'

'Are you sure?'

'Quite sure, *signora*. Just think: how could they trust you? Or us, for that matter? They would suspect a trap. For example you could have a radio on you.'

James returned with a small bowl of ice and a bottle of mineral water. On a sideboard, he poured the whisky. He handed the glass to the visitor. 'Will you tell me how much water?'

The Colonel put the drink on a pillar table by his arm. He moved slowly, with deliberation. Carefully, he placed the tumbler in the exact centre of the round table top. He looked up. 'Sachetti – the man you stopped this morning – still insists he knows nothing. Nothing at all. He is an extreme Communist. He dislikes foreigners. He is sticking to that. This afternoon, *La Nazione* – one of our newspapers, *signora* – received a telephone call from a woman. She claimed the same: Sachetti is innocent. Having said that, she threatened there would be trouble – unless he was released tonight! I thought I had better tell you as quickly as possible, before you hear it elsewhere.'

'What kind of trouble?' James was alarmed. 'Will you let him go?'

'It's not the *carabinieri*! The police hold him! I have no authority in the matter. As for the threat – the woman did not say what would happen. However, if Sachetti really has nothing to do with the kidnapping, the threat cannot possibly affect your children. I think this is obvious. Nevertheless, I wanted to point it out, to spare you – I hope! – the additional worry. Altogether, the whole thing makes little sense –'

'But do you, Colonel, believe he knows nothing?' James cut him short.

'My opinion is he knows either nothing or only very little. Very little. I hope to see him myself tomorrow.'

James shook his head. 'Did you understand, Claire?'

'I think so. Roughly.'

For a short while, they sat in silence. The freshening evening breeze fanned one of the French windows, which – open but not fastened – gave onto the balcony. The Colonel put down his drink. 'I believe we shall hear very soon now from the kidnappers. The Sachetti incident may prompt them. Of course, if Sachetti knows something after all they may well try to silence him.'

'Kill him?' James asked.

'If they can get to him.'

James got to his feet. He paced up and down, stopped, sat down again. 'If there is trouble – what could it be?'

'I believe that's an empty threat. In any case, what are we to do?'

'Do you believe – they are members of the Red Brigades?' At last, James had asked the question.

'They may be.' The Colonel shot an uneasy glance at Claire. 'I fear they are no ordinary criminals. The way they ambushed our men is something you learn in the army – or abroad, where they train terrorists. Nevertheless, they almost bungled the abduction. The planning was poor.'

'I have been thinking the same,' James agreed. 'They must have meant to take all of the children. And Caroline.'

'Of course – '

'Colonel, do you believe the children are in the mountains? Around here?' Claire asked suddenly.

'I think so – now. We have no evidence at all, *signora*, that they left the area.'

James had not heard the Colonel's earlier exchange with Claire. He realised that the officer understood – probably also spoke – English.

'The man on the roof.' The Colonel turned to James. 'At the Palio. We interviewed your assistant in Rome.'

'What did she say?'

'Basically – I understand – that she saw less even than you. She never looked through the viewfinder. Where's the cameraman?'

'In Norway. He's working for someone else.'

The Colonel looked unhappy. 'Are you absolutely sure he didn't film the man?'

'Absolutely. I saw the rushes. Every single frame we got. Francesca saw them too. Glyn never filmed the man.'

The Colonel smacked his thighs. 'A pity! Just think! We have pictures in our files. We could have tried to compare them.' He pulled out an oldfashioned fob watch. Its gold lid sprang back. 'I must go. I have another meeting.' He got up. 'Before I forget! The *signorina* Ceccarelli gave us a message for you. She has cancelled her holiday. She will come back as soon as she is finished in Rome.'

Quickly, James went to the study and got the letters. He explained what they were. Maybe a little surprised, the Colonel took them. Claire rose. The officer kissed her hand. James took him to the front door. The sun was about to drop behind the vineyard above the house.

'I will deliver the letters tomorrow. At the funeral. Thank you for writing them.' The Colonel descended the steps and walked up the drive towards the helicopter. One of his men opened the door for him.

Watching the aircraft rise over the road, James suddenly thought of Pasquale. Was he back? Anna would know.

She was with Claire, helping to transfer her things to the room David and Suzanne had been staying in.

'Anna, is Pasquale back?'

'He must be. I heard the tractor – '

'He's back? Why didn't you tell me? Did he say anything?'

'I have not seen him, *signor* James! I only heard the tractor. A short while ago. The *signorina* Kazue went to look.'

James nodded, slowly, as if it was difficult to understand what he had just heard. Distractedly, he eyed Claire. 'Do you prefer this room?'

She stopped, her hands in her bag. 'I thought – I felt – I shouldn't be occupying one of the children's rooms.' She could not say that in Thomas' room she had felt as though she had taken it from him for ever.

'Of course. I understand.' He backed to the door. 'I'll go and see Pasquale. I'll be back soon.' He turned and rushed upstairs. It did not occur to him to ask Claire whether she would have liked to have come with him.

Twenty

DESPITE HIS IMPATIENCE – and because it would keep him busy for longer – James decided to walk rather than take the car to Anna and Pasquale's house. All the way round the ravine, he listened for the tractor. He could not hear it. A thought struck him. What if it was a trap? Anna had heard the tractor. She had said that she had not seen it. From the house, she could not possibly have done so. Nor had she seen Pasquale, of course. Kazue had gone out to meet him. Had the tractor noise been devised to lure some one from the house?

He tried to rid himself of the thought. It was far-fetched, fantastic even. Nevertheless, was it not wiser to be careful? Should he go back and tell the guards of his suspicion?

It was an idea, not a suspicion. He had to go on. He accelerated his step. Afraid, suddenly, for Kazue, he ran. Heedlessly, he dashed downhill.

He stopped where the track came out into the open. The house and its outbuildings looked as they always did on a sunny evening. The open yard between them was tidy as usual. From afar, it was not possible to see whether Pasquale's van was parked in its shed or not.

Again, he tried to listen. His pulse pounded in his throat. He heard his own rasping breath. He saw the donkeys, grazing near their usual place. Undisturbed, heads down, they tore into the lush grass under the olive trees.

He got off the track. Across the open slope – well away from the house – he aimed to describe a descending half circle, down to the far top of the vineyard. There, if attacked, it would be easier to escape. He would let himself roll, down the steep rows of vines. There were olive trees at the bottom. Around them, the grass was always deep. If necessary, he would find easy cover there. He would be able to cut back, through the ravine finally, to his own house.

Scanning the sunburnt slopes around, he advanced. A dull,

mustard yellow, they gave off some of the heat they had soaked up earlier. Dust and the scent of dry grass rose in his nostrils. Underfoot, the parched blades rustled. He slipped. On his side, he slid until he grabbed hold of a clump of hogweed or some other similarly tall stems.

His heels found a footing. He pushed himself off the slope. More slowly, choosing where he placed his step, he got down to the vineyard, near its uppermost, west corner.

He looked down.

He looked across.

Level with him, in the far corner, Pasquale stood listening to Kazue. The tractor, nose up, stuck out from the vines just below them. Kazue was about to finish her description of what had happened in Siena, in the morning.

Pasquale spotted James. He waved his hat. Kazue turned. They watched him approach. A curious look was in Pasquale's deep eyes. For a moment, they rested on his side, which was still dirty from the fall.

James was in no mood to give the half expected explanation. 'I didn't know you'd come back! We had a visit from Colonel Amorini. How was your trip?'

'All right, thank you. I covered the ground.'

'And – did you find your friends well?' Awkward, unsure what to ask, he put the question.

'One of them had died. In the winter. It's a shame! Nobody had told me!' Pasquale's voice rose just a little. Immediately, James assumed the man must have been of importance: another possible source of help in the recovery of the children now lost.

'Two were not at home.' Pasquale went on. 'I talked to their sons.'

'You mean – you talked also to the dead man's son?'

'I did.'

'Will they help us?'

'They will. If they can. We shall have to be patient.' Pasquale paused. 'You must not let your hopes rise too high! The *signorina* tells me of that man – Sachetti. Do you know where he's from?'

'Carpignalle,' James promptly recalled, somewhat to his own surprise. 'At least, that's what I think he told the police.'

Pasquale shook his head. 'I don't know any Sachetti. Not up there.'

'You mean – you don't know any Sachetti anywhere? Or not up

there?'

'I'm not sure I've come across the name. Not here. Not there.'

'What did the Colonel say?' Kazue asked.

'No progress.' James shrugged. 'But a woman phoned *La Nazione*. This afternoon. She said there'd be trouble if Sachetti wasn't released by tonight!'

'What kind?'

'She didn't say. The Colonel seems inclined to think it's just a threat. The woman said Sachetti has nothing to do with the kidnapping.'

'In that case,' Pasquale interjected, 'the threat doesn't concern Emma or Tommaso. It's against the police, I suppose.'

'That's more or less what the Colonel seems to think,' James confirmed.

Pasquale looked at the sky. 'I should watch out a little, nevertheless. The weather may break again. It's been very hot.'

'The Colonel really seems to believe now the children are still around here.' James ignored the change of subject.

'That's good!' Pasquale gave an encouraging smile. 'That improves our chances!'

'If your friends hear anything – how shall we know?' James asked.

'They will send a message.'

'Will they really do that? Or should you go and ask again?'

'They will send a message. You can be sure.'

Pasquale brought the conversation back to the vineyard. Only a few days ago James had asked him whether it could have been extended on one side. The idea had been to plant some *colorino* grapes. Occasionally they are added to the other varieties traditionally used to make Chianti.

'I asked one of my friends for advice,' Pasquale said. 'He would let us have some vines – good ones! – if we want them. I can do the terracing in winter. We'll have to hire a machine.'

James suddenly looked very dejected. 'It may not be mine any more! Have you not thought of that?'

'We have!' Squarely, Pasquale looked his landlord in the eye. 'But we don't believe it, *signor* James. You are here for good. You belong here, with us! Don't you feel it? In your heart?'

On the way back to the house, James began to think about what Pasquale had said at the end. Later, unable to rid himself of the subject, he talked to Kazue about it. Did Pasquale know something already that he had not told?

Kazue guessed he did not. At the same time, she felt – and said so – that Pasquale had spoken from a deeply held conviction which, although emotive, nevertheless was based also on experience and, therefore, was likely to prove right.

James knew that there would have been no point in pressing Pasquale for an answer he had not volunteered in the first place. Besides, he was inclined to agree with Kazue's interpretation. He decided that in the morning he would return to the vineyard to work there. That way he would also be close to Pasquale. In his dreams, which seemed to fill the short periods when he was not lying awake, Pasquale's remark kept turning over and over, painfully, changing shape all the time, giving, allowing no relief at all.

Twenty-one

'THE HELICOPTER!'

The children! Something had happened to them! Frenzied, James' imagination reacted to the aircraft's sudden noise as he yelled out the words. He ripped off his straw hat. Tossing the pruning shears inside, he threw it to the ground. On all fours, he clambered to the top of the vineyard.

'I'm taking the van!' he shouted to Pasquale.

Further down on the slope, Kazue realised that she could not keep up with her friend. Breathless, she stood and watched his frantic climb.

The helicopter was still in the air when he reversed the van out of its shed. Instantly frustrated by the vehicle's lack of power, he set off up the track. At last he reached its end. From the road, he saw the Colonel pass through the gate. People – mainly reporters – milled round the officer, trying to stop him, without success.

The *carabinieri* cleared the way for James. The reporters recognised him. They began to shout. They hammered on the roof of the passing van. In the rush he had not rolled down his window despite the midday heat. 'The children! Your children!' he thought he heard them shout.

'I'm here!'

Ashen, out of breath, he found the Colonel in the sitting room, standing by the window. Anna had left the visitor there.

The officer, in a dark uniform he had not seen before, bowed.

Claire had entered behind James. He had not heard her. Anna had gone to get her.

The Colonel pulled an envelope from his jacket. He opened it.

'I have brought this!' He put a photograph on the sideboard next to him.

Claire darted across the room.

The picture showed the children. It was a Polaroid. The *carabinieri* had wrapped it in cellophane.

Side by side – Emma on the left, Thomas on the right – the siblings sat on rough, upright chairs. Their hands lay on their knees, palms down. Wooden – eerie in their lack of all expression – they faced the observer. The flashlight had made their eyes look red, opaque, quite dead. Their cheeks were blotchy. Behind them, the front page of Tuesday's Communist newspaper *L'Unità* – little more than twenty-four hours old – had been pinned to the wall.

Claire picked up the picture. She held it at face height, as though she could have talked to her children through it. James peered over her shoulder.

'The television people in Florence received it this morning. A few hours ago. They also got a telephone call.'

The Colonel produced a piece of paper from the envelope. He unfolded it. He cleared his throat.

'The price for the children's release is two thousand million *lire* each. Grey has until Monday. For each day's delay, we will send him a finger. We will begin with the boy.'

Gasping, Claire began to sway.

James caught her by the shoulders. Gently, from the side, he helped her to a chair.

'Is that – is that the whole message?' he asked, still trying to comfort her.

'It is.'

'Four thousand million *lire*? By Monday? That's impossible!' Suddenly he shouted. 'It's not possible!'

'How much money is that, James?'

'More than two million pounds!'

'We don't have – '

'They expect you to negotiate, *signora*! Please believe me! All of these cases are settled for less than is asked. Some of them at mere fractions!'

'But how? What can we do? What are we to do now?'

Dazed, James heard her voice break with despair. Indeed, where were they to begin? How, practically, could they respond to the demand? Compared with what they would be able to offer, it was absurd. Yet it was potentially lethal, all the more so because they had no hope of meeting it as it stood.

'We must go to London, Claire,' he replied at last. 'It's too late today. Tomorrow we'll take the first plane. We'll get some money. As much as we can! Then we can negotiate.'

Disbelieving, she shook her head. She buried her face in her hands. The photograph fell to the floor.

James bent down to pick it up. Holding it, he shut his eyes. He put it on the sideboard, where the Colonel had put it first.

'I take it you are not insured?' the Colonel asked hesitantly.

'Insured against what? Kidnapping? I thought that had been made illegal, to stop the business. A long time ago!' James snapped.

'Mr Grey! We're in Italy! Of course, people still insure themselves against it. Mainly through London underwriters, I understand.'

James shrugged.

'You may wish to appoint someone,' the Colonel went on. 'To help you negotiate.'

James had heard of go-betweens. 'Anyone you know?'

'There are – lawyers. Let's call them that. And certain other people who claim to have experience in these matters.'

'So – you don't recommend – '

'I can't say I do! I merely want to remind you that such people exist. I am bound to warn you, most negotiations are extremely tortuous. Dangerous. Painful in every respect! I know of cases where the relatives suffered more than the hostages themselves. Ultimately, the relatives became the true victims. Just to make contact with the abductors can mean an endless drive along a prescribed route – for days and days, literally, all over the country – waiting, looking out for the signal. You may wish to save yourself at least from that. On the other hand – if you can face it – you may negotiate a much more favourable deal on your own.'

'Will you – would you advise us?'

'I will do what is in my power. Certainly.'

James nodded. 'I'll do it. I'll try. Don't you agree, Claire?'

'Yes.' Barely audible, she gave her approval.

'I must go!' The Colonel took the photograph from the sideboard. 'I missed the funeral itself. At least I must be there afterwards.'

'May I keep the picture?' Claire asked suddenly.

The Colonel was embarrassed. 'I'm afraid, *signora*, we still need it. We may be able to find out where the film was bought.'

'I see.' She bit her lip.

James took the Colonel to the kitchen. He did not want to show himself at the front door. From the noise at the gate he gathered that the number of reporters had increased.

'The deadline! It's not enough time! Will they really start to cut off – '

James did not finish his question. Deliberately, he had refrained from asking it in front of Claire.

'Unfortunately, it's not a very original threat, Mr Grey. It has been used – carried out, I'm afraid – more than once. How long will you need?'

'I called my lawyer yesterday. He has started work. But all we have left is tomorrow and Friday. The banks – everything in England shuts on Saturday!'

The Colonel had thought about the problem on his way to Terrarossa. 'Tomorrow you will be travelling. You are left with Friday only,' he corrected. 'I suggest this: we make a statement – after your departure. We say you are on your way to London to raise the ransom. That at least sounds positive. We'll say nothing at all about the amount itself. But we will point out the difficulties as regards time in detail: your need to travel so far, the weekend. They must understand that. They must accept that nobody can raise millions of pounds – that's the point: pounds, not *lire!* – in one single day! You agree?'

The plan sounded plausible. Eagerly, James accepted the proposal. 'Thank you! Thank you for taking so much interest! Without you I don't know what we'd do.'

The Colonel gave an embarrassed smile. 'Somebody else would help, I'm sure. In fact, several of my men are taking a very personal interest, Mr Grey. They want to help. Now – I wish you and Mrs Rudd a successful journey. Of course, we will continue to guard your house.'

James returned to the study.

Immobile, Claire sat on the same chair. Tears fell from her eyes. Behind the tears, her eyes stared through the open window, over the hills.

'Claire?'

She did not react.

The noise of the departing helicopter taking off made a carafe dance on a side table.

'At least we know the children are alive, Claire!'

'They'll kill them, James! We haven't got enough money!'

'We'll negotiate, Claire! I'm sure we'll satisfy them somehow.'

'Two million pounds! It's so much more than we have! On Monday, they'll cut off one of Thomas' fingers! Don't you understand? On Tuesday, one of Emma's!' She shut her eyes. 'I feel so sick, James!'

'The Colonel's going to ask for more time, Claire. We talked about it on the way out. He'll do it tomorrow. You've heard what he said. It's a matter of negotiation. They won't do anything as long as they believe they'll be paid. Everything here is subject to negotiation. You know that! Just remember when we bought this place. Please, believe me, Claire! Don't make yourself even more ill than you are already!'

He helped her up. Slowly, holding her tightly round the shoulders, he walked her downstairs.

'The Colonel didn't think they'd allow me to join the children. Can't I stay here? While you go to London?'

He opened her door. He had hoped she would come to London with him to help raise the ransom. He feared that alone, with only Anna and Max at Terrarossa, she might be more wretched still.

He shook his head.

'You must help me, Claire. We must go to London. Together!'

Twenty-two

JAMES KNOCKED ON Claire's door an hour later. Lightly, he tapped on the old pine panels. He waited. There was no answer.

He knocked. He heard only his own breath. Concerned, he entered.

'Claire? Can I do anything for you?'

She lay quite still.

Disturbed, he approached.

Her eyes were open.

'Can I get you something?'

She shook her head.

Carefully, he sat down on the edge of the bed. 'I must go to Siena, to get us on the plane tomorrow. Kazue's going back with us. She returns to Japan on Monday. I'll be calling Richard. Shall I ask him to give a message to Tony? That we're coming?'

'I want to stay here,' she whispered.

'You must come, Claire! It'll help you to be with Tony.'

'I can't ask him for money. He's got his own children. I must stay here!'

'Asking him for money's not the point! There's nothing for us to do! Not here, not anywhere. Not until we have some money! Only then will we be able to begin!'

She remained silent. Her eyes were dry now.

'I'll call on Caroline if there's enough time. Would you like to come with me?'

She shook her head.

'Don't let this destroy you, Claire. The children will need you when they're back. Whole!'

'I – I'm fighting – I'm trying to convince myself – I want to believe they'll be back. But I can't! I can't!' Sobbing, she buried her face in the pillows.

'We *will* get them back! You mustn't doubt it, Claire! We *will*! We'll lose them only if we don't believe we can succeed. You must hope!'

'How can you be so sure?' Screaming, she sat up. 'Because you brought them here? Lost them?'

'What do you mean?' Stung, he jumped to his feet. '*I* lost them? If you hadn't left me, you would have been looking after them yourself!' he shouted. 'It could have happened anywhere! There's danger everywhere!'

'Danger? Not this kind of danger! Only in Italy could such a thing have happened! And you know it!'

'Why didn't you object to them coming here, then? You know as well as I do nothing like this has ever happened here before! Especially not to foreigners!'

He stormed from the room. He slammed the door behind him.

'James? Why are you so angry?' Alarmed, Kazue tried to stop him in the kitchen.

Pretending not to take any notice of what was going on, Anna continued to roll out some dough on the *pasta* slab.

'She blames me now! It's my fault! All my fault!'

He shut himself in his study. Drained, he paced up and down for a long time until he had recovered his composure. From the writing table, he picked up the list of telephone calls and errands he had jotted down before he had gone to see Claire. He went outside.

Kazue did not want to accompany him. She thought it would be better to leave him alone.

The reporters were still at the gate.

Unable to pass, he stopped the wagon and rolled down his window.

'Mr Grey, we hear the ransom is two thousand million for each child. Are you prepared to pay that much?'

'We will pay.'

'But how much? That's a different question. Can you pay that much?'

'I'm not prepared to answer your question. No comment.'

'Will you be going to London?'

James recognised the questioner. He was one of the London journalists who had asked for exclusivity.

'We will. In due course.'

'When is that?'

'I don't know. Not yet. Now I'd be grateful if you let me pass. I have some urgent business in Florence.'

Ignoring all further questions, he put the car into gear and let it roll forward. The guards cleared the exit. In the rear mirror he saw the reporters getting into their own cars. He accelerated to the brow of the hill where he disappeared from their sight. Before they could see him again, he had turned into the side road, through the hills to Siena.

Claire stayed in her room for the rest of the day. She could not bring herself to join the others for supper.

Taking up less than a quarter of its seats, James sat with Kazue and Max at the kitchen table. Anna had taken a tray of food to Claire's room before she had left for her own house.

'Are you sure? You really don't mind if I stay on, James?' Max asked.

James started. 'No. No. Not at all. In fact, I'm really quite glad you're staying. I'd be grateful if you could go and visit Caroline once or twice. I wasted such a lot of time at the telephone office, I never got round to seeing her.'

'Of course. I'll be glad to. When are you leaving?'

'We must leave at noon. I want to leave the car in Pisa rather than at the airport.'

'You must not get so angry with Claire,' Kazue said to James when they were alone.

'I know. I'm angry with myself now for losing my temper. It's just – from the beginning I felt as if she thought I had no right to grieve. Maybe it's because I feel so guilty – '

'You're not guilty, James! She can't really think that. She has the children most of the time. And you *are* divorced. These things are bound to influence the way she feels.'

'I hadn't thought of it that way. You may be right. Still, if both of us let all our fears take over, what could we hope to achieve then?'

'That's true. You must hope.'

'I have hope! Although – last night after you'd gone to sleep, thinking about what Pasquale had said – I hardly dared to shut my eyes in case it went away. Hope is so elusive. Yet, without it, everything I'm living on collapses. Without hope – what is there to hold on to?'

Twenty-three

THUNDER ROLLED IN the distance for most of the night. At daybreak, rain began to fall. It spread over the hills from the north. Its constant, splashing sound awoke James before five.

Unable to sleep any longer, he slipped from the bed. Carefully, he covered Kazue with the thin quilt which had slipped to the floor.

In the grey morning light, he looked at the reflection of his face in the bathroom mirror. The stitches in his eyebrow had gone. The cut was still visible. Deep rings lay under his eyes. His cheek bones and nose appeared more prominent than usual. He had lost weight. He switched on the light. Quickly, he shaved and showered. In his kimono – a gift Kazue had brought – he went to the study.

From the various stacks of papers on the writing table, he prepared a list of things for Francesca to do. The second *Palio* was only three weeks away: equipment had to be hired; arrangements had to be made for travel and accommodation of the film crew; new camera positions needed to be negotiated with the owners of stands and houses in the Campo.

He heard Anna arrive at seven. In the kitchen, he asked whether Pasquale had received a message by any chance, in the afternoon or evening?

Anna shook her head. 'It's still early days, *signor* James! It may still come! These things take time!'

Max came up the stair.

'I would like to buy one of these.' He pointed at Anna's umbrella which, wide open and green, lay on the brick floor. Its wooden handle, thick and red, stuck in the air.

'I don't think you'll need one,' James said. 'It's lighter already.'

'What do you mean? The rain or the light?'

James was disconcerted for a moment. He did not see the mild joke his friend had attempted. 'Both,' he replied curtly.

'Claire seems asleep still,' Max said, taking no offence. 'She was in an awful state last night.'

'Did you speak to her?'

'I tried to, twice, I told her you must help each other – not fight. She's got to go to London with you.'

By nine, the rain had stopped. A few minutes later, one of the guards called James to the radio. As he stepped outside, he saw that a number of reporters had gathered at the gate.

'We have lost Sachetti,' the Colonel opened the conversation.

'Lost him?'

'Exactly! He jumped through a window, approximately one hour ago. My men could not keep up with him. They lost him.'

'But – that's awful! I had hopes – '

'I know. I'm sorry! He was about to be questioned again. He obviously did not enjoy his interviews. I am telling you so that you don't hear it from others first.'

Despondent, James looked at the reporters. He was almost certain they had heard of the escape. Why would they have come otherwise?

'We may catch him again while you're away,' the Colonel went on. 'We have your number in London. I'll call you if anything significant happens.'

James faced the reporters. Their first question confirmed that they had been told.

'Mr Grey, are you concerned about Sachetti's escape?' The journalist was from an Italian paper.

'Of course I am!'

'Did you think he was connected?'

'I don't know. I was waiting for the police – or the *carabinieri* – to find out.'

'The fact that he escaped: does that not make it more likely that he was connected with the kidnap?'

'Possibly. But what did he know? To me, that would have been the important question.'

'Are you afraid he might try to take his revenge on you?'

James shrugged. 'If he connects, I don't think he'll want to kill the golden goose. At least, not until the ransom has been paid. If he's innocent, he'll probably prefer to stay well clear. It's the children – only the children – I fear for.'

James noticed one of the London reporters who had asked for

99

exclusivity. All the while during his exchange with the Italian journalist, the British contingent had been trying to get their questions answered.

'We have been asked about granting a newspaper exclusivity,' James said, raising his voice so he could be heard by all. 'If anyone wants to bid for the exclusive rights to what Mrs Rudd or I may have to say from now on, they should contact my lawyer in London.' He gave Richard Hall's name and address.

'When will you be going to London, Mr Grey?'

'Will Mrs Rudd be staying here?'

'We shall see,' James said and walked away.

'Today, Mr Grey?'

He ignored the callers. He had barely reached the house when he heard the first cars start. Sachetti's escape at least had the benefit of drawing the reporters back to Siena. But what, he asked himself, did it mean?

He looked for Max. The painter was in the loggia, sorting out his drawings, having laid them out on the floor.

'Sachetti escaped. I just heard.'

'He escaped? How?'

'The *carabinieri* let him jump through a window. It's a bloody scandal!'

'I thought that only happened *deliberately*.'

'What do you mean?'

'When they throw them out. To get rid of them.'

James was well aware of his friend's deep mistrust of the police, of anyone, in fact, who wore a uniform. 'I think you had better watch out during the next few days,' he said, steering away from the contentious remark. 'Be careful, especially when you go out.'

'You don't think he'd attack us?'

'I don't know, Max. There was something strange – crazy – about him. It worries me. I'll talk to Pasquale before we go.'

James went inside. He knocked on Claire's door.

She sat at the dressing table, fastening back her hair.

'Are you ready?' he asked. 'I'd like to leave as soon as I've been to see Pasquale. Sachetti jumped from a window.'

'Is he dead?'

'He ran away. He escaped.'

'Escaped? Had they found out anything?'

'I gather not.'

100

'Do you think – ?'

'I have no idea!' he cut her short. 'Nobody seems to know anything any more. Did you sleep?'

'A little. I knocked myself out in the end. James, I'm sorry about what I said yesterday. I don't mean to blame you.' Embarrassed, she turned a hair-grip in her fingers.

'It's all right.' He tried to smile. 'I understand. I'll go and see Pasquale quickly. Then we can leave.' Even more ill at ease than she, he retreated.

Pasquale was putting the donkeys out to grass when James arrived at his house. Their long reins gathered in either hand, he led the animals towards the olive grove.

'You were right about the weather. Are they well?' James pointed at Pasta and Eeyore.

'They are. They'll be a little stronger by the time the children are back.'

'Anna says you have still not heard anything.'

'Not yet.'

'Sachetti escaped. A couple of hours ago. I'm afraid he may turn up here.'

'I'll watch out then. When will you be back?'

James gave a despondent, helpless shake of the head. 'Monday night – I hope. But I doubt it. The weekend is the problem.'

'Townsfolk! I suppose nothing makes them work!' Pasquale held out his hand. 'I wish you a safe and speedy return.'

Pensive, James drove back to the house. Pasquale's quiet confidence was indeed food for thought. Should he accept it as more than that?

Claire and Kazue waited with their packed bags in the kitchen. Anna had made some coffee for them. Max sat at the table. He was arranging a bunch of wild flowers he had picked a little earlier.

'Can you drop me off in Siena?' he asked. 'I'd like to visit Caroline.'

'I wanted to avoid the town,' James replied, not meaning to refuse.

'I'll take the bus then. Don't worry! I rather like watching the locals.'

'You know?' Unexpectedly, Claire broke her usual silence. 'When she was a child nobody told her any stories. She loves telling them.'

'Caroline?' Max asked.

'Yes. Caroline. She had a most unhappy childhood. Apparently, her parents thought stories were out of date.'

'That reminds me,' James interjected. 'Did you speak to her father?'

'Tony got hold of him in the end. I told her. He didn't seem very perturbed.'

James put the bags in the Chevrolet. Anna and Max came outside to say goodbye. A few minutes after eleven – considerably earlier than he had planned – James set off with Claire and Kazue. The sky was clear again and luminous, its blue lighter and more brilliant than it had been on previous days. Grey, dissolving, a few last clouds drifted over the valley.

'We should have a clear view today,' James said as they climbed towards the top of the long ridge which stretched to the north from Terrarossa. A little used road ran along it towards Castellina, partly in the open, then plunging again into dense woods.

'There's Siena!' Kazue pointed from the back seat over James' shoulder. Brick red and brown – burnt sienna in fact – the ancient city lay spread over its three hills in the distance. Gently, it curved from many ragged sides towards the highest point, the dome and bell tower of the cathedral. Pointing out the Palazzo Pubblico – the old town hall – and the location of the Campo, the Torre del Mangia stood thin but clearly visible among the many other towers.

'I remember.' Claire could not accept the beauty of the picture.

They descended to Castellina, went on to San Donato and joined the fast road to Florence. They arrived at the garage near the centre of Pisa in good time. Kazue found a taxi while James spoke to the parking attendant. At the airport, a British Airways Trident was being refuelled. James checked in. They were waved through customs. A stewardess waited for them on the air side. 'We're keeping the first row for you,' she said. 'If you don't mind, we'd like to board you last. So you can keep quite separate.'

The plane, the first of the day to London, was almost full. Soon after takeoff, the captain sent his compliments, asking whether there was anything he could do. James asked if it would be possible to avoid going through the arrivals hall at Heathrow.

'Have you thought about the ransom?' Claire asked James.

'Have I thought about it? I've been doing sums all night! The longer I do them, the more I wonder how long it's all going to take.'

'I imagine – you have a little more now than when we separated?'

102

'Most of it went into the house. And that, I'm afraid, isn't exactly saleable after what's happened.'

Kazue slipped across the aisle to sit on the other side where there were two empty seats.

'It all depends on how much I can borrow. I only hope some friendly banker believes in my continuing success as a producer. I needn't tell you there's less in it than most people believe.'

'What about David?'

'He's offered to help. Basically, he's the wrong kind of banker. He deals with multinationals – not individuals.'

'He *was* involved!' Claire insisted.

'Sure. That's why he offered to help. I'll call him on Saturday. He said he'd expect my call then.'

The stewardess offered drinks, tea or coffee. They asked for coffee. They fell silent.

Through the loudspeaker system, the first officer pointed out Mont Blanc.

'I don't know what Tony's going to say,' Claire said.

'I'm sorry for him. He must be wondering what to do. I know, he has his own children. On the other hand, you're his wife!'

'It's awful he should be drawn into it.' She paused. 'He's very fond of Thomas – and Emma – although she's quite unpleasant to him at times.'

'I didn't know!' Surprised, James turned to her. 'Do you think he'll want to help? When he married you, did he accept that the children would be living with you?'

'He did. Nevertheless, it's – oh – I – I just don't know what it'll do to our relationship!' She closed her eyes tightly, biting her lip.

'Are you – are you two having problems?'

She gave a faint nod, her eyes still shut.

'I'm sorry, Claire.' For an instant, he touched the back of her hand.

'Mummy can't help,' she said after a while. 'She only has her cottage. It's horrifying what inflation's doing to the pension Daddy left her with!'

'I wish I had rich parents! I really do!'

'You always did.'

'True. But now – we could *really* use them!'

James' parents had died in the war, when he had been only a few months old. An uncle, on his father's side and now also dead, had

103

attempted to bring him up. Finally, he had spent most of his early years in boarding schools, each more disastrous than the one before.

'I've come to the conclusion that if we can raise ten per cent of the money — we'll be lucky,' he said quietly.

'Ten per cent! Is that all?'

'That's all.'

She began to cry.

'Do you realise that to borrow a hundred thousand pounds costs at least twenty thousand a year in interest? Where's it all to come from?'

The stewardess announced that they were about to begin their descent into Heathrow. James looked out. The sky was quite clear. Automatically, he tightened his seat belt and returned the back of the seat to its upright position. He looked at Claire's. She had never moved it.

An assistant ground manager met them at the gate. James realised as he stepped from the plane that he had no recollection of any of the passengers. He wondered whether they had recognised him or Claire, if they knew what had happened at Terrarossa.

They were shown to one of the special suites in Terminal One usually reserved for VIPs. A porter brought Kazue's case a few minutes later. Two officers, one from immigration, the other a customs man, entered. They only glanced at the passports offered and left again. James asked for a taxi. Soon a black cab pulled up outside. James noticed the inquisitive look as the driver held open the car door for his new passengers.

On the M4, the traffic out of London had already begun its build-up towards the evening peak. On the Hammersmith flyover, the cars in the two westbound lanes crawled along at walking speed.

The taxi dropped Claire outside her home on Campden Hill.

'I'll telephone you in the morning,' James called, watching her unlock the door.

The remaining part of the journey, to Covent Garden, took longer than it had taken from Heathrow to Claire's house. The rush hour traffic had reached its peak. Silent, James and Kazue watched it flow past. At Hyde Park Corner, they were stationary for some twenty minutes.

The driver slid aside the glass division. 'When we get out of this mess, which way to you want me to go, guv?'

'I don't mind. Whatever you think best. I'd go down the Mall, through Trafalgar Square, then up Charing Cross Road.'

The partition slid shut.

At last they got to Neal Street. James pointed out an old brick warehouse. Its top floor had been converted into his flat. Through the open window, the driver reached back and opened the door for Kazue. James got out on the other side. He took her case from the front compartment and walked round to the driver.

'How much?' he asked.

'I'm not taking any money today. Not from you. I wish you and the children the very best of luck!' The cabbie let in the clutch. Clattering, the taxi drove off.

Twenty-four

'It's MEASLES! You've caught measles! Look!' Eagerly, Emma pulled aside the dirty collar of her little brother's shirt. 'Spots!'

'I can't see!' The voice was thin. Tears burst from his drowsy eyes. Streaming, they wet his blotchy cheeks. His nose ran even more than it had done before this outburst, the fifth if not sixth of the afternoon.

'You mustn't worry, Tommy!' She buttoned his shirt up again, including the collar. 'I had measles two years ago, remember?'

'I don't,' he whimpered. 'I'm not going to die, am I?'

'Of course not!' Emma realised how frightened he was. 'I didn't die, did I? Nobody dies of measles! All I remember is it's best not to read anything when you have measles. Mummy kept the curtains shut even during the day. Silly darling!' Patting him, she pulled the blanket to his chin.

'I'm cold. We haven't got anything to read anyway.'

Dragging shackled ankles, she shuffled over the stone floor. By the glassless window, her own blanket hung over a rough, upright chair. The woman had put it there to dry. The thunderstorm, which had made the roof of the old mill drip in the morning, had soaked it.

Supporting herself on one hand and arm, Emma reached to feel the blanket.

'It's still damp, Tommy. You'll catch a chill if I put it on you.'

'I've got a chill!' Suddenly, his teeth chattered. 'I'm cold!'

Emma pulled on the blanket. The chair toppled. Crashing, it hit the floor.

'Ma che succede?'

Threatening by her very stance to hand out yet more of her painful cuffs on cheeks and ears the woman stood in the door.

'Thomas has measles!'

106

Silent, the woman advanced. A flick of the wrist ripped the blanket from Emma's hand.

'Thomas is ill! He's cold! *Freddo!*'

The woman turned. Distaste – hate – darkened her narrow face. The blanket dropped to the floor. Suddenly, she lashed out. Blows rained down on Emma's head. Crying out loud – piercing the roar of the mill stream, which rushed past under the window – she fell to the floor.

'*Fermati!*'

Barba pulled the woman back. Angry, he shook her by the shoulders. He pushed her, towards the door.

'Okay?' Barba bent over the sobbing girl.

'I've got measles!' In his corner, Thomas was sitting up.

'He is ill!' Emma pushed herself up from the floor.

Barba was not sure he understood. He knew that the little boy had been crying for most of the afternoon.

'He needs a doctor!' Emma pleaded. She sniffed. 'I know he's got measles! I had them myself.'

Barba held out a handkerchief.

Hesitant, Emma took it. 'He's got spots. On his chest.' She pointed to the place on her body. 'Spots. Have a look!'

With uncertain fingers – while the woman stood sullenly in the door – Barba undid the small buttons on Thomas' shirt. Frightened, fighting to hold back his tears, the little boy looked up at his captor's suddenly concerned expression. Emma came shuffling across the room to watch the examination.

Barba puffed up his cheeks. He had understood. His big hand covered Thomas' forehead.

'I'm cold.'

'*Freddo?*'

Thomas tried to nod. The strain made his head hurt.

Barba got up. He crossed the room and picked up the blanket. Instantly, he felt its dampness.

'No good!' he growled, righting the chair. He threw the blanket over it.

'He's cold. He has a temperature!' Emma insisted. 'We must keep him warm!'

'*Ho capito!*' Barba gave a nod. 'I return!'

Making the woman go in front of him, he left the room.

107

Twenty-five

'THAT OFFICER — the Colonel as you call him — we saw him on the box. Twice, I think. He seemed perfectly sure of what needed to be done. Are you saying he's not competent?'

'I don't know, Tony! James thinks highly of him. I'm not convinced. I can't make him out. He always agrees with James. Nothing can be done! Not until we have some money! They ignore the deadline!'

Tony Rudd got up to make himself a second drink. His wife's intense — feverish, he thought — account of her time at Terrarossa had alarmed him. Several times she had implied that no one — apart from her — was taking sufficient interest in the children's return.

'They're bound to take it seriously, Claire,' he objected. 'But, of course, what else can they do but try to win extra time? The kidnappers are in a very strong position as long as they hold the children.'

Tony's younger son entered. Tall, with the powerful frame of a rugby fullback — his father's spitting image — he bent over Claire and kissed her on both cheeks. 'I'll be back by eleven,' he said to Tony and was gone.

'I've put Hansport on the market.' Tony put his glass on the arm of the chair he had been sitting in. 'The boys agree.'

Stunned, Claire looked at her husband. 'You mean — in order to help?'

'That's right.' He sat down. 'As you say, we can't afford to waste time!'

'Are you sure, Tony?' She knew how much the small farm, which had been in his family for many generations, meant to him.

'Quite sure.'

In disbelief, she shook her head. Never would she have dared to ask him for a sacrifice even remotely similar.

'Wouldn't it be easier for you to sell this house?' she asked at last.

'It would, of course! But I've got to work. We need a place in London. The children – all of them – need to go to school.'

She saw the logic of his decision. With trembling hands, she opened the box on the coffee table and took a cigarette.

'You shouldn't start smoking again, Claire. You know it doesn't do you any good.'

'I'll stop in time.' Puffing, she lit the cigarette. 'How much can we raise?'

'I hope – oh, about a hundred and fifty thousand. Provided I can persuade the Inland Revenue to accept Hansport as our principal home – under the circumstances.'

'I don't understand – '

'If they don't, we'll have to pay capital gains tax.'

'Could you sell this house instead?'

'I'd use it as an argument. But it wouldn't be a very good one. How much can James get together?'

'He said we'll be lucky if we can raise ten per cent.'

Tony tried to evaluate the sum she had implied. Instinctively – he was an accountant by profession – he felt that James had been conservative. 'I think we should be able to do a little better than that,' he said at last. 'If we have to.'

'James put all of his money into Terrarossa. He says it'll be difficult to sell now.'

'I thought so. Nevertheless – it must be possible to borrow money against it. You had better call him.'

'He said he'd telephone me in the morning.'

Tony shrugged. He did not want to say that, in his opinion, she should call James straight away.

'You didn't say – how is he?' Tony asked after a while.

'At first, he was strange. Foreign. Almost Italian. But cold, without emotion. Max says it's a façade. Something he puts on in order to cope.'

'I can understand that. You used to say he was impossibly temperamental. I suppose he's trying to suppress that.'

'Maybe. He did frighten me when he got so angry.' She took a fresh cigarette. She put it back when she saw Tony watching her.

'Of course, you hadn't seen him for quite some time. He may have changed.'

Claire wished he would stop talking of James. 'We all change, in time. That's what happened. But at Terrarossa sometimes I felt like I had never met him before at all! It was as if I'd never got to know him. He made me feel redundant. Absolutely superfluous!'

As she spoke, Tony's conviction grew that she was exaggerating her sense of isolation at Terrarossa. He wondered whether – maybe subconsciously – she was trying to please him. His concern for her mental stability returned. How would she stand up to the time ahead? If the worst were to happen: what then?

'Then is it wise for you to go back? Really?' Softly, he asked the question, hoping she would not take offence at the implicit suggestion.

Speechless, she eyed him.

'I only meant to say, Claire, that – in the end – you may be able to contribute more to the children's return from here. You may be more useful,' he tried to explain.

'I must be back by Monday!' She jumped to her feet. 'I must go back! I couldn't stay here! Not with Thomas and Emma down there! Not now, Tony! Never! Never! Think what they're going to do to them!'

Indignant, angry, she stormed from the room.

Twenty-six

RICHARD HALL – like his friend, in his later thirties but shorter, stockier and with dark hair above thick, tortoiseshell spectacles – arrived outside James' flat at half past seven. A carrier bag from Harrods' food halls hung from one of his hands.

'I thought you'd rather stay in than go out again. I bought you some food.' Still in the doorway, the lawyer handed over the bag.

Grateful, James thanked him. 'Will you stay? Judging by the weight there's enough for a minor army.'

'If you want me to. I need a drink! I was stuck in bloody Knightsbridge for nearly half an hour.'

'What took you over there? Knightsbridge isn't your part of the world.'

'I had to see a client. That's why I bought the food – '

Kazue emerged from the bathroom. She was wrapped in an enormous robe – one of James' – made from white towelling.

James turned. 'Kazue, meet Richard!'

Smiling, she held out a finger. 'I'm wet, please excuse me! James has told me how much you have helped him already. I will join you as soon as I have changed.'

In a kitchen cabinet, James found a bottle of gin. 'The usual?' he asked. 'I'm not sure where I put the angostura.'

'In the spice cupboard. Unless you moved it.'

'I didn't. Please, help yourself!'

Directly, Richard found the bottle. He shook it over the tumbler James had taken from another cabinet. 'I've got to tell you, old chap, straight away. There's no chance we're going to wrap it all up tomorrow. Not that I'll give up. I'll keep on trying. But I know we're bound to run into the weekend. You had better prepare Claire.'

James gave a dejected nod. 'I've been trying not to remind her – '

'Of the deadline?'

111

'Yes.'

Richard poured gin over the few drops of bitters he had not shaken out again from the glass. 'I wouldn't have thought she'd be able to forget.' He turned on the cold tap. 'You know, sometimes it's better to talk about these things rather than be silent. They don't go away because you refuse to talk.' He held the glass under the tap. Instantly, the drink turned a brownish pink.

'I'll be speaking to her. In the morning,' James said, leading the way to the living room.

'I gather there was a call from one of the papers while I was out.' Richard let himself fall into a chair. 'They made an appointment for tomorrow.'

'Any idea how much we might get?'

'I haven't. But if we manage to get the others to counterbid, we'll soon find out. Don't you worry! I'll squeeze them hard! As much as I dare, anyway. You'll be seeing your bank manager in the morning. I made you an appointment for ten o'clock.'

'What else? Did you speak to the estate agents?'

'I did. And it's none too good!'

'I thought there'd be problems.'

'I know. As regards Terrarossa, we've got nothing so far. One of them said maybe. But we'd have to pay for him to go and see it first. The others were entirely negative. Nobody'd want to know – imagine buying a house where a thing like that happened!'

'What about the flat?'

'That's easy! In fact – if you really want to sell – you should get about ninety thousand. Pretty quickly. But remember you need a place you can work from. And a home, too.'

'I'm aware of that. My work's in Italy.'

'Okay. We can't sell Terrarossa anyway. That's that, then. So we've got ninety thousand here, minus mortgage and costs – '

'The mortgage is about twenty-two.'

'I know. Twenty-one, five hundred. I checked. Which leaves us with, say, sixty-four to -five. Plus your portfolio. The bank manager wouldn't tell me anything about it. He insisted he'd need your personal instructions. Even under the circumstances. Deadline or no deadline.'

'He's new.' James saw why his friend was so pessimistic about raising money before the weekend. 'I never met him. I told you, there's about ten, maybe eleven thousand. We'll find out. I've no idea what happens when a whole bunch of shares is sold outright. Taxes, commissions, what have you – '

'It may be wiser to use it as collateral.'

James frowned. 'We already have Terrarossa for that. There's a limit to what I'll be able to pay in interest.'

Kazue stood in the door. 'Is that food? In the Harrods bag? Shall I unpack it?'

Blank, James looked at her.

'Your friend asks whether she should unpack the stuff I brought you,' Richard intervened.

'Oh!' James' face came to life. 'Yes. Yes, please. Richard's staying to eat with us.'

Amused, Kazue gave a little bow. Then she returned to the kitchen.

'I say!' Suddenly, Richard seemed embarrassed but, having started, he was going to continue. 'I hope you don't think I'm frivolous. Your friend is the most stunning woman I have seen. Anywhere. In all my life!'

Disconcerted, James almost smiled. He shook his head. 'I – I suppose so. You know I don't know what I'd have done these last few days without her. She was – all the time – she was there. Simply there! To comfort and help me. I only wish she didn't have to live so ridiculously far away. She's got to go back on Monday.'

For a moment, they sat in silence.

Richard picked up their previous conversation. 'You mentioned selling the Bentley. I know it, of course. But I don't know the model.'

'It's a 1957 Flying Spur. It's in good shape. I last saw one advertised for fourteen thousand, I believe.'

'Presumably you wouldn't sell to a dealer?'

'It's better to advertise it. Inquiries to you.'

'Okay. Where is it?'

'I keep it in a garage. Just round the corner.'

'What about Claire? How much can she raise? Have you talked about that?'

James shrugged. 'We did. She said – she couldn't ask her husband for anything.'

Richard sighed. 'Nothing? She must have some money left – from your divorce settlement!'

'There wasn't very much. Remember, she didn't ask for anything. Not that there would have been much anyway.'

'He is quite wealthy, isn't he?'

'I suppose so. I'm not sure.'

'You *will* speak to her?'

'Yes. In the morning. I'll let you know of course – '

For the time being, little else remained to be said. They joined Kazue in the kitchen where, soon afterwards, they sat down to their meal. Kazue talked to Richard. Forcing himself to eat, James spoke only once, when the conversation touched on a recent film.

'You look dreadful, old boy!' Richard said when they had finished. 'It's time you got some rest. You're white as a sheet.'

They agreed that James would call as soon as he was through with the bank manager. Then Richard left.

'I hardly know any lawyers,' Kazue said, clearing away the dishes. 'They're quite rare in Japan.'

'You're lucky! And more reasonable in your use of the law, I suppose. Richard's good, though. There are few lawyers who understand money the way he does.'

'Has he made progress?'

James shrugged. 'Not enough! It isn't his fault. But we're not going to get it all together by tomorrow. Not unless there's a miracle.'

They went to bed. Overtired, James could not sleep. Over and over, he heard Richard run through the figures they had discussed. Would Claire come up with anything? How much? His mind switched to Sachetti. Maybe he had been caught again. Terrarossa was so far away. Tomorrow was Friday. The day after, Saturday. Only a week since Emma and Thomas had been taken. Who was looking after them? The woman who had shot at him, at Valcortese? The children's picture. Their small bodies. On the chairs. Country chairs. Their eyes. Dead. Red because of the flashlight. If only Pasquale and his comrades could help! He drifted. He knew he was drifting. He was almost asleep. Richard's voice woke him up again. Monday was the deadline.

'Can't you sleep?' Kazue asked.

'Did I wake you?'

'No. I was trying to think – how I could contribute some money. Shouldn't you take a sleeping pill? You hardly slept last night – '

'You need some sleep too.' Confused, he got up, to find the pills. Kazue had offered financial help before. But he knew that she could not afford it. She was not rich. She had to support her ageing mother

114

and an aunt who lived with her.

He had left the tablets at Terrarossa.

'Maybe I can help a little,' she said in the dark. 'If you relax.'

Methodically, she began to massage his shoulders, lightly at first, then more deeply, penetrating with increasing strength.

'I thought you were an art dealer. That's how you can make money. You're better than the masseuse at the Myako. The one who tried to sort out my back.'

She gave a little laugh. 'Not very successfully, I remember. My mother taught me.'

He winced as he was about to say what a lucky man her father must have been.

'Now – turn over! I really should have started on that side.'

He rolled onto his back. Her hands returned to his shoulders, then the chest. Gradually, her rhythm slowed. His muscles eased. His breathing became more regular and light. He fell asleep.

Twenty-seven

AT EIGHT IN the morning, Claire rang to tell James of Tony's offer to sell Hansport. Amazed, he listened. She told him the price Tony hoped to get.

'I don't know what to say! That's wonderful! Please tell Tony I thank him with all my heart! It makes such a difference!'

'Did you speak to Richard Hall?'

'He was here last night. He said I had better warn you that we're unlikely to get it all done today.'

'Tony said the same.'

Relieved, he went on. 'I gather we may have an offer from one of the papers later today.'

'We had a call last night. Tony told them to get on to Richard Hall. There are some reporters outside now.'

'It's probably best if neither of us says anything until we've decided on a deal. Do you agree?'

'I couldn't bear to talk to them anyway. You'll have to do the talking. Tony's already gone to the office. He'll be in touch with you later. About transferring the money. Do you mind?'

'Not at all! I'll be in and out, though. If there's no one here, ask him to leave a message with Richard's secretary, please.'

They rang off.

For an instant, James reflected on how calmly Claire had accepted that they might not be able to get everything done by the evening. Suddenly, he felt betrayed, lonely – as he had done after she had left him for Tony. Of course, Tony's offer was good news indeed! He thought her attitude must be due to that. He wondered whether he should book their return flights. For when? It was better to wait until the picture was a little clearer.

He presented himself at the bank a few minutes before ten. He was shown immediately to the manager's tiny office. A bald man –

short, in a grey suit – rose from behind a grey desk and held out a limp hand.

Eyeing each other with some circumspection, they sat down.

Directly, James explained that he had decided to sell his flat, his portfolio and the Bentley. He would not be able to obtain a good price for Terrarossa for some time. He wondered whether it would be acceptable as collateral for a substantial loan?

The manager pushed himself away from the desk. The wheels on his chair squeaked. 'The problem as I see it, Mr Grey, is that the property is not only difficult to dispose of now. It's in Italy. Abroad.'

'You wouldn't consider, then – '

'I didn't say that. However, my branch would not be able to deal with it. It would have to go to head office. Do you have life insurance?'

'Nothing substantial. Why?'

'If you take up a loan it must be secured. Real estate can be difficult to handle as collateral. Under certain circumstances.'

'You mean – if I were to be killed?'

The manager squirmed. 'It can be awkward – '

'Quite. I understand.'

'I'm sorry, Mr Grey. I'm afraid you're most unfortunate. Most unfortunate. You see – as much as one would like to help – the money has to be found on the normal commercial market.'

'I know that! I'm not asking for a present! Not at the price money is today!'

The manager sighed. 'You know it's not us who set the lending rate. God knows, I think it's too high. Far too high! Maybe – if I may suggest – you might be better off raising the loan in Italy anyway?'

James decided to change the subject. He asked about the sales value of his portfolio.

'When would you wish to sell?'

'Today, of course! We have a deadline!'

'You have consulted your accountant?'

'No! Why?'

'I am thinking of the tax situation, Mr Grey. It may make a significant difference whether you pay capital gains tax in one year or the other.'

'The last accountant I used was the Munich contact of my London accountant. I was on a contract there for a couple of years. My tax status is somewhat – a little confused at the moment.'

'In that case, Mr Grey, I would advise you not to sell but to clear up the matter first and take up a loan for the time being.'

'How much would that cost?'

'Two per cent over base rate. That's the best I can do, Mr Grey. Really.'

'How much can you let me have?'

'I thought you might ask!' With a satisfied smile, the manager opened the buff file which lay in front of him. 'I did a little homework, after Mr Hall's telephone call. Incidentally – I hope you understand – I couldn't release the information he sought. Not without your authority.'

The manager pulled a slip of paper from the folder. 'Now then! I tried to evaluate the various items as generously as possible. I could offer you – twenty thousand on the terms I mentioned. That's rather more, of course, than the portfolio's worth. But we *do* like to help. You have been with us for a long time.'

'Thank you. I need an additional eighty thousand. Before the day's out!'

The manager rocked back on his chair. He looked startled.

'My flat's valued at ninety thousand. Minus a mortgage of twenty-one. As I said, I'll sell the Bentley. That's an additional fourteen.'

'Have you got a buyer? Has the flat been surveyed?'

'It's on the market. From today. Mr Hall handles the sale. He has my full authority to act also in banking matters.'

The manager was unwilling even to consider the idea of advancing more than he had offered. The proper motions – all of them – would have to be gone through first. 'Please ask Mr Hall to call me on Monday. If he can produce the necessary papers, I shall see what can be done.'

'On Monday? I need the money today! I told you, without it we can't even begin to negotiate! Time's of the essence! Haven't you heard? *They're going to cut off the children's fingers!*'

Taken aback by the outburst, the manager hardly dared to look at his agitated client. Nervously, he tried to think of what to do. He shut the file.

'So you're refusing to help – '

'Please, Mr Grey! Not at all! If you remind me of Mr Hall's number, I'll still call him this morning. But I shall have to speak to my superior. It'll depend entirely on head office, Mr Grey.'

118

James gave him Richard's number. He signed a paper, authorising the lawyer to act on his behalf *vis-à-vis* the bank. He thanked the manager for his help. He had little hope left that Richard's forecast could be bettered.

'Raising the money's more hassle than getting kidnapped!' Grimly, James made this observation when, back at his flat, he telephoned Richard.

'Of course it takes time! What do you think? Unless you want to give it all away and pay through the nose in the process! I'm taking most of it off you anyway! What're you complaining about?'

'The bloody slowness of it all! Have you heard from the bank manager?'

'He was on the phone a minute ago. We'll get the hundred thousand – '

'Today?'

'I wouldn't bank on it.' Richard gave a sarcastic snort. 'I'm preparing the papers now. I'll be seeing him and his boss immediately after lunch.'

'You *are* trying?'

'Of course I'm trying!'

'Have you heard from the newspapers?'

'They're outside. Another lot's coming at twelve. I'm pleased for you about Tony Rudd's contribution. Now, I must get on, if you don't mind.'

James rang Claire next. He told her of his meeting with the bank manager. 'It's all so slow! How's Tony doing?'

'You haven't heard from him?'

'I was out.'

'I'll call him. Unless he's tied up, I'm sure he'll speak to you straight away.'

Kazue had gone out, to shop and confirm her return flight. James sat down to write the advertisement for the Bentley. He wondered how he could check on the asking price when the telephone rang.

'James! Good morning. I hear you're still hoping to get it all agreed today. I'm having a go. But I don't think it's realistic.' Tony Rudd's friendly voice boomed in the telephone earpiece.

Silent, James took in what he had heard.

'James? Are you there?'

'Yes. Yes, Tony. I'm sorry! I was just thinking. I suppose you're right. It's difficult to accept. Tony, I must thank you – in fact, I don't

119

know how to thank you. If ever I can make it up to you – at least in money – I'll do so.'

'I'm sure you'd have done the same. After all – I hope you won't mind me saying this – it's in the family. Even if a little unconventionally so. I gather you're having a tough time, especially with your bank.'

'Not tough! Slow!'

'Banks always are! I reckon, you'll do well to get away Monday night James.'

'That's the deadline!'

'I'm aware of it! Though Claire tells me you have asked for an extension.'

'The Colonel has. At least, that's what we agreed.'

'They've got to see that you need more time! I'm sure they must be intelligent enough to grasp that! I'm confident I'll get my lot on the way on Monday. Does your lawyer have your Italian bank address?'

'He has.'

'I'll speak to him. We'll transfer the money so you can draw on it there – as you need it. How're you planning to go about it?'

'What?'

'Negotiating.'

'I thought we'd say through the media when we're ready. Presumably they'll respond, set up some kind of meeting. At the meeting, I'll offer a down payment, with a promise of more on safe release of the children.'

'You really expect they'll meet you?'

'They've got to. Somehow. Negotiation seems the accepted form.'

'Hòw much will you offer?'

'I don't know. Ten, fifteen thousand to start with. No more.'

'And after that?'

'I'll try to keep it low so that – ultimately – we're not forced over what we can get together. I've no doubt they're extremely greedy. They'll try to press for more than they can realistically expect.'

'I'm sure you're right there. But – for heaven's sake – be careful! If anything were to happen to you, our chances could be slim indeed.'

Their conversation came to its end. 'I'll be in touch!' Tony promised and hung up, before James could thank him again.

He returned to the advertisement. A call to a car magazine helped him to set the price and, at the same time, make the booking. By half past twelve, he had nothing left to do but wait.

For the better part of an hour, he paced up and down in the living room. He tried to visualise Richard's meetings. Should he have asked to be present? He was sure the lawyer preferred to act on his own. The tone of their last telephone conversation confirmed it. I must let him get on with what needs to be done, James thought. 'I realise it's no good upsetting everyone.'

Kazue returned.

'Have you booked your flight?' he asked, wondering when he would be able to make the reservations for his own and Claire's return to Pisa.

'Ten past twelve from Heathrow. On Monday.'

'Via Anchorage or Moscow?'

'Anchorage. Moscow still won't accept Jumbos. What are you doing?'

He shrugged. 'Nothing! Just waiting. Everybody tells me I won't get out of here before Monday!'

'I am sorry, James. At least we can be together. Do you mind? Would you like to go out? A walk would do you good.'

'I must stay here. In case Richard finishes after all.'

'Have you had anything to eat? I bought some food.'

'I'm not hungry.'

She left him alone. He continued to pace up and down. Nobody called. Slowly, painfully so, the hours of the afternoon dragged by.

Exhausted, Richard arrived at a quarter past five.

'I thought I'd better come here straight away. To tell you in person. They wouldn't even consider working overnight at the bank. Let alone the weekend. You won't be able to leave until Tuesday morning. I'll need you to sign the various papers on Monday.'

'Tuesday? Are you crazy? What's the problem?'

'There is no problem. They're just lazy! Mentally as well as physically. So they're hiding behind Bank of England regulations and similar rubbish. It's the most appalling rigmarole I've ever gone through!'

'I must get back, Richard! I can't wait that long!'

'You'll have to. You have no choice. I need you on Monday.'

James rushed to the telephone. 'What's the name of the man you saw? What's his number? I'm going to ask the bastard what the hell he thinks he's playing at!'

'You'll do nothing of the kind, James! All you'd achieve is to blow our chances completely! Irretrievably! Besides – I bet he's gone to the country by now anyway.'

'But – '

'No but! If you do that, you'd better handle everything yourself. I'm warning you! I'm going to have a drink.'

Eyes shut, James tried to come to terms with the sudden confirmation of what he should have expected and prepared himself for. Tuesday! Tuesday! Not even Monday!

Richard returned to the living room.

'What about the newspapers?' James asked quietly.

'The first lot offered forty grand. The second only thirty. Even that took some pushing. But you won't like it either. Both of them insist their people more or less live with you. Just to make sure they pick up every last little secret of your souls.'

'They're probably more concerned to keep the competition out.'

'Whatever. What do you want to do about it?'

'I don't know. Claire couldn't cope with them. She told me as much. I'm not sure how I'd react. They could upset the negotiations – once they're on the way.'

'How do you mean?'

'If they went into detail about both families. Saying what Tony owns and so on. Before we know where we are we'll get eaten up by demands. You should have seen the reports in the Italian papers! Catalogues of everything! Even ransoms demanded and paid! An amateur could have extrapolated the going rate in this case.'

'If you feel like that, why the hell didn't you turn them down in the first place? I wasted hours with them! You even asked them to bid!'

Bad-tempered – irritated by his friend's erratic behaviour – Richard let himself fall into a chair.

'I had to find out what we might get! I didn't know Tony'd help. Now we may be a little closer to what would be acceptable – going by what I read. Maybe we can leave the possibility open until later.'

'You do realise, James, the later you let them in, the less any paper will be willing to pay? Unless the story takes a nasty turn?'

'I do! But we must have a more realistic base now! Tony's money plus my hundred thousand plus whatever I can borrow with Terrarossa as collateral – '

'It's still peanuts, James! What's it going to amount to? Twenty per cent of the demand? Less than that! I needn't tell you – if these chaps are sharp, even only a little so – they'll squeeze you and Claire and

Tony like lemons! Until every last little bit you called your own is either sold or in hock. You may save the children's lives. But what about yours? Working on your case, I realise how many victims there are. You'll end up crippled, all of you! Mentally, physically, financially!'

'There's no need to rub it in, Richard. I got the message. Some time ago!'

Hard suddenly, stubborn, James sat down by the telephone. He had to call the Colonel in Siena to tell him of the delay. After that, the return flight had to be booked. Claire, too, had to be told of the new situation.

Twenty-eight

THE TELEPHONE RANG early on Saturday morning. Kazue took the call. It was David Wright-Garrison.

'I thought I'd try you in London. We got back late last night. We didn't feel like staying anywhere. How're you doing? Am I too early?'

'James is very upset because he cannot return to Italy until Tuesday. Everything is very slow.'

'Is there anything I can do? May I speak with him?'

Kazue knocked on the bathroom door. Under the shower, James had not heard the telephone ring. He emerged dripping wet.

'How was your trip?'

'Mainly hot! I'm calling to find out whether there's anything I can do.'

'I need to borrow as much as possible with Terrarossa as collateral. The bank here doesn't want to know.'

'How much is the house worth?'

'I have no idea. Right now it's quite unsaleable, of course.'

'I guess so. If we don't know how much it's worth under normal circumstances, maybe we should look at it the other way round: how much do you want to borrow?'

'That depends on what I can afford. Here in London, I can raise approximately a hundred thousand pounds, just by selling what I have. I suppose I could afford about twenty thousand a year, to service a loan.'

'You mean pay interest?'

'Yes.'

'What about repaying the principal?'

'When I can sell Terrarossa.'

'How would you be able to work? Don't you need a base in London?'

124

'Not really.'

'What about your future? Do you have anything big coming up?'

'You know what I'm working on. It's for the next two years, almost. It is quite big. After that – I don't know yet.'

'And you'll be based in Italy.'

'That's right.'

'Are you sure you can afford twenty thousand? Are you leaving yourself with enough to produce the programmes?'

'I think so. The only thing I couldn't do would be to pay the interest in advance. The way my cash flows, I'd need to pay at the end of each year.'

David had enough information. He promised to do what could be done over the weekend. But he held out no hope that he would be able to obtain a firm offer before Monday afternoon or evening.

As he replaced the handset, James realised that he had not asked David about Suzanne and the girls. Should he call back? The telephone rang. Half expecting it to be David – maybe he had another question? – he picked up the handset. The caller said he was an estate agent.

'I hope you don't mind me troubling you so early, sir. I saw the reports. I am deeply sorry. Would you consider selling your property?'

'You mean Covent Garden or the house in Italy?'

'Covent Garden, sir. I know the property. I might have a cash buyer. I imagine – under the circumstances – this could be of interest?'

'How much?'

'Well, it's difficult to say. You understand, of course, I have not seen the property recently. Fifty thousand, perhaps? For a quick sale?'

Without a word, James hung up. Seconds later, the telephone rang again.

'Mr Grey, it appears we were cut off. I offered fifty thousand pounds. In cash. Are you interested? I could let you have the money within a month.'

'I cut you off! The flat's worth at least ninety thousand. To crooks like you I wouldn't sell for double that!'

James put down the telephone.

It rang again.

'Now look, Mr Grey! I'll not be called a crook! You retract that!'

125

'You are a crook! You can have it in writing if you care to collect it in person. Now get off my line or I'll give your name and disgraceful attempt at exploiting our situation to the press!'

He slammed down the handset. He realised that the agent had said his name only at the beginning. He could not recall it. His fists clenched tightly, he circled the telephone. It remained silent. He looked around. Soon the flat would not be his any more. Three biggish canvases – by young and relatively unknown artists – would have to go to friends. Inexpensive, they would nevertheless be nearly impossible to sell. They would have appeared out of place at Terrarossa.

Kazue called from the kitchen. 'Are you going back in the bathroom?'

'I'm finished, thank you.'

'Will you have some breakfast? You didn't eat last night.'

'Just a cup of coffee, thanks.'

He looked through the kitchen door. She was pouring coffee beans into the grinder.

'What are you going to do today?' she asked.

'Wait, I suppose.'

'Won't you come out with me? At least for a little while?'

He shook his head. 'I had better stay. Just in case. You go out. I'll wait here. I'll be all right.'

Twenty-nine

'YOU MUST DRINK, Tommy! You haven't had any water for two days! You'll die if you don't drink!'

Agitated, Emma looked down at her brother.

His eyes had slid shut again. Delirious, he twisted and turned on his makeshift bed. With bound ankles – despite her pleas, Barba had refused to take off the shackles – he kicked away the blanket she had put back so many times.

'You must drink! You must!' Close to tears, she tried to make him understand.

His eyes dull, with huge, dilated pupils, fluttered open.

'You must drink! Please! Sit up, Tommy!'

'Caroline? Mummy?' Barely audible, the names came through his cracked and swollen lips. 'Mummy?'

'Mummy's not here, Tommy. We're in Italy! Daddy will come and get us out. You must drink! Please!'

Panting, he shut his eyes again. His thin face was flushed. Compared with the rest of him, the measles had left it relatively unmarked.

Something had to be done! But what? If only she could think of something! No one had come upstairs all morning. She knew it was Saturday. Much earlier, before the sun had touched the tree tops she could see from the window, she had heard new voices. They had mingled faintly with the noise of the rushing mill stream, almost drowned in its roar. Counting Barba and the woman, at least five people, maybe more, she thought, were downstairs.

Once more, she tried to reason with Thomas.

She could not get through to him.

She did not dare to call for help. She knew she would only be gagged again.

Even Barba had shown little further interest once he had made a better bed for the patient – two extra blankets, which he had put on the floor. He had brought an enamel mug of water and a couple of aspirins, sealed in metal foil.

'*Una soltanto*,' Barba had said, pointing at the pills.

'*Si*! I know. Children must take only one at a time,' Emma had replied.

Suddenly she recalled watching her mother when Thomas had been very small, maybe a year old. He had refused to take his medicine, some liquid which had to be given with a small, plastic spoon.

Claire had held Thomas' nose. Unable to breathe, he had opened his mouth. Grabbing him from behind, she had popped the spoon in. It had worked.

That was the thing to do!

Emma put the mug of water closer to the side of the bed. With dirty finger-nails, she tore through the foil and extracted one of the aspirins. She put it on the floor by the mug.

She slid to the side of his head. From behind, with both hands, she lifted his shoulders. She pulled in her bound legs. Kneeling, she propped Thomas up in front of her. With one arm – still from behind – she held him round the chest, leaving her hand free to reach up to his nose.

She groped for the mug.

'You must drink, Tommy! I have some water. Cool water. Poor darling! You're so hot!'

She pinched his nostrils.

He struggled.

She tightened her grip round his chest.

Moaning, he opened his mouth. He gasped.

Quickly she put the mug to his lips.

He struggled.

The water splashed. It wet his lips and tongue. Suddenly, he seemed to understand. He began to drink.

He had drunk about one third of the water when she took it away.

'I've got some medicine,' she whispered. 'To make you better. Will you take it for me?'

She slipped the aspirin in his mouth. 'Swallow, Tommy!'

She put the mug back to his lips.

Spluttering, he spat the pill out. It stuck on the blanket.

'Please take it, Tommy! It'll get the fever down. You'll feel much better when you're not so hot.'

She tried again.

Again, he spat the medicine out. The pill had dissolved to little more than half its original size.

Emma was about to try for the third time when she felt herself being watched.

She looked up.

Stonefaced, the woman stood in the door. Some lengths of string, two blindfolds and two gags hung from her hands.

Thirty

THE DOOR BELL made James jump. The newspaper he had been trying to concentrate on sailed flapping to the ground.

'Who is it?' Tense, he listened into the earpiece of the entry phone.

'It's Tony! Tony Rudd! May I see you for a minute?'

Dumbfounded, James pressed the button to open the downstairs door.

Out of breath, the visitor arrived at the top of the stairs.

'I thought you'd gone to Hansport with Claire and the boys,' James greeted him on the landing.

'They went ahead. I'll be taking the train at six. Since I was nearby, I was hoping you wouldn't mind if I dropped in on the off chance.'

'You're more than welcome! Can I offer you a drink?'

Tony looked at his watch. 'It's a little early for me. I'd love a cup of tea, though.'

They went in to the kitchen. James filled the kettle and switched it on.

'Chinese or Indian?' he asked. 'I think there's both.'

Tony did not have a preference. 'I ruin it anyway. I still use lots of milk and sugar. I – from school – I never got rid of the habit.'

'Indian then.' James rummaged in one of the cabinets. 'How's Claire? She seemed quite reassured when I told her the Colonel was going to make the announcement on Monday anyway.'

'That's really what I hoped to talk about. I hope you don't mind, James. I'm desperately worried about her!'

For a moment, James looked at the man who had motivated Claire to ask for the divorce. They knew each other by sight only, from the few occasions when they had met handing over the children.

'That makes two of us,' James said. 'Don't misunderstand, please!

130

I – I think I've come to terms with the divorce. Still – you must understand – somehow I still care.'

'Of course you care! That's natural!'

Faintly, the water in the kettle began to seethe. James heated the pot under the hot tap.

'I'm terribly afraid she's going to break down!' Tony went on. 'At the moment she puts on a brave face. But I wonder how she'll fare once you're down there again? Please! I don't mean that as any kind of put-down. I know you feel at home there.'

'Do you want to come? I did suggest it, right at the beginning.'

'You'd only have another displaced person round your neck, James. Claire's so deeply hurt – I don't see how she'll cope. It's her – her mental stability that concerns me so. I'm frightened, James! I fear she may not make it! She told me she felt lost when she was with you. Useless. I suggested she shouldn't go back. What do you think? Honestly?'

The water was about to boil. James drained the pot. He spooned out the tea from a tin caddy. He switched off the kettle and poured the steaming water into the pot.

'Let's sit in the living room.' He motioned the visitor to go ahead, while he put the tea and whatever else was needed on a tray.

'Please.' James pointed at a group of brightly coloured armchairs which surrounded a white coffee table.

They sat down.

'I share your worries.' Flatly, James made the statement. He pushed a cup and saucer towards the guest. 'She may have mentioned it. I said she must stay whole. The children will need her more than ever when they're back. I tried to put myself in her position. But it's impossible for me to judge what would be less painful for her: to stay here with you? Or to go back? Where at least she has the illusion of being near to the children. It's true she's now a stranger at Terrarossa. She behaves like one. But wherever she is, there is little for us to do but wait.'

Increasingly pained, Tony had listened. He shifted in his chair. He shook his head. 'It's – I – I wish she were less of a black-and-white person. A couple of weeks ago, we had a row. About something quite ludicrous. Really of no importance. Yet she thought – because of it – that I wouldn't be willing to contribute to the ransom. She expected – nothing. If only she could pray! She has so little hope!'

'I've been tempted to pray.' James poured the tea. 'I stopped

131

myself. It seemed rather dishonest when I don't pray normally.'

'But you have hope! Claire told me how confident you were. Strangely, that's one of the things which upset her even more.'

'I'm aware of it. There's a fine line. If you're seen on the wrong side of it, you look as though you're not hopeful but uncaring, callous. I'm only trying to deal with the situation we're in. It occurred to me – it's a situation where the father has to take charge. Where there's violence, a woman is at a basic physical disadvantage.'

Tony reached for the cup he had never touched. Methodically, he added milk, then sugar. He stirred for the better part of a minute.

'I wonder whether she accepts that.' At last, he put down his spoon. 'I believe you may be right. Nevertheless, she's a mother – something you and I can observe but never feel. She's a mother who has lost her children.'

'Kazue – my friend – said the same. I feel with Claire – the loss negates her identity as a mother. But what are we to do? We're in a situation which cannot be controlled. We can only control ourselves. So that we may cope with it.'

For a while, they sat in silence. Pigeons cooed on the roof outside one of the open skylights. Dust particles caught the rays of sunlight which fell into the room. Not far away, a clock struck five o'clock.

Their conversation revived for a few more minutes. It touched on Hansport and the one hundred and fifty thousand pounds. Tony was confident that the money would be available for transfer as he had said, on Monday afternoon. James explained his decision not to accept an exclusive deal with a newspaper, at least not for the time being. Hearing what it would have entailed, Tony agreed that the decision was right. He was in no doubt that Claire could not have put up with a constant press escort.

'I made the reservations,' James said. 'We're on the first flight, Tuesday morning. Unfortunately, all they had was first class.'

'I'll try and speak to her one more time. So far she's adamant. She's got to go! May I call you if she changes her mind?' Tony got up.

'Of course! If I can help – I'll do whatever you think best. She's your wife now. You know her. I don't, really – not any more.'

Richard telephoned soon after Tony had gone. He was about to leave for King's Lynn, to see his parents. 'I'm taking your paperwork with me. I'm back tomorrow night. Unless anything unforeseen happens, I'll see you Monday. Try and rest!' He gave his parents' telephone number and rang off.

The front door opened and Kazue let herself in. She was laden with shopping bags.

'My God!' James exclaimed. 'Is there anything left in the shops?'

'I think so. It is not much.' Smiling, she slipped into the bedroom.

He was standing at the window, looking down at the empty street, when Kazue approached from behind.

'Shut your eyes!' she said.

He shut his eyes.

'Hold out your hand, please!'

Turning, he held out his hand. Something light – so small he could not tell its shape – fell into it.

'Now you may look.'

A tiny parcel lay in his palm.

'Am I – am I to open it?'

'Of course!'

He tried to undo the wrapping paper.

'It feels so light! I can't guess!' He fumbled with the paper. It felt stiff, because of its small size. Its colour was a deep navy.

Amused, Kazue watched. Twice she held out a hand to help. Each time, she retracted it, without him noticing.

At last, he tore the paper off. A tiny jewel box was in his fingertips. He pressed its lock. He lifted the lid. On a cushion of blue velvet lay a cameo of the Madonna. A smile played on her lips. Over a rich, deep brown background, her head dress had been carved from a beige, the face itself from an even more luminous, near white layer of the stone.

'She's beautiful!' He kissed Kazue's cheeks. 'Thank you! Thank you!'

'She's Italian. Maybe from the *settecento*. She'll protect you!'

'I'm not sure I'm entitled to her protection – '

'Just believe in her a little! She'll be with you!'

Thirty-one

'OUR LAST DAY!' Drowsy from the sleeping pills Kazue had collected for him, James sat up in bed. The bright light in the window hurt his eyes. 'What's it like?'

'It's beautiful! Sunny. You must get out today. It will do you good! Last time, you promised to show me the white cliffs. Couldn't we go there today? Please?'

He remembered telling her of Beachy Head and the Seven Sisters. His instinct was to stay at the flat. Reason told him that there was little point – none – in staying indoors all day. He knew she was longing to go out. It was not fair to keep her virtually imprisoned with him.

'If you want to.' He was committed. 'We'll go.' He swung his legs from the bed. 'May I have some coffee, please? To wake me up?'

Quickly, he shaved, showered and dressed. It was not yet ten when they walked to the garage where he kept the Bentley. The narrow streets of Covent Garden looked homely in the warm light of the morning sun. Yet there was hardly a sign of life to be seen. 'It can't stay so quiet much longer,' he said. 'Since the market moved out, everybody's trying to live here.'

At the garage, they had to wait for the car to be brought out.

'Where did you find the Madonna?' He felt the cameo in his pocket.

'A shop in Bond Street. I go there every time I'm in London. But I found it by chance.'

'I read once that the Japanese mix their religions. Is that true?'

'A little. Is it not a good thing to do?'

'Pragmatism! Even in religious matters!' he teased. 'I believe in God. I don't want to belong to any of the churches, though. I feel it's wrong that they all try to exclude each other. It seems an excellent idea to me, to share a little of one's beliefs.'

A pale silver grey, the Bentley appeared on the ramp. Silent, it rolled down the slope. The long fastback coachwork dwarfed all other cars on the ground floor.

'Did she start all right?' James asked the garage attendant.

'No problem, sir. We put the battery back yesterday when we heard you was in town. A shame, sir! We're very sorry!' The man got out. He pointed at the tachometer. 'She's ticking over just beautiful!'

James opened the door for Kazue. He waited until she had settled in the red leather bucket seat and shut it again. From his side, he helped her to put on the safety belt. 'These cars were built a long time before belts became standard,' he explained. 'It'd be rather painful if you hit that wooden dash board.'

He clicked the automatic gearbox into drive. Lightly, he depressed the accelerator and let the car roll forward towards the exit. 'It always takes me a little while to get used to this long bonnet.'

The garage attendant had gone out into the street, ahead of them. His help proved unnecessary. There were no cars about.

They drove down to the Strand and on to Fleet Street, past St Paul's and the Tower. A portable road sign blocked access to the bridge. 'A new weekend feature.' James turned back to London Bridge. They crossed the Thames and followed it downstream, to the Cutty Sark in Greenwich. Through the park, past the observatory, they drove over Blackheath and headed south into Kent.

An hour later, they were crawling through Tunbridge Wells, at little more than walking speed. 'I'm sorry it's so slow. We're not the only ones who thought of going to the coast.'

'I'm glad you made the effort, James. This is all new for me.'

'You'll like the cliffs. On a day like this, they really are white! I wonder how much has fallen off since I last saw them?'

'What falls off?'

'The cliffs themselves. Every now and then, a piece drops off. Onto the beach below.'

'Is there a beach? I thought the water came right up – '

'Beach is the wrong word. It depends on the tide how far the water comes in.'

'So – the people who jump off Beachy Head don't fall into water?'

'I don't think so. How do you know about that?'

'Some time ago, I read an article. About beautiful places, which seem to attract a disproportionate number of suicides. Like Mount Fuji.'

Silent, they travelled on, going south through the lush hills and woods of East Sussex. Not far from Eastbourne, they turned west for a few miles, then south again into one of the shallow valleys which shape the rolling South Downs. 'There's the sea!' Kazue had caught a glimpse of it. Over the end of the valley – for a fleeting moment – it shimmered in their view. James' flat hand circled. It fell, in a chopping move. 'The cliffs cut clean through all this.' Smoothly, the round hills rose on either side of them. 'When I was little, I imagined an enormous giant, who hacked off England from France, to let in the sea.'

'Was he English or French?'

'English, of course!'

It was lunchtime. People stood and sat with their drinks outside a public house. Some of them stared at the rare motorcar.

They reached the shore at Birling Gap. He shuddered. 'The mess people have made of this place! I can't understand why these ramshackle huts are allowed to stay.' He turned east. At the next low point in the undulating coastline – where one of the troughs in the Downs came to its abruptly precipitous end and the road curved only yards from the cliff's edge – he pulled the car onto a narrow and little used parking space.

They got out.

The sea air embraced them. Balmy, it carried up to them the soft sounds and faintly salt scent of the water. A deepening scale of glistening ultramarines, the sea spread out from under the sheer white walls. Tiny fishing boats dotted the lazy swell of its tranquil mirror surface. Of infinite depth, sky and sea had merged without horizon. Together they curved to contain the immense picture.

James held out his hand and they began their walk towards Beachy Head. The highest of the cliffs they could see, it stood some two miles ahead. Three, maybe four troughs in the downland separated them from it. The dense turf, strewn with countless little flowers, felt soft under foot. Constant, a slow measure of time, the swell rolled onto the shore. Far out, the tide was low.

'How high are we!' Kazue changed to his other side, where she was closer to the edge. 'The colours are so strong!'

Climbing steadily, they gained height on the first cliff. They lost it again in the next trough. Their second – much steeper – ascent made

136

them hot. Only the lightest of breezes fanned their glowing faces. Huge fair-weather clouds billowed in the distance. Seemingly immobile, they towered over the land to the east. Fat, impeccably white seagulls launched themselves from the cliff's edge. When the sun caught the orange beads of their eyes they were glassy without hint of expression. On translucent wings they soared and glided in the white light. Ridiculously, their whining cries and quick, quacking cackle contrasted with the silent elegance of their flight.

At the top of the third cliff, Kazue asked to sit down. Beachy Head was still half a mile away, at the end of a gently rising plateau. People walked on it. 'They all do the same – go to the top and mill around there.' James sat down by the edge.

'Can you smell the sea?' Kazue asked.

'And the land. Have you noticed the many, many flowers we've been walking on? You should see the gorse when it's in bloom! There are whole fields of yellow! Over there.'

The sun in their faces, they sat still for a while, looking out over the sea and the cliffs of the Seven Sisters. The strident song of larks hung high in the air over the gorse fields he had pointed out.

He lay down. On his back, he stared at the cloudless blue above. He closed his eyes.

'This is so beautiful!' Kazue said quietly. 'Can you not look at it?'

He shook his head. 'I want you to see it. There are few places where what we can see is so vast. So elemental. The depth of the landscape rivals that of the sea. Not down! Outwards! The light travels. It changes. The colours are so big! My eyes could never get enough of the surfaces and shapes.' He spoke softly, as though to himself.

'I came here the day after Claire had asked me for the divorce. I was stunned. Desperate. I sat not far from here and looked out over the sea. Grey clouds drifted over it. Shafts of light fell between them. Suddenly, I felt content. I tried to fight the feeling. I felt guilty being content. But it took over. I felt peace – deep peace – something I had never experienced before. Maybe it was similar to what the mystics describe. Later I thought so. Now my mind is numb. Sick. This time, I dare not focus on what has happened. I am terrified of concentrating on the children. I am afraid of my own imagination.'

'Do you want to go on? Is it too painful for you to stay?'

'We'll stay – as long as you want to stay. Wherever we go, I can't escape.'

Later, they went to a point where they could look down onto Beachy Head lighthouse. Hand in hand, they stood at the edge of the chalk and flintstone walls which rise almost six hundred feet over its red and grey tower. Then they walked back to the car. In Eastbourne they stopped for tea at one of the old hotels along the sea front. Hidden in a corner of its once grandiose hall, they remained unnoticed, so much so that James had to get out of his chair to find a waitress who would serve them.

They left the resort well before the mainstream of Sunday trippers began their return to London. They took the car back to the garage. It was just after six when they arrived outside James' home. A small group of reporters was at the door.

'Mr Grey! We understand there's been another attack. Did you know?'

'What? What happened?'

'We're not sure. Has no one phoned you?'

'We were out!'

'The reports say a couple of *carabinieri* were killed this morning. At your house.'

'At Terrarossa?'

'That's what the reports say.'

James unlocked the door. He rushed upstairs.

He had left the number of the *caribinieri* headquarters in Siena on a piece of paper by the telephone. His first attempt to dial the number failed. The second time, he found it engaged. Immediately, he tried again.

He got through.

He asked for Colonel Amorini.

The telephone clicked. A male voice answered. It was not the Colonel's.

James said his name. Again, he asked for the Colonel.

'I am Rossi,' the voice said. 'I'm on the Colonel's staff. I'm afraid Colonel Amorini's out.'

James began to explain who he was.

'We have met, *signor* Grey,' Rossi cut him short. 'At your house.'

Vaguely – for an instant only – James associated the voice with a young officer who had assisted in taking the first statements after the children's abduction.

'I hear two of your men – '

138

'We lost one. The second too, probably. Unfortunately, he is not expected to live – '

'So – at the house? They're safe?'

'They're fine. Colonel Amorini tried to telephone you. It happened on the road to the village. Soon after eight. They had just been relieved from guard duty.'

'Where were the other two?'

'We had decided to reduce the guards to two over the weekend, while you were away.'

'Do you know –'

'We know nothing. Nobody saw or heard anything. The bus found the car in the middle of the road. Our men were still inside. Both of them had been shot in the face – point-blank. I believe they may have been talking to the assassins.'

'It couldn't have been Sachetti?'

Rossi paused. 'Sachetti? Hardly! They would have recognised him. They would have been warned.'

Their conversation was at its end. James thanked the officer for speaking to him. Pensive, he hung up.

'James?'

He did not hear.

'James? Is it – bad?'

He looked up. 'I don't know, Kazue. I don't understand what it means!'

'What happened?'

He repeated the little he had learned. 'It sounds like some of the political attacks we read about. I don't understand! How do we fit in?'

'Maybe they're just after money?'

He shrugged. 'I would have thought there'd be much richer sources than us. They're so vicious! What will they do to the children?'

The door bell rang.

James answered the entry phone.

The reporters wanted to know whether he had telephoned Italy.

'One man has been killed. The other's critical. They were guards. It happened on their way from Terrarossa. Nobody seems to have seen or heard anything.'

'What else? Can you –'

'I've told you all I know.'

Seconds later, the door bell rang again. Dismayed, James looked at his friend. She went to the door.

'Mr Grey? Please, would you mind – '

'Mr Grey has nothing further to say. Please, leave him alone now!' Kazue said and hung up.

The door bell rang for the third time.

Furious, James dashed to the entry phone. He ripped the handset from its hook. 'What is it now? We told you we've nothing to say!'

'Telegram, sir,' a voice announced flatly.

He dropped his arms. He stood quite still. He hung the handset back on its hook. As fast as he could, he rushed downstairs. He opened the front door.

A lad from the post office stood before him. In a half circle, the reporters pushed and shoved behind the messenger.

'I'm sorry I shouted at you.' James took the envelope the young man held out to him. 'As for you,' he addressed the journalists, 'I really can't help you! I told you all I know. Please go away!'

'The telegram!'

'What's in the telegram?'

'Won't you tell us? Please!'

He ran upstairs.

He tore open the envelope. Fumbling, his shaking hands unfolded the telegram.

'All safe. Pasquale has message. Max,' it read.

Stunned, he stood in the room. He held out the telegram.

'A message? That's good, James! It must be!'

'But – what is it? I want to know! I must know!'

'If it's important – wouldn't he tell the Colonel?'

'I'm not sure he trusts him. There's nothing I can do. I'm stuck here until Tuesday. Stuck! I must tell Claire!'

Thirty-two

THEY HAD FINISHED their evening meal.

'Would you mind if we had some music?' Kazue asked.

'Music?' James got up. 'Of course not! I never thought of it. I'm sorry I'm so inattentive! What would you like to hear?'

'Could we have one of the quartets?'

He opened the box of Beethoven's late string quartets that she had given him during her last visit. 'Which one shall I put on?'

'You choose!'

'The one in the middle then. Each time I think I have mastered the numbers, I find I mix them up.' He extracted the record from the box and slid it out of its sleeve. 'A hundred and thirty-one,' he read from the label.

He waited for the opening bars. He adjusted the sound and returned to his chair. Tense, he sat quite upright. He thought of his conversation with Claire. She was going back to Terrarossa with him. Outside, the sky over the roofs was deep, inky blue. A motorbike started in the street below. Its noise died in the distance.

The first side came to its end. He did not move.

'May I turn it over?' Kazue asked.

'I'm sorry! Yes. Please. I was far away.'

'Would you rather we had no music?'

'It's soothing. It's just – I can't concentrate on it.'

She turned the record over. The *presto* began. She lowered the volume and sat down by one of the skylights. Only a pair of wax tapers lit the room. Her soft profile was pale against the sky.

'I'll be very lonely without you,' he said when the movement was over and the following *adagio* was past its quiet opening. 'I know – you need to be independent. More so than I. Very selfishly, I wish you could stay! Though – every day you did stay must have been a sacrifice – '

141

'Not at all, James! You must not think that. Maybe – now Claire seems a little more confident – you'll be able to help each other more?'

They fell silent again. He forced himself to listen to the music.

'We are both so tied to what we do!' he suddenly exclaimed. 'Now I'll never be able to come any closer to you. I'll be tied for ever!'

'Not for ever, James.'

'But how – '

'Time will free you. It heals! It's so much stronger than we can believe.'

Thirty-three

MONDAY. Dull and humid, the day had dawned over London.

The estate agent whom Richard Hall had appointed rang at exactly nine o'clock. She had a potential buyer for the flat who wanted to view it as soon as possible. James explained that he would be out for most of the day. He suggested the agent arrange the inspection for Tuesday, when he would be gone.

At ten, he went to get the Bentley from the garage. A few minutes later, Kazue came downstairs with her luggage and they set off. They travelled in silence. The traffic became lighter once they had reached the west end of Cromwell Road. It was just after eleven when they arrived at Heathrow.

Kazue did not want James to wait after she had checked in. Suddenly, tears were in her eyes. She embraced him. 'Please take care of yourself! Write to me!'

She tore herself away. Quickly, she climbed the stairs to the departure level of the terminal. Without turning, she waved her hand overhead. She was gone.

James returned to his car as a traffic warden was circling it, book in hand, ready to write a ticket. She was about to address him when she saw that he was crying. Embarrassed, she turned away, slipping the book into a pocket of her jacket.

Slowly, he found his way out of the airport. In the roundabout on the far side of the tunnels, which lead to and from the passenger terminals, he was about to turn towards the M4 when he remembered the long tailback he had seen on its city-bound lanes. He decided to take the old A4 instead. His sudden change of direction almost caused the car behind to run into him. Sharply, its blaring horn reminded him that he was driving and not alone on the road.

At the first lay-by he stopped. He killed the engine. He slumped over the wheel, head down, eyes closed.

'You must not crack, Grey! You can't afford to crack!' he said aloud. 'You cannot let yourself go to pieces!'

He restarted the engine and waited until the road behind him was clear. He drove on.

He returned the car to the garage. On his way back to the flat, he stopped at a newsagent's. He bought some of the daily newspapers. Walking along, he tried to see whether there was anything new in them about the attack on the *carabinieri* guards. There was nothing he did not know already. Two of the papers reported that both men had died instantly.

He was still unlocking the door when he heard the telephone ring.

'I tried you before,' Richard Hall opened the conversation.

James explained that he had only just got back from taking Kazue to the airport.

'I'm sorry she couldn't have stayed with you longer. Our appointment at the bank's at three.'

'Are there any problems?'

'I hope not.'

'Where do we meet?'

Richard gave the address and the name of the man they were going to see.

'Have you spoken to Tony Rudd?' James asked.

'A minute ago. His bank's transferring a hundred thousand tomorrow – '

'What about the rest?'

'Wednesday, he hopes. You should have a couple of hundred thousand at your disposal by then.'

'What about that life insurance the bank manager said I should have?'

'I don't think he really thought through that one. As a matter of interest: I did ask a broker friend of mine. He reckons you'd be more difficult to insure than a couple of Formula One racing drivers together.'

'Thanks for asking. You cheer me up no end.'

'Well – there you are. Consider yourself on a par with the famous. But I'm sure you're winning, old chap. Never forget that!'

Thirty-four

'ALL THIS IS to do with me?'

Incredulous, James pointed at the stack of files Richard had put on the seat next to him in the lobby of the bank's head office. To James, they seemed out of all proportion.

'Yes, the whole lot! Leases, guarantees, letters of transfer of authority and, I'm afraid, a new will. An addendum to it, to be precise.'

'My will?'

'In case you get killed. They're most concerned that the bank should be repaid first.'

'What if I'm killed before the children are released?'

'I've taken care of that. Don't worry – and don't lose your temper! Don't forget, it's part of their job to be conservative. In fact, they're really quite generous now. Under the circumstances I got them down to one per cent over base rate.'

'How much is that then?'

'Fifteen per cent. But remember, it may go up.'

'Seriously, Richard. What happens if I'm killed?'

'I'll take over. With Claire and Tony. I was your executor before. I assumed you wouldn't mind if I continued.'

The commissionaire in charge of reception came up to them. He asked them to go to the fourth floor. They would be met there.

'Into battle then!' James got to his feet.

Richard shook his head. 'It's not a battle. You sign, I talk. Please!'

A young secretary met them on the fourth floor. Smiling, she greeted them and showed them to a conference room at the end of a long corridor. Three men were waiting for them there. One of them was the manager of James' branch. The other two were considerably younger, younger even, James thought to his surprise, than himself.

Shaking hands with the visitors, the bankers introduced

themselves. 'I look after the legal work,' one of them said.

Richard put his files on the table and began to hand paper after paper to the bank's lawyer. Apart from the officer's occasional short questions there was silence as, together, the two lawyers read through them.

James looked around the panelled room. A portrait of the Queen hung over the fireplace directly opposite him. Paintings of old-fashioned gentlemen hung on the other walls. A telephone, a full water jug and a tray of glasses sat on a sideboard in one of the corners. The smell of furniture polish hung in the stale air.

'That's fine!' the bank's lawyer announced. 'If Mr Grey could sign now, we're in the clear.'

Surprised by the sudden and – so it seemed to him – easy outcome, James said he did not have a pen on him. Smiling, the branch manager offered his. One by one, Richard passed the papers and witnessed them where necessary after James had signed. He collated them and handed them to the bank's lawyer. They all rose. They shook hands. James was now able to call on a total of one hundred thousand pounds through his bank in Siena.

On their way down in the lift, the friends agreed to meet for dinner at Richard's club. They parted outside the bank. The sky promised rain. James decided to walk back to Covent Garden.

Thirty-five

DAVID WRIGHT-GARRISON telephoned James at six o'clock.

'We tried earlier. We couldn't get through. Any progress with your bank?'

'I got a hundred thousand this afternoon.'

'Was it expensive?'

'One per cent over base rate.'

'That's good! You can't expect to do better than that.'

'Have you been able to – '

'I have. I stuck out my neck a bit. I got two hundred and fifty thousand dollars but I need the papers for the house and a few signatures.'

'That's tremendous, David! What's it going to cost me?'

'Well – fifty thousand is from me and Suzanne. We'll lend it to you until you actually sell. The rest's at my bank's minimum rate, twelve per cent right now. Could you stop over with the papers on your way back to Italy?'

'I'm most grateful, David. But I've got to get back! The deadline's today!'

'Of course! I didn't think of that. Can I deal with your lawyer?'

'I was just going to suggest that. He's a close friend. He's handling the entire legal and financial side anyway. Would you mind?'

'Of course not! What's his name?'

James gave Richard's name and address.

'If you brief him – maybe he'd like to call me in the morning. I have to go out after lunch. We should be able to do most of it by Telex and courier. I'm sure we'll sort it out between us.'

James remembered to ask David about his family. They were well. Rachel was still a little nervous.

'She'll be all right in time,' David said.

'Please give her my love. And Sarah and to Suzanne.'

David asked when he would be returning to Italy.

'We're on the first flight tomorrow morning. Pasquale received a message! He may have picked up something about the children's hiding place.

'That'd be wonderful, James. But be careful! We saw the news about those two poor devils – '

'I know. There seems no end to the violence. Keep your fingers crossed! Think of us!'

Thirty-six

'A GLASS OF champagne, madam? Sir? While we're waiting?' the Alitalia steward asked.

Claire refused. James asked for a cup of coffee. On their own, they sat in the first class cabin. Muzak poured from the loudspeakers overhead.

'I noticed some empty seats in economy. Why did they make you book us in first class?' Claire asked.

'I guess if all the people with economy reservations had turned up, the plane would have been full. I didn't want to risk travelling on stand-by.'

The steward returned with a tray and two cups of coffee on it. 'Won't you have some coffee, madam? I am very sorry about the delay.'

Hesitant for a moment, she accepted the cup. James asked for an Italian newspaper. From an overhead locker, the steward produced two of Monday's editions.

'What are they saying?' Claire asked looking over James' arm.

'The second man died.'

'Do you think it was revenge?'

'For what? For having killed two men in the first place?'

'No. On the state, the way terrorists seem to think.'

'God knows! Anyway, how would we connect with the Italian state?'

'You do. You live there.'

'I suppose so. Although it seems a bit tenuous – I always considered myself detached. Without rights or interest in local politics.'

'Tony taught me to be more aware of what's going on around us. Especially in the community.'

'I'm not very good at that. I imagine that to a committed

revolutionary I must be something of a red rag. No! That doesn't work! Red's *their* colour.'

The plane was pushed from the gate. It rolled back.

'I guess,' he went on, 'if you look at it through terrorists' eyes, two possible motivations look quite plausible: they need money for their movement and they're taking it from people who stand for – or at least seem to accept – many of the things they're fighting against. People they can hurt into the bargain. With David's children – or himself – it would have been even more obvious.'

The plane stopped. After a short halt, it started to taxi. Claire looked at her watch. She put it back one hour.

'You used to consider yourself a socialist when we met,' she said.

'Most people did at university. I mean, we had the ideals. But you know very well that I never really fitted in. I still don't want to be committed.'

'So what are you now?'

'Now? A poor man! Nothing – I hope – you could label. You know I'm selfish. I'd like to be part of society. But only if I can do what I want to do. Partly because I believe – really! – that we do best what we like doing most.'

'What do you contribute? What do you give the Italians?'

'Nothing! But I don't take much either. I suppose my programmes entertain some people. Occasionally, they offer ideas. I create a few opportunites for people to work. Even at the house. I'm not a political animal. I rarely grumble. I'm an observer. It amuses me to observe and record – for example, how corruption works. It can be quite a dynamic system.'

The plane had come to a halt at the start of the runway. James looked out. Several other aircraft were waiting for their turn to take off. The steward pulled the curtain between the first class and economy cabins to one side and fastened it back. With a glance, he checked that their seat backs were in the upright position. The whine from the engines rose in pitch. The plane rolled forward. It turned onto the runway.

'I don't like this at all!' Claire said.

The noise increased to a fierce howl. The smell of kerosene entered the cabin.

'Hold my hand, please!' She put her hand on the small table between their seats.

'It feels strange to touch you. I remember you used to like flying.'

150

The pilot released the brakes. The plane began to accelerate. Claire's grip tightened. Bouncing, juddering, the aircraft raced down the runway. At last it lifted off. A whirring and thumping noise from under the floor indicated that the landing gear was being retracted. A 'ping' and the no-smoking sign went off.

Claire's grip relaxed. She turned to James.

'I said, I remember you liked flying. What happened?' he asked.

'I do usually. It's – I'm so concerned we get there – '

Behind them, the steward closed the curtain again. Then he disappeared up front into the galley.

Over the Channel, they were offered breakfast. James asked for another cup of coffee which was all he wanted. Claire inclined the back of her seat and closed her eyes.

James changed to a window seat on the other side of the aisle. He looked down. The air over France was clear. The sun stood dead ahead. Barely audible, the engines hummed at the back of the plane. Watery and bright beneath, a deepening blue above, the sky filled the windows. The rushing sound of the slipstream told of the plane's steady progress through these cold and empty regions.

Over the Alps, Claire crossed the aisle to sit next to him.

'I've been thinking about that Italian businessman,' she said. 'He told his wife and daughter's kidnappers he wouldn't pay a penny for their return.'

'He didn't say that. He said that he'd only pay after their safe return. At least, that's what I recall.'

'Did he pay?'

'I don't know. I never read about the outcome.'

'What do you think of his approach? In principle?'

'I couldn't do it. Never. I wouldn't dare to negotiate like that!' Violently, he shook his head.

Despite their late departure, they landed only twenty minutes behind schedule.

A dull grey sky hung over Monte Pisano. It stretched to a faint silver line far out on the sea. Solid clouds hid the sun. The air was humid and warm.

Two *carabinieri* cars came right up to the plane. Several officers and customs men awaited Claire and James on the tarmac. Moments later, the couple were whisked away to the centre of town, the cars' sirens blaring and lights flashing, travelling very fast.

James retrieved the Chevrolet from the garage and they set off out

151

of town again, one *carabinieri* Alfa Romeo in front, the other behind. They followed the route they had taken when Claire had first arrived. After Florence, where they turned due south, they caught up with the back end of a solid thunder storm which had passed over them less than an hour earlier.

In the hills the road was still awash. They slowed down. James opened his window to let in the fresh smell of the rain, humid earth, trees and grass.

'I'm glad we're not going so fast today,' Claire said. 'Do you think there were reporters at the airport?'

James shrugged. 'They'll soon catch up with us. All I want to know is what Pasquale has to say.'

She nodded. 'I've been trying to push it out of my mind.'

Surprised, he looked across at her. 'I was just thinking the same. It's been driving me insane!'

They arrived at Terrarossa a little before three. Apart from the guards, there was no one at the gate. The two men had taken shelter in their jeep. Now they got out. They saluted.

James parked the wagon. He walked round and helped Claire from it. Together they thanked their escorts and invited them into the house. Politely, the *carabinieri* refused. They turned their cars. For a minute or two, they stopped at the gate. Then they were gone.

Max and Anna welcomed them in the door. A fire filled the kitchen with the warm scent of burning olive logs. Max had placed a chair on the hearth stone, under the fire hood, where he had been reading an old travel guide to Tuscany. He had found the book in the study.

Anna laid out bread, salame and *pecorino* on the table. From a *damigiana,* she filled the terracotta jug with wine. 'Pasquale has gone to see if the hail has done any damage to the vines. He was waiting for you. He'll be back soon.'

'Caroline's back,' Max said. 'She's having a rest.'

'How is she?' Claire asked.

'She seems much better. They sent her back yesterday. But she's to stay in bed for another week or so,' Max replied. 'She'll be glad to see you back.'

'I gather the second man died,' James said.

'The Colonel told us yesterday. He's been very kind to us,' Max said. 'He came to see us immediately after the attack had been discovered.'

152

'Did he help you with the telegram?' James asked.

'He did. In fact, he tried to telephone you but you weren't in.'

'So he knows about the message Pasquale got?'

'Yes. Someone saw a woman. I believe the *carabinieri* are checking – '

'Where?'

'Where?'

Claire and James had asked the question at the same time.

'I forget the name. Not far from here, I believe.'

Wishing that Pasquale would come back soon, James went to his room. He unpacked his bag. He went to the study next to see whether there was any mail. Reading a note from Francesca, he did not hear Pasquale until he stood in the door. Anna had made him take off his muddy shoes before he even entered the kitchen. In his socks, he shook James' hand.

'Are the vines all right?' James asked.

'They're fine. The hail was only light.'

'I gather a woman was seen – '

'Yes. At Campana. On Saturday. She was buying newspapers and several packets of cigarettes. Different kinds.'

'Did you get a description? What she looked like?'

'I told the Colonel. He said they would interview the man who had served her.'

'Have they done so?'

'I don't know. I imagine so – '

One of the guards appeared in the still open door. 'Colonel Amorini would like to speak to you, *signor* Grey.'

Quickly, James followed the man.

'Welcome back! I wish I could say to happier circumstances. How did you get on with your financial matters?'

'I'm ready to negotiate. Did you tell the media?'

'I did. As we agreed. The statement went out at noon yesterday.'

'We were horrified to hear about your men – '

'We still don't know how it happened. It would seem we're in this together even more than we thought. Pasquale Neri told us about a woman – '

'I know. Do you think – '

'I do. The description fits yours. We started to comb the area immediately.'

'Did you find anything?'

'Nothing. Not so far. But we haven't given up. Not yet!'

Disappointed, flat, James returned to the study.

Pasquale was still there.

'I have a second message,' he said, still standing in his socks.

'What is it? Tell me! Quickly!'

'The message is – you should go and ask the Count di Lando to help you.'

'Michele di Lando?'

'That's right. At Montenano.'

'Who says so? Why, Pasquale?'

'I can't tell you.'

'Did you tell the Colonel?'

'No.'

'Why not?'

'You don't need the Colonel to ask the Count for help. To look for the woman, that's something else.'

'And you can't say who told you? Or why?'

'I can't. I don't know.'

'You mean – you don't know whether you can tell me? Or you don't know?'

'I don't know. I was told not to ask.'

'What if this advice was given with bad intentions, Pasquale?'

'It was given to help you. That I know.'

Thirty-seven

ARE YOU SURE you don't want to come with me?' James asked Claire in the morning. 'We could do the bank first if we go straight away.'

'I wouldn't be able to say anything, James! If Pasquale could take me, I'd like to go to the bank though. Afterwards I can spend some time with Caroline. Max wants to go out.'

In the study, James wrote a short letter to the manager of his bank in Siena. He was certain that the banker would remember Claire from the days when they had bought Terrarossa.

'I've written a note for you to take to Verga. I'm sure he remembers you very well. Please ask him to decide on the denominations. I have no idea what would be acceptable.'

'Claire took the letter. 'How much am I collecting?'

'I thought fifty million. In two lots.'

'How much is that?'

'It depends on the rate of exchange Verga will let us have. I said in the note that I'd like to see him about that later. Roughly, it's between twenty-eight and twenty-nine thousand pounds.'

At ten o'clock James set off for Montenano. The guards stopped him at the gate. Sheepishly, one of them asked where he intended to go.

He hesitated. Should he tell a lie? 'To Montenano,' he replied at last. 'Why do you ask?'

'An order from Captain Rossi. It's easier to protect you if we know where you are.'

'I see!' The simple explanation nearly made James laugh. He kept a straight face. 'Please don't tell the journalists if any of them come.'

The guard shook his head. 'They've all gone to the funeral.'

'Your colleagues' funeral?'

'*Sissignore*. This morning.'

155

'I didn't know.' James' face darkened. 'Nobody told me. I am sorry.'

He rounded the ravine and began his descent to the bridge. Beyond the valley Montenano shone in the limpid light of the morning. Pale, its ramparts stood in the east. A single tower rose above their massive walls to the left of what might be the tiled roofs of some lower buildings.

The view evoked a picture of the castle in his memory. Thomas had drawn it, challenged to a competition by his sister. An impossibly steep hill crowned by walls. A tall tower. A long horizontal flag. Black trees covered the slopes. A knight sat on a horse in the foreground. His lance topped the tower. Plumes waved from his helmet.

Emma had protested. The knight, so she had complained, was pure fantasy.

'Did you agree to draw from nature?' James had asked. 'Exclusively?'

'We didn't!' Thomas had insisted.

'You said you were going to do a picture of that castle!' Emma had objected, pointing at Montenano. 'I can't see a knight!'

James could not recall how – if at all – the dispute had been settled.

Descending to the valley, he lost Montenano from sight. He crossed the bridge and turned left. Automatically he followed the familiar road. He wondered whether it had been wise to let Claire and Pasquale go to the bank without an escort. Pasquale had more or less insisted they did not have one. It was better, he had argued, not to attract attention to the money transport. His van was unobtrusive.

Half an hour from Terrarossa, James turned south. Climbing all the way – steeply in places – the minor road followed a narrow, winding valley. It cut deeply through the hills. Oaks, cedars, pines and chestnuts overhung it. They limited his view. Protected from the sun, he switched off the air conditioner and rolled down his window. Birds sang in the trees. A stream, hidden in thick undergrowth rushed on its way to the Arbia. The air was soft. Still humid, it was fragrant with the rich scent of the forest.

He had planned to arrive at the castle at eleven o'clock. Calling without an appointment – a stranger – he hoped the hour would be acceptable. Only a few minutes early, he reached the entrance to the

156

castle's grounds. The road seemed to fork. The drive led straight on through massive, stone gateposts. The road itself turned sharply to the right. Then it disappeared to the left behind another corner. The local wine growers' official sign pointed at the gate. 'Castello di Montenano,' white letters announced on blue. A red circle contained the black cock of the *Consorzio Vino Chianti Classico*.

He drove slowly up the gravelled private road. For more than half a mile it zigzagged on the steep hill. Trees blocked his view, up and down. He imagined himself on foot, a petitioner on the last leg of his journey rehearsing nervously the speech he would make at the feet of his liege lord and master.

The ramparts' sheer height and massive strength astonished him. A colossal black iron portcullis barely reached a third of the way to the top of the walls. It barred the entrance. In front of it, the drive ended in a terrace which was wide enough for a single car to turn on it.

He stepped from the wagon. He gaped up at the walls. Above them he saw only the sky. Where he stood, on the castle's north side, the walls cast their deepest shadow. The air was cool. A faint breeze made the tree tops rustle in the stillness of the place.

Behind the portcullis and the deep gateway it blocked lay a steeply rising coutyard. A second set of walls surrounded the cobbled space. It was empty. A weather-beaten grey wooden gate led on from it.

To the left of the portcullis was a small metalled door. A bronze bell pull hung at its side. He hesitated. He pulled the handle to the lowest point of its travel. He let go and watched as it rose slowly to its former position. He could not hear any sound. Disconcerted, he wondered whether he should have pulled the handle more sharply.

He waited.

He pulled the handle sharply a second time.

Grating, a key turned inside the door. It swung slowly inwards. A tall man stood in the frame, his hand on the door, ready to push it shut again. His hair was grey.

'What is it you want?' The voice was low.

'I am James Grey. From Terrarossa. My children have been taken. I would like to ask Count Michele di Lando for help.'

'You have no appointment.' A pair of pale grey eyes looked James squarely in the face.

'I know. There was no time to write.'

'Terrarossa,' the man repeated. 'Please wait.'

The door shut. The key turned inside.

For more than ten minutes James paced up and down, wondering what – if anything – would happen next.

The key grated. The door opened.

'Please enter,' the man said.

James stepped inside. He watched the man lock and bolt the door. A plain table and a dusty wooden chair stood in a corner of the stone chamber they were now in. A window and a door, both shut, gave on to the gateway behind the portcullis. A spiral stone stair led upwards from the chamber opposite the front door.

'Please follow me.'

The man began to climb the stair. They were inside the wall. Through it, small loopholes provided light at the spiral's every other turn. From a landing – no more than two feet square – a dark corridor led to another chamber. In its dim and distant light, James thought he could see the lifting gear for the portcullis.

From the next landing, they crossed to the interior walls. Inside them, they descended. A straight stone staircase led to the ground. Through a low arched doorway, they stepped out. They were in the courtyard of the castle.

The sun stung his eyes. Dazed, James stopped.

He blinked at a white villa.

Near the far end, to the right of the courtyard, the house stood elevated on a stone terrace. A vast but shallow roof covered its two floors. Clear and simple in its lines, its proportions and style were of the Tuscan Renaissance. The castle's tower, built of grey stone, much older than the house, rose on the left, where it connected with the east walls and ramparts.

'I never expected this!' James exclaimed, still rooted where he had stopped.

The man smiled. 'Is it the house which surprises you?'

'Everything! I imagined it would be all enclosed.'

On two sides – east and west – the walls dropped away steeply towards the south side where they were no more than the edges of an extensive platform. On it stood the castle's entire superstructure. A formal garden – he saw what looked like a small maze in its foreground – lay to the side and behind the house. Beyond it all, a stupendous landscape of hills and forests, vineyards and fields rolled into the vast distance towards an uncertain horizon.

'You came to an entrance we don't use any more,' the man said.

'There is a more convenient way up. On that side.' He pointed south.

'I didn't know. I followed the sign.'

'There is one also on the other side.'

'Do many people ring the bell?'

'It does not work. We disconnected it.'

'Then how did you know I was there?' Assuming the bell had been silenced in order to discourage unwanted visitors before they could even be noticed, James asked the question.

'I saw you.'

Side by side, they had crossed the part gravelled, part cobbled courtyard. In front of the house, they climbed a paired flight of curved stairs. Three tall casement windows gave on to the terrace at their top. The one in the centre stood open.

They entered the house.

'Please wait here for a moment.'

Alone James looked around the hall. The room, square in plan, was quite empty. Grey and white marble slabs formed a diamond pattern on the floor. Age had softened its contrasts and lines. The high walls were white. A pair of doorways broke their plain surfaces. Facing each other, they led to either side of the house. Fine cornices matched the honey colour of their stone lining. Carved beams supported the ceiling. In between them its panels had been whitewashed. The casement windows shed cool north light into the room and on its floor.

Quick sharp footsteps approached from the left. Presently a young woman came through the doorway.

'I am Laura di Lando,' she said in English.

James bowed. He took the hand she held out. He said his name.

'My father is out. He should be back shortly. Please come with me!' She turned towards the doorway she had just come from.

Behind it – a continuation of the hall in style – was a small vestibule. A marble staircase flowed from the upper floor. Tall double doors stood open to reveal a formal room of considerable proportions.

'It's such a beautiful day after the rain! I have been sitting on the terrace. Do you mind if I speak English? I don't often get the opportunity here.'

Glancing back at the visitor only once, she threaded her way through the room and around some of its rich furniture. As

159

resolutely as she had crossed the hall, she guided him towards the French doors on the south side.

'It is quite perfect.' Clumsily, he meant to compliment her on her English. He did not realise that his remark could have been attributed equally well to the quality of the day. Two, three steps behind, he was aware that he had no recollection of her face. He guessed she was in her mid-twenties. On thin, high-heeled sandals, she appeared slim, uncommonly tall. Her naturally blond hair fell loosely over the back of her neck. A pair of tortoise shell combs held it immaculately over small ears.

'Please, Mr Grey. Will you sit?'

A gesture of her hand indicated a group of cane chairs and a round table. A bright blue cloth covered the table to the floor. Newspapers and letters lay in a white basket tray. Next to them a little silver bell sat on the cloth. A deep canvas awning protected the airy place from the sun.

He waited for her to sit first.

'My father and I were very sorry to hear about your children. Have you had word from the kidnappers?'

'Not yet.' He sat down abruptly. He looked at her across the table. 'We announced we're ready to talk.'

'Yes – we saw.' From the curtness of his reply she concluded that – already – she had gone too far. 'May I offer you a drink? Or some coffee? I am sure my father will not be long.'

He accepted coffee.

She lifted the bell. Lightly, it rang in her hand.

A young man appeared in one of the doors. He wore a white jacket. His hands sported white gloves. He listened attentively to the simple order. He bowed and backed away.

'My son once drew a picture of your castle.' For an instant, James shut his eyes. 'I suddenly thought of it. On my way here. He drew a fortress. I expected to come to a fortress. But this! It's a villa! It reminds me of Sangallo.'

She smiled. 'The house is considerably younger. I suppose the architect tried to copy him.'

'Do you know who he was?'

'A local man. Of modest talent only. We know very little about him.'

A telephone rang in the house.

Its ringing silenced James. Its persistence made him increasingly

160

uncomfortable.

The ringing stopped.

He was trying to think of something to say when the servant reappeared.

'A telephone call for the gentleman,' he announced.

'For me?' James jumped to his feet. 'I – I am extremely sorry! I did not presume to ask anyone to call me here. In fact, hardly anyone knows – '

'Paolo, show Mr Grey to the telephone! Quickly!'

Ashen suddenly, he followed the servant into the house. The telephone was in a small room, not far from the vestibule.

He grabbed the handset.

'My apologies for disturbing you! I wanted to be quite sure where you were.' Faintly, the Colonel's voice came over the crackling line.

'Where are you? What's going on?'

'I cannot tell you. Not now! Please stay at Montenano until we pick you up. I'm sending the helicopter. Maybe you could tell di Lando that I hope to have his permission to land inside his walls.'

The telephone clicked.

Perplexed, James eyed the dead receiver in his hand. He replaced it slowly. For a moment longer he stood quite still.

On his own, he found his way back to the terrace.

His coffee had been served. A silver jug, sugar basin, tongs and spoon sat on the table next to a plain white cup.

'You look disturbed!' Concern showed in her voice. 'Have you had bad news?'

'I don't know.' He did not want to sit. 'I have no idea what it means! Colonel Amorini – of the *carabinieri* – is sending the helicopter. To pick me up.'

'Here? At Montenano?'

'He wants to land inside. Is that possible?'

'Of course! My father used to hire a helicopter company to spray the vines. They landed here sometimes.'

He recalled the way the Colonel had referred to the Count. 'Does your father know Amorini?'

'They are friends. Amorini's father worked for my grandfather. In a way, they grew up together.'

'What did he do?'

'Amorini's father? I'm not quite sure. There were so many more people here when my great-grandfather and after him my

161

grandfather modernised the estate.'

An old-fashioned car horn sounded from the far side of the house. 'That's him!'

Laura got up. A smile softened her clear features. 'My father believes the horn on his old car sounds funny. He likes to blow it – only here – when he leaves or arrives. I'll go and tell him of your visit. You may not have much time.'

Through the doors, he watched her cross the great room. He turned to the stone balustrade. Waist high, it contained the garden side of the terrace. Unable even to guess at what the next few hours might bring, he looked into the distance. He had no eyes for the intricately balanced pattern of hedges, gravelled paths, flowers and ornamental bay and orange trees, which lay before him.

Michele di Lando was halfway across the terrace when he heard his step.

He turned.

A tall man held out his hand.

'My daughter tells me you are about to leave again. What can I do for you?'

Disconcerted by the direct address, James took the hand. It felt firm. He tried to re-order what he had intended to say. The Count seemed friendly, even less reserved than his daughter. White hair topped an open outdoor face. The smile, although faint, was warm, sincere.

'I have a man helping me at Terrarossa,' James began. 'His name is Pasquale Neri. He is one of the old partisans.'

'I have heard of him.'

'You have?'

'A good man. We could have done with many more like him.'

'After the children had been taken, Pasquale went round the province to ask his surviving comrades for help. So far, two messages have come back to us. One of them is straightforward. A strange woman was seen. The *carabinieri* are still following up on it. The other message is very different. It says I should ask you for help.'

'Me? Why?'

'I don't know.'

'Well – didn't Neri say?'

'He didn't. Or, rather, he can't. He says he cannot tell where the message comes from. He was told not to ask. But he is sure that it was sent in good faith.'

162

The Count shook his head. 'I want to help you. I am not taking lightly what a man like Neri has to say. But where am I to begin?'

'I don't know! That's why I'm here.' Dejectedly, James looked at the man who – in terms of age – probably could have been his father. 'I've tried to think. Maybe – could it mean the children are hidden on your land?'

'I own not only the land here at Montenano, Mr Grey. Some of my property is quite far away. Fragmented. A bit here. A little bit there. Does Amorini believe they're on my land?'

'He doesn't know of this message. Not yet. I have not seen him since my return from London yesterday afternoon.'

'But – do you know whether Amorini believes the children are still in this area?'

'He seems to think they may be hidden in the woods. At least, he said so. A few days ago.'

'What facts do you have to support the suspicion?'

'The car in which my daughter was taken away had yellow mud on its wheels.'

'Yellow? There is yellow earth here. But also in other areas – it's not exactly rare. Outside Chianti too – '

'If the car I saw had been travelling far or at all fast, the mud would have been thrown off its wheels. You may recall the storms – on the two days before my children were taken. The Saturday before last.'

'I remember. I was concerned for our vines on the first day. We got rather more of the storm over here than you did near Siena. I remember very well! However what you say does not rule out the gangsters going further afield. After they took the children.'

'Except – the *carabinieri* put up roadblocks very soon. Also I cannot believe the kidnappers had planned to go far. They had intended to take my friends' children as well. Four in all.'

'Four children! I had not realised that!'

'My friend is an American banker. I believe the kidnappers were far more interested in his children than in mine. They tried to take him hostage instead, later – '

The sound of the approaching helicopter stopped James in mid-sentence.

'We had better go outside.' The Count invited his visitor to step through the door first. 'We have reverted to simpler methods but for

was still struggling with his harness when they lifted off. They some time we hired a helicopter to do part of our spraying. Do you know where they're taking you?'

'I don't. I have no idea what's going on! Is it all right if I leave my car where it is?'

'It may be safer inside. If you like I will have it brought round.'

In the hall, James handed over his car keys. They went as far as the front terrace.

The helicopter climbed on its final approach to the castle. Suddenly, its full noise fell into the square and the aircraft came swooping over the east ramparts in a dipping, spiralling curve. For an uncertain moment it hung in the air, swinging from side to side. Stabilising, it began to come down. Dust flew away from the downwash in a circular cloud. Caught all at once by the walls on three sides, the roar of the turboshaft engine and the beat of the rotor reverberated deafeningly in the courtyard.

'I expected it to come in from the other side!' the Count shouted. 'From Siena!'

James gave a nod. He screwed up his eyes. Despite his distance from the landing place, dust had got into them.

The helicopter set down. The rotor flapped at idling speed. A *carabiniere* jumped from the cabin. He ducked. Straightening the bottom of his jacket, he came running across the square.

'I am Rossi.' The young officer – James had recognised the face immediately – saluted. 'Colonel Amorini expects you, Mr Grey.'

'He knows that,' the Count interjected. 'Where're you taking him?'

'I'm not supposed to say, *signor conte*. But I'm sure you won't tell. Camilliano.'

'Camilliano? I have a little land there. What the deuce is going on?'

'I am really not allowed to tell.' Embarrassed, Rossi bit his lip. 'Please understand!'

'I wish you a good flight then, Mr Grey.' Displeased, the Count eyed the officer.

'Remember me to that secretive chief of yours! In future, if you are going to mess about on my land maybe he'd like to let me know. And don't forget – you've got to bring Mr Grey back here. We're looking after his car.'

With Rossi's help, James climbed into the back of the helicopter. Hunched behind the pilot, he tried to find room for his knees. He slipped out sideways, over the west ramparts. In a steeply rising turn, they came back over the north gate and walls.

He looked down. The Chevrolet was where he had left it. The Count, still on the terrace, gave a single wave. Laura and the grey-haired man who had let James into the castle stood with him. Immobile, faces turned up, they watched his sudden departure.

Thirty-eight

IN THE MARKET square, Pasquale heaved the two well-worn baskets which served to take shopping to Terrarossa into the back of his van. Carefully, he pushed them against the back of his seat. There, they would not slide about. At the bottom of the first basket – under bags of fruit, vegetables, pasta, bread and cheese – lay two parcels. They had been wrapped in printed paper, red type on white. Verga, the bank manager, had sent out for it to a friend who owned a small bookshop. The parcels looked alike, as though they contained maybe a dozen paperbacks each. Worth exactly twenty-five million *lire* apiece, each had been made up with a combination of fifteen hundred used banknotes of ten thousand *lire*, plus a further five hundred notes each of double that denomination.

He locked the tailgate and opened the passenger door for Claire. Anxious to get away, she slipped into the hot compartment. She pulled the door shut before he could help her.

They set off. In the busy streets, alive with the traffic of workers on their way home to lunch, the insignificant vehicle went barely noticed. Soon Siena lay behind them. They were on their way back through the hills to where they had come from some two hours earlier.

Vaguely – certainly without the benefit of real contentment – Claire experienced a feeling of satisfaction. For the first time, she had contributed practically to the long and tortuous process of getting the children back. She wound down her window all the way. Warm, the wind caught her hair. Through half closed eyes she gazed at the great heat-hazed landscape ahead. Long ago, Montenano had dissolved in its shimmering veil. If only James were to return with a promise of fresh help, the day might turn out the best she had endured since the abduction.

The guards stopped them at the gate.

166

They talked excitedly through the window at Pasquale. Several times they pointed east.

Increasingly alarmed, Claire could not follow the rapid exchange.

'What are they saying?' She knew she would have to summon all the Italian she could still muster if she was to find out. '*Che cosa dicono?*'

'They say Colonel Amorini suddenly left the funeral. Something is going on. In the hills. East of here.' Pasquale tried to speak slowly, so she would be able to understand.

'In the hills? The Colonel?' The Italian word for funeral – she did not know the one he had used – confused her.

'Yes. Amorini has gone to the hills. Over there.' His hand pointed east.

'Why?'

He gave a shrug. 'They're not sure. It seems quite a few men have gone there. Also the helicopter. They saw it fly past. They must be on to something. That's all they know.'

'The children? Have they found the children?'

'They don't know, *signora!*'

'But James has gone to Montenano!'

'They know that. Maybe they'll contact him there. There's nothing we can do here.'

Angry suddenly, she got out of the car. If only she could have spoken the language with more authority! She would have demanded an explanation over the radio! Unbearable tension had gripped her body. She needed air. Taking no further notice of the men, she hurried down the drive. Then she remembered that Max had gone out to draw.

Pasquale caught up with her in the kitchen. Silent, he lifted the baskets on to the table. He began to unpack them.

Anna came up the stair.

'*E questo il denaro?*' She pointed at the two parcels.

'*Lo è.*'

Easily, Anna's hands grabbed a parcel each. She turned towards the interior of the house.

Puzzled, Claire had observed the laconic exchange between husband and wife. Suspiciously, she followed to the study.

Anna put the parcels on a chair. From her apron, she produced a long key. Over a side table, let into the wall, was the ornate door of an old safe which James had found in a junk shop. Despite its obviousness – white and gilt garlands contrasted with the bottle-green background – Claire had never noticed it.

Anna unlocked the door. She pulled it open. Apart from some papers on an upper shelf, the safe appeared empty. She put the parcels in. Comfortably, they fitted into the back of the lowest compartment. The door grated in its frame as she pushed it shut to lock it. She returned the key to her apron.

'*E sicuro qui!*' Anna smiled.

Speechless, Claire stared at the woman. It was obvious that James had given the instructions for what should be done with the money.

But he had not told her, Claire!

Just as she was beginning to feel closer to him and – above all! – involved practically in securing the children's release, he had left her out. Completely, she felt, and not even thoughtlessly so.

Even angrier – a mass of furious emotions and humiliating frustration – she stormed out. She shut herself in her room. She had no thought for Caroline who was still looking forward to her visit.

Thirty-nine

UNLESS JAMES MADE him take off his helmet again, there was no way he could have asked Rossi to explain what was going on. The officer had donned the shiny shell the very moment he had taken his seat beside the pilot. Busily, he spoke into its built-in microphone either to his colleague – several times the pilot looked expectantly across at him – or the ground, or both.

The noise inside the cramped cabin was intense, painful to the ears. James tore the corners off a tissue he carried in his pocket. Twisting and crumpling them, he made himself a couple of ear plugs.

He had never heard of Camilliano nor could he remember seeing the place on a map. He guessed that it lay to the northeast. Monte Luco and Monte Calvo – two of the highest peaks in the area – stood straight ahead.

They flew low, maybe a thousand feet above the undulating landscape. To his untrained eyes, the dense woodland appeared impenetrable. The vibration, pitching and yawing of the aircraft made it difficult for him to focus. He began to feel sick. He looked ahead instead of down.

They skirted the western flanks of Monte Luco. They dropped into a valley. Houses appeared in front of them. Rossi turned. 'Camilliano,' James read from his lips. Less than ten minutes since their departure from Montenano, the helicopter set down in the centre of the hamlet.

Grateful for the shortness of the flight, James got out. He unbent his knees. Only now – in the hot but clean air – he realised how strong the smell of kerosene had been in the cabin.

Nervously, he looked around. Several jeeps were parked under a group of trees.

A personnel carrier stood nearby. Alone, a man in camouflage

169

uniform sat on the ground in its shade.

He realised that his ears were still plugged. He picked out the paper balls. Stuffing them into his pockets, he felt the cameo of the Madonna. He took it out. Firmly, he clasped it in his hand.

'Colonel Amorini is over there.' Rossi pointed to the other side of the cars.

A group of officers clustered round the Colonel. He wore headphones. Immobile, he bent over the side of an open jeep.

Hesitant, James went nearer. No one spoke. He heard the hissing and crackling of the radio. The operator's hands hovered over the controls.

Unnoticed, James observed the men. If only someone would speak to him, explain what was going on! He heard himself breathe. His pulse throbbed in his throat.

The operator's fingers flew into action. Rapidly, they adjusted the controls. The men drew together, closer still, their heads bowed. They listened intently, as if wishing something on, forcing it to happen.

James clenched the Madonna. His knuckles whitened.

'They've gone!' the radio's loudspeaker announced. 'The place is empty. They left the cars behind.'

Furiously, the Colonel ripped off the headphones. He threw them into the jeep. He turned, pale with anger. Under the moustache his mouth was shut tight. His jaw jutted. He stamped up and down.

'Somebody warned them!' he snarled. 'Somebody gave us away!'

He saw James. He stopped in front of him. 'I'm sorry I thought we had a chance. I needed you here in case we were able to take them by surprise. I wanted to have your permission.'

Dumbfounded, James opened his mouth. His eyes stared, incredulous. The sudden collapse of the suspense and the realisation that they had been close to freeing the children were more than he could come to terms with at once.

The Colonel put an arm round his shoulder. 'I wish I could offer you some comfort, make a promise. Let's go and have a look! At least it doesn't matter if we make a lot of noise now.'

The flight to the top of the valley and on to the far side of Monte Calvo's foothills took only a few minutes. Rossi sat with James in the back. Twice the officer tried to point something out to him. Each time he failed to see what Rossi was indicating. The pilot circled. He brought the helicopter down in a triangular clearing. Wood cutters

170

had been at work in it not long ago. Neat stacks of logs lined a stony forestry road. A couple of jeeps were parked in one of the corners, under trees in whose shade the track disappeared.

The men who were with the jeeps stood to attention.

'How far is it from here? Exactly?' the Colonel demanded.

'Four and a half kilometres, sir. Do you wish to see the map, sir?'

'Give it to me! Let's go! Quickly!'

James got into the first jeep with the Colonel. Rossi followed in the second vehicle. Silent, they rode along while the Colonel studied the map. On the steep track their progress was slow. The midday sun lanced the half-light of the forest with colonnades of near-vertical rays. After the helicopter, the jeeps' purring motors seemed stealthful indeed.

Some ten minutes later and deeper into the forest, they forded a stream and climbed up on to a plateau. A scout in battle dress stood on the track. He guided them on to an even narrower path.

At walking speed, they entered an area of thick undergrowth. The path softened. The air smelled damp. They crossed a short stretch of black mud.

The track began to climb again. Its surface hardened. The scout jumped into the first jeep and they went faster. Rocks stuck through the dark soil. Patches of pale and mossy stone showed between tall trees.

They came to an old clearing. Bushes and crippled trees stood about. At the far end, screened by them and almost totally overgrown, hid the remains of a stone cottage. Several men were busy searching the ground around it.

Built, maybe, by a charcoal burner sometime in the last century, the house was as simple as could be. Rough stone walls contained two rooms. Identical in shape and size, they had dirt floors. The entrance was a hole in the wall. Less than mansize in height, it opened into the first room. Stones had broken from its ragged edges. The roof consisted of a few remaining slates which lay on rotting timbers. It sagged. Thick overgrowth provided the cover.

Behind the Colonel, James entered the first room. His eyes adjusted quickly to the poor light. Rubble and earth filled the only window. Some sticks lay in a corner. The remains of a fire were on the floor against a side wall. It had obviously not burned often or for a long time. Dank, musty, the air was stagnant in the empty room.

The second room was darker yet. Green light came through its overgrown and glassless window frame. A bird rustled noisily in the twigs outside. It chirped and flew away on whirring wings.

'Nothing! Absolutely nothing!' The Colonel looked up at the broken rafters of the roof. 'Let's take a look at the cars.'

The sergeant in charge of the scouts took them round the back of the cottage. A silver-grey Alfa Romeo and a pale green Fiat were parked side by side.

'Is this the Alfa Romeo you saw?' the Colonel asked.

James looked at the front wheels. The yellow mud had almost gone. 'I think so.'

The Colonel turned to the sergeant. 'Have you found anything?'

'We're still looking, sir. I don't think they were here for long. We discovered a path. It leads down to Castiglione. Castiglione del Bosco, sir.'

'Can you tell whether they walked on it?'

'I think so, sir. We found footprints further down.'

'How many people? Can you tell?'

'I reckon two men and one woman, sir.'

'None of the children?'

The sergeant looked uncomfortable.

'Well?'

'Only one, sir.' Nervously, the man glanced at James.

'Only one?' James stepped forward. Terrified, he turned from the sergeant to the Colonel and back. 'Are you sure?'

'They may have carried a child,' the Colonel interjected. 'Which child's are the footprints?'

'I'm not sure, sir. It's difficult to say without knowing the shoe sizes – '

'All right. Let's go and have a look. Maybe Mr Grey can help us. Where is that path? Maybe you'd like to lead the way.'

At first neither the Colonel nor James could see where the track began. Only after the sergeant had walked straight into a bush and parted it with his arms could they see its faint outline. Gradually it widened. For a short distance, it disappeared again. As they descended, the ground grew damper. They reached the place where the footprints had been found.

James looked at the path. It was so narrow only one person could pass at a time. The passage was twenty-five, maybe thirty feet long. In the drying mud, footprints could be seen all along its length. The smallest ones were Emma's, he had no doubt.

172

'Can you tell anything?' the Colonel asked.

'Those are my daughter's footprints.'

'Look carefully, Mr Grey! I assume your son's must be smaller – '

'Much smaller.' Holding on to the bushes along the path, James worked up and down the short stretch. However hard he strained his eyes, none of the prints could have been Thomas'.

'Nothing?'

'Nothing.'

'They may have separated the children,' the sergeant suggested. 'It wouldn't be unusual.'

'That's right!' the Colonel was quick to agree. 'They may well have done so. If you think about it, it's a kind of self-insurance if they keep their hostages in different places.'

James saw the point. Desperately, he wanted to accept it, believe in its reality. But all the time, he had imagined the children staying together. It was difficult to rid himself of the assumption.

'What – what if they killed him? They threatened to cut off their fingers!' he cried out.

'Why should they, Mr Grey? Tell me!'

'He wasn't here!'

'You don't know! Not for sure! As we said, they may have carried him – '

'He's good on his feet! He can walk for miles!'

'All right! So he wasn't here. I'll be brutally frank with you. You know – we all accept – that the chances for the children's survival are only even. But unless something were to happen, something which would persuade their captors to rid themselves of the burden of keeping both children – because of, I don't know, uncontrollable circumstances I cannot imagine – they will kill either both or neither. Why should they have killed the boy at this stage? Why? I have not forgotten what the man said to you at Valcortese. It's engraved in my mind too. But it makes no practical sense! If anything, he must be easier to hold. He's smaller, weaker, not old enough to even think of planning an escape. As for the deadline, you have done everything they demanded of you. Have you not?'

James had no reply. He had a single fact only: Thomas had not walked through the mud. Maybe someone had picked him up just for the short stretch? It was possible. How could he argue? His fears – not his reason – insisted that something had gone wrong. He knew the *carabinieri*'s forensic experts would soon be going over the place in minute detail. Maybe they could confirm that Thomas had been held at the house? Whatever, he had to hope! He had to believe that his son was still alive.

He looked up from the path. 'I'm sorry. I don't mean to doubt you. Please forgive me. I want you to be right!'

Forty

THE HOURS OF the early afternoon were torture for Claire. Their silence made her feel even more isolated than when she had shut herself away.

Suddenly wishing for company, she left her room. She knocked on Caroline's door. There was no reply. She went outside through the loggia.

The sun seemed to have come to a halt in the glaring sky. Its white heat compelled rest, stillness. The guards below the house – increased to four since the last incident – had each taken refuge under separate olive trees. The two men at the gate sat on the ground in the narrow band of shade afforded them by their jeep. On and off, a tractor sounded from a distant vineyard. Each time it reached the top of a row its engine rattled, accompanied by the clanging of its metal tracks when it turned. Then there was silence again.

She decided to have a swim. She swam up and down methodically, counting every length. Why was James still not back? She gave up her counting. She began to persuade herself that he would return with good news. Maybe he too had gone to the hills? Maybe he would return with – the children, her mind went on to say – but she dared not admit that. She chased the tormenting thought away. Out of breath suddenly, she climbed from the pool and went inside.

Max returned at four. He found Claire on the terrace. Fists clenched, she was pacing up and down. With every other step, she beat the outsides of her thighs. Distracted, she only glanced at him. For an instant, she slowed down. Staccato, she told him what she had learnt from Pasquale and the guards.

'I suppose James is with them,' he said when she had finished. 'It may mean something good. Can I do something for you? I'm going to make myself some tea. Would you like some?'

She shook her head.

'Have you seen Caroline? How is she?'

'She's asleep.'

'Would you like to go for a walk? We could pick some flowers.'

'It's too hot.'

He sighed. 'I suppose so – '

'How long have you been here?' she asked.

Not sure what she meant, he looked at her. 'You mean now? I've just – '

'No. Altogether.'

'Since the eleventh. A couple of days before Caroline and the children arrived. You sent me the book. Remember?'

'I forgot.'

'Why do you ask?'

Again, she shook her head. 'I don't know. It's just – it's – everything's ground to a halt! Time's dead!'

Before he could find anything to say – how much he wanted to comfort her! – she had rushed inside and downstairs, back to her room.

Forty-one

DRAINED, SEEMINGLY WITH nothing left to say, they arrived back at Camilliano. Still in the jeep, James had told the Colonel of Pasquale's second message and the Count's reaction. The *carabinieri*'s various vehicles had gone. Only the Colonel's driver and a young lieutenant were still waiting, standing by his car. Apart from an old woman, the hamlet was deserted. Dressed entirely in black, she was tending her small garden.

'We had better go and talk to di Lando,' the Colonel suddenly announced. 'In any case, we've got to get you back there – '

A short conference with Rossi, who was to take the helicopter back to Siena, and the Colonel was ready to leave.

'Slowly now!' he said to the driver and got into the back of the car, after James.

The lieutenant took the front passenger seat. The heat of the afternoon had reached its maximum. With all windows down, they set off across country towards Montenano. No one spoke for a while.

From Camilliano they went to Barbiscio and on to Gaiole where they joined the road from Montevarchi. They turned west, towards Siena. They encountered other cars only twice. Few people were about.

James could hold back no longer. 'How did you find out?'

'Ah!' The Colonel had long expected the question. 'One of my comrades,' he emphasised the word sadly, 'told me.'

'You mean – one of Pasquale's comrades?'

'No. Just one of our local contacts. Basically, we used a little routine method. We drew a rough circle round Terrarossa, a circle whose radius represented the maximum distance we estimated they could have covered before our roadblocks went up. We pinpointed the areas particularly suitable to hide in. We asked around, door to door.'

The lieutenant turned to the Colonel. He had a call from headquarters on the radio.

'Is it important?'

The young officer shook his head.

'Say – Rossi's on his way back. I'd be grateful if he could deal with the problem.' The Colonel turned to James again. 'An old man from one of the villages went to pick mushrooms. On Monday. The rain brings them on. That night, he told a friend that he had seen something unusual. He had seen the cars. Instead of alerting us, the friend went to have a look for himself. He thought perhaps the old man was a little crazy. That was yesterday. Our man got the information from him.'

'So you heard only this morning?'

'That's right. At the funeral. Hence the rush and this half-baked operation.'

'Do you think – as you said – someone warned them?'

'I doubt it now. In fact, I'm sure they had planned to leave. The footprints looked quite old to me. It's the usual practice for kidnappers to keep moving, at least at the beginning.'

James shut his eyes. He tried to imagine what the scene would have been like had the children and their captors still been at the cottage. The Colonel had mentioned taking the place by surprise with his, James', permission. If it came to a similar situation again how would they assess the danger? What would they decide?

They arrived at the junction where James had turned towards Montenano in the morning. He opened his eyes. Blinking in the bright light, he reflected that he was on the same stretch of road, travelling in the same direction for the second time within a few hours although his car was still at the original destination.

'I thought Laura di Lando was very attractive,' he said, intending to get back to talking about her father again.

'Her mother, too, was very beautiful,' the Colonel replied.

'Is she dead?'

'She was killed in a car crash. Very nearly eleven years ago.'

'Here?'

'It happened in Rome. Di Lando's sister lived there. She died in the same accident. In fact, it was last year, at the tenth memorial mass, that I last saw Laura. Di Lando suffered terribly from the loss.'

'Is she his only child?'

'Indeed. They are a very small family now. The only other close relative is his nephew. His dead sister's son.'

'Does he live at Montenano?'

'Not any more. I believe he is still in America. He's a student.'

'A student?'

A glint of irony was in the Colonel's eyes. 'I don't think Enrico's the type who'd turn against his family's values.'

Embarrassed, James looked out through the window. The sun had travelled west. The valley seemed even deeper and fuller of shadows than in the morning. They passed the gate he had entered earlier. Without a trace of hesitation, the driver continued on the road.

'I went up there.' Grateful for something to say, James pointed at the sign by the roadside. 'I was misled.'

The Colonel smiled. 'I guess di Lando reckons this way he gets rid of one half of his unwanted visitors. It's quite difficult to get inside the castle if you're not invited.'

'He didn't seem unfriendly – '

'On the contrary, he's a perfectly pleasant man. But he is also very rich, which makes it necessary to be equally discreet.'

'I imagine he and his daughter must be prime targets themselves?'

'Of course! The rich are at risk everywhere in Italy.'

A few minutes later, under the south side of the castle, they turned through a stone gate which was identical to the one they had passed. But the slope above it was almost bare. Higher up, it steepened into ramparts and walls. Burnt yellow grass rustled drily in a freshening breeze. Under the wind it bent and sprang back only to bend again. In long drawn waves, the movement flew over the round hillside. Two orderly lines of cypresses zigzagged to the top. Between them, they watched over the drive.

The entrance through the walls was similar to the one James had seen in the morning, too. The driver stopped the car, got out and jerked the bell-pull. James noticed that he pulled the handle twice in rapid succession before he let it go. Slowly, it returned to its previous position.

The driver was behind the wheel when the portcullis began to lift. Inside, they climbed steeply between two walls to the top of the platform on the west side of the house. An old Lancia Lambda, its black cabriolet top neatly folded back, was parked there. Beside it stood James' wagon. Incongruously, it dwarfed the old car.

179

A servant, middle-aged in grey livery, showed the visitors to the library in the southwest corner of the house. A vast bookcase lined the only windowless wall from floor to ceiling. Tall library steps had been pushed right up to it beside a window at the far end of the room which faced south. An antique globe, brown with age and some fifteen feet in circumference, was the centrepiece of the room. Several tables covered with books, old and new, stood between the windows. Armchairs had been arranged in a corner where one of the French doors stood open on to the west terrace.

'A surprise!' Michele di Lando exclaimed. Vigorously, he shook the Colonel's hand. 'Have you seen your car, Mr Grey?'

'I have. I'm afraid, next to your beautiful car, it rather spoils its style.'

A faint smile acknowledged the compliment. Serious again, the Count turned to the Colonel. 'What happened? Did you find anything in Camilliano?'

'News spreads fast in this part of the world,' the officer observed drily. 'We were too late. By several hours.'

'Too late for what?'

Briefly, the Colonel explained what had led them to Camilliano and the hills above it.

'I don't own any land in the direction you describe.' The Count looked at James.

'I knew it wasn't yours,' the Colonel said. 'However, we can't afford to take lightly what Neri said about asking you for help, di Lando.'

'I agree entirely. I've been racking my brain ever since Mr Grey called this morning. How do I fit in?'

'I believe,' the Colonel replied, 'the connection may not be your land. Maybe it's someone you know, perhaps have only met. You know, the way the message is worded suggests to me that someone may be trying to be tactful. Save you embarrassment.'

'But why? Do you think my butler has done it?'

The Count was still speaking when the young servant who had been in attendance in the morning entered the room.

'*Deus ex machina!*' the Count exclaimed. 'Forgive me, Mr Grey! I didn't mean to be flippant. Will you take something? Tea? Coffee? A Drink? And you, Amorini?'

James asked for tea. The Colonel wanted coffee. A silent bow. The servant turned and made for the door.

180

Pensive, the Colonel followed him with his eyes to the far end of the room. 'I think it's quite obvious who it is we're dealing with. After the attacks on my men.'

'Exactly! That's why I'm at such a loss! If they were local no-goods, malcontents, one could try to run down the register. Could one not? It can't be all that long, can it?'

'It's long enough! Have you been threatened recently? Or Laura?'

'Nothing! I cannot even remember a poison-pen letter. Not for a year. I would have told you. Incidentally, Mr Grey mentioned this morning you were checking up on a woman. Can you tell me something about her?'

'She was seen at Campana. She was young. She may have been the woman who took part in the actual abduction.'

'What did she look like?'

'Small, dark, unremarkable.'

'And her voice?'

'The man who served her said she spoke well. Like an educated person.'

'There was nothing educated about her when I encountered her,' James interjected. 'I thought most Tuscans spoke well. Or did he mean her manner?'

'He didn't think she was a local. That's the whole point. She was a stranger. He said that. For the rest, I assumed he meant her manner. Buying cigarettes and newspapers does not normally entail deep conversations.'

'Did he say where he thought she might be from?' the Count resumed his questions.

'I asked him. Very carefully, in fact. I wanted to avoid putting anything in his mind. Maybe Roman, he volunteered after a lot of prompting by Rossi. But really he was only guessing. I am quite sure he had no idea what distinguishes an educated Roman from – I don't know – a Paduan.'

'So? Where does that leave us, gentlemen?' Expectantly, the Count eyed his visitors.

'Nowhere! Just about nowhere!' The Colonel walked away, to one of the windows.

The servant entered. He carried a tray.

'Put it over there, Paolo!' The Count pointed at the group of armchairs by the open French door. 'We'll help ourselves.'

Paolo set down the tray. He left as quietly as he had come.

Silent, the Count served James. He took a cup of coffee to the Colonel who had not moved from the window. Then he helped himself to some coffee.

The Colonel turned, into the room.

'I'd like you to sleep on the whole thing, di Lando. Maybe something will occur to you. Or to Laura. People you met in the past. They may have come here. By the way – Enrico – is he still in America?'

'He finished. He got his degree a week ago.' The Count turned to James. 'Enrico is my nephew. He went to MIT to do postgraduate work. He's an engineer. I was very pleased with his results. I sent him a little extra money: he wanted to travel a little – in Mexico – before coming back to Europe.'

'Can you contact him?' the Colonel asked.

'I'm afraid I have no idea where precisely he is. Nor when he'll be back.'

'I must go.' The Colonel put down his cup. 'Thank you for your hospitality. Every time I leave my office, people pile papers on my desk.'

'I too had better go,' James said. 'Claire – the children's mother – must be wondering what happened to me.'

'We could have called Terrarossa on the radio,' the Colonel said.

'I didn't think – '

'Do you want to do it now?'

'I'll be home quite soon. A sudden call might frighten her even more.'

Together, the three men went outside. The sun was over Siena. Terrarossa stood clearly visible in its softening light.

'Now you can see my house.' Turning to the Count, James pointed west.

The Count shielded his eyes with both hands. 'You have a wonderful position, Mr Grey. Your view must be as good as ours.'

'One last question,' the Colonel interrupted. 'How many people do you now employ in your forests?'

'Specifically in the forests? One overseer and two assistants. But they don't spend all of their time outside. They're managers, really. They deal with all the subcontractors who cut what we decide to sell.'

'Have you asked your people to help by keeping their eyes and ears open?'

182

'I am going to ask them myself. I shall visit some villages this evening, the others tomorrow. I'll ask everyone worth asking. Rest assured.'

Forty-two

JAMES RETURNED TO Terrarossa at half past five. He was still in his car when Claire appeared in the front door. Silent, she watched him get down from the Chevrolet.

He was at the bottom of the steps. 'I hope you didn't worry. I was suddenly – '

'The mountains?'

Surprised, he looked up at her. Suddenly he realised the state she was in.

'I'm sorry, Claire! Who told you?'

'The guards told Pasquale. They wouldn't say what was going on. Tell me! What happened? Is it good? Or bad?' Anxiously, her eyes were fixed on him.

'Neither, Claire,' he replied quietly. 'Let's go inside. I'll explain.'

'Nothing?' Disbelieving, she would not move, blocking tho entrance. 'Nothing at all?'

'I'll explain. Don't worry. Please!'

He wanted to put his arm round her shoulder, to calm her, comfort her.

Irritatedly, she shrugged him off.

They entered the kitchen. From the balcony, he heard Caroline's voice.

He went straight out through the sitting room. Irritated himself now by Claire's unexpected welcome, he decided that he might just as well tell the others what had kept him away for so long at the same time.

'James!' Max jumped to his feet. He saw Claire's grim face. 'I was about to give you up. Claire's been through absolute hell waiting for you.'

'I got the picture.' James snapped. He addressed Caroline. 'Have you been up long? How do you feel?'

184

In her dressing gown, she sat in an armchair Max had brought out for her. She had made herself a turban with a blue headscarf, to cover her bandages. 'Only since it got a little cooler,' she replied, pleased about the inquiry. 'It's good to be out.'

'It's good to see you up again. I'm sorry I kept you all in such suspense. I didn't think you'd know. I had no idea you'd worry.'

Methodically, he began to relate his day's events. For Claire's sake he toned down the probability that the operation might have succeeded. Hesitating for a moment, he chose not to mention the footprints at all. He finished with the Count's promise to go out and ask for help before the day was over. Most of the time he had stood with his back to Montenano. He was unaware of it, though. Warmer, brighter than in the morning light, the castle shone in the early evening sun.

They were silent. High in the sky the swifts flew in wide circles, feeding for the night.

Claire cried quietly. The missed opportunity and the Count's evident inability to help straight away combined to produce in her a bitter disappointment. The fact that at least nothing terrible had happened in the hills brought her no relief. Less hopeful than ever and with the feeling that James had betrayed her, she took herself away, downstairs, back to her room.

Forty-three

A TERRIBLE BOOMING voice woke everyone at Terrarossa in the middle of the night.

'Grey! Get up! Are you ready, Grey?'

Through a megaphone the voice bellowed from the other side of the ravine. It called several times. Eerily in the night it echoed.

At once, James was on his feet. He pulled the kimono over his shoulders, pushing open the doors to the balcony. He stumbled out.

From the *carabinieri*'s jeep, a searchlight came on. Erratically, it ran along the road. Over the bend, it caught some of the tree tops.

A rifle shot shattered the light.

'The next shot kills! Do you want to try?' the voice mocked.

'I am ready!' James called out. 'What is it you want me to do?'

'Put the money in your car! Go to the bridge! Follow the instructions!'

Instantly, he went back inside. He switched on his reading light and got dressed. From the bedside table, he took the cameo of the Madonna. He put it in his pocket. He went to the study next. He unlocked the safe, took out one of the parcels and locked it again. On his way out, he passed through the kitchen.

'Anything we should do?' Max whispered in the dark.

'Stay inside! Don't go out in the dark!' James put the parcel on the table and switched on a single light over a work top. 'I'll tell the *carabinieri* that you're up.'

In their night clothes, Claire and Caroline huddled on the hearth stone. They looked frightened. The dim light made their faces very pale. Wrapped in his striped bath robe, Max stood by the window looking out towards the top of the ravine.

James detached his keys from his belt loop. He separated the car keys from the others.

'I'm not taking these.' He put the rest of the bunch on the table.

He picked up the parcel.

'Please take care!' Claire called after him.

He put the money on the floor behind his seat and started the car. He switched on the sidelights. The clock in the dash board showed twenty past two. Slowly, he rolled up to the gate. The guards were by the jeep. One of them was very young. He was busy at the radio. The other man peered into the dark through a pair of field glasses.

'Can you see anything?' James whispered.

'Not a thing!' the man replied. 'I think they've gone.'

'Did you hear a car?'

'No. They must have left it further down.'

The young man took off his headphones. 'I can't get a reply,' he whispered.

'Why's that?' James asked.

'Nobody's at the other end. I keep on trying.'

'Listen!' James whispered. 'I'm going down to the bridge now. I'm taking twenty five million *lire*. Maybe one of you could try and follow me to the corner. You may be able to see which way they'll make me turn.'

The older man nodded. 'I'll have a look. In two or three minutes. Good luck!'

James put on the headlights. With dipped beams, he drove off. From the far side of the ravine he looked back at Terrarossa. A faint light shone in the kitchen windows. He had forgotten to tell the guards about the women and Max. It did not matter. The light said enough. He started the descent. He put the headlights on full beam.

He drove carefully. White in the powerful headlights, the road seemed no different than it was on other summer nights: dry, potholed, so dusty that the grass and flowers which grew on either side appeared furry, an opaque, silvery grey.

He passed the road to Valcortese. Still a hundred yards from the bridge, he slowed to walking speed. He rolled his window down all the way. The air was warmer in the valley than it had been at Terrarossa. He heard the gently rushing water of the Arbia.

Headlights ablaze, he drove on to the bridge. As far as he could see, nothing was out of the ordinary. There was no sign. He moved so slowly now that the bridge remained silent under the car's weight. Its loose planks did not rumble under the heavy wheels. Once, twice, pebbles flew, squeezed, suddenly catapulted by the grip of the rubber treads.

'Switch off your lights!'

The command came from his left, as he was about to roll off the bridge.

He switched off the lights and stopped.

'Go on twenty metres! Then stop!'

He let the car roll forward. He stopped.

Steps came from behind.

'Open the door! No! The other one!'

He had been about to open his door. He leaned to the other side. He unlocked and pushed open the passenger door. The interior lights came on.

'Switch that light off!'

He pulled the door shut. He felt for the switch, flicked it and pushed the door open again.

A gun pointed at him. A dark figure stepped up, right foot first, then left. The smell of stale tobacco, damp earth and the scent of the humid air by the river entered the car with the intruder.

'Look straight ahead!'

He had already seen lace-up boots, jeans, a battle jacket, bare hands, a distorted face pressed flat under a stocking pulled over the head.

The figure changed the pistol from one hand to the other and back. The passenger door slammed shut.

'No lights until I say so! Understood?' Inside the car, the voice sounded muffled, even angrier than it had done from a distance.

James gave a nod. He had no doubt: the voice was that of the man he had met at Valcortese.

'Turn left at the junction! No indicators! Don't use the brakes until we're out of sight from the top!'

He put the car in drive. It crept forward. As he began to turn, he placed the toe of his left shoe on the left edge of the brake pedal. At the same time, he depressed the accelerator with his right foot. Smoothly, the car gathered speed.

Out on the road, he placed the car in the centre. He drove slowly, at some twenty miles per hour. There was no moon. The clear night was bright enough, lit by its stars, for him to see at the low speed. He knew that soon they would be out of sight from Terrarossa.

'Switch on the lights! Go faster!'

As the dashboard lights came on, he looked at the clock. The time was now twenty-five minutes to three.

'How are the children? Is the boy all right?' Urgently, he asked the question.

The man did not answer.

'Please! Can't you – ?'

'Shut up! Drive! You'll know soon enough!'

They drove in silence for the next few miles. Softly the big engine rumbled through the night. Ahead, the nearest village in the valley was still several miles away.

'Slow now! Turn right! Here!'

The track looked so narrow that James was not sure he could negotiate it. Bushes brushed and scratched along the sides of the Chevrolet's big body. They entered an area of low trees and dense undergrowth. A strip of high grass in the centre of the track suggested that it was seldom disturbed.

Flat and straight at first, the track began to climb, then forked. A flick of the gun told him to turn left.

They entered an old quarry. The car bumped on its uneven floor. At its end, they began to climb again, across an open slope and back into the forest. There was less undergrowth here. The trees were taller. The track turned so often that James was no longer sure whether they were going east or south.

'Stop here! Switch off the motor and the lights. Stay in the car!'

The man vanished into the dark.

Peering, James' eyes adapted to the nearly lightless place. Pale patches among the trees indicated stone or sand on the forest floor. The trees, with straight thin trunks, were mainly pines. He looked up, out of his window. Stars shone through the tree tops here and there. He leaned over to see the clock. It was nearly three.

'Get out! Bring the money!' Another man – James had not heard the voice before – called from further up the track.

He turned in his seat. His heart pounded. He picked up the parcel and opened the door. He stepped down on the track. It felt soft, sandy. He walked into the dark, towards the voice.

'Stop!'

The man who had come with James was right behind him.

'Drop the money! Raise your hands!' he commanded.

James put the parcel by his feet. He raised his hands.

The man came closer. His clothes rustled.

Hands ran down James' sides and legs and up, into his groin.

The man backed off.

'How much money have you brought?' the other man asked and a dark figure, maybe fifteen, twenty feet in front, stepped out on the path.

James hesitated. Suddenly he feared that his strategy was totally wrong.

'How much?' the man insisted calmly.

'Twenty-five million. As a down payment.'

'How much?' The voice was incredulous.

'He said twenty-five million,' the man behind mocked. 'Are you joking?'

A shattering blow to the side of his head, instantly followed by a kick in the back, sent James sprawling to the ground.

'On your feet!' the man in front ordered.

Dazed, James got to his knees.

'On your feet!' the man behind hissed. 'Or do you need a little help?'

A kick from the side threw James to the right. Slowly, he got back to his knees. He stood up.

'Get back! On the path!' the voice in front, still calm, ordered. 'Faster!'

James took up his original place.

'Now then,' the man in front said, 'explain! What are your children worth to you?'

'Everything!'

'And what is everything?'

'All I can give! No less!'

'Stop your rhetoric! How much?' the man behind shouted.

'Five hundred million – maybe a little more – '

Two rapid kicks to the back of his knees made James fall forward. Several blows to the sides of his chest took away his breath. He tried to push himself off the ground. Suddenly in front, his attacker kicked him in the stomach. He doubled up. His head dropped to his knees. A kick deep into his side knocked him headlong to the sandy ground.

'Are you playing games with us, Grey?' the front voice asked quietly, still without expression.

'He must be!' the man behind mocked. 'He doesn't seem to understand we'll kill his darling son and daughter.'

'Are they,' gasping, James was back on his knees, 'are they all right? Is the boy all right?'

190

'Ah! You knew he was ill! He's not well. You had better hurry! Get him a doctor!'

'What's wrong with him?'

'I thought you knew. How should we know? Tell me: if he doesn't die anyway, which child should we kill first?'

'And how would you like us to do it? Slowly? Maybe strangle one right in front of the other?' the man behind added.

'Please!' James's voice broke in despair. 'How can you be so cruel? What's wrong with Thomas? Please tell me! Let me arrange for a doctor!'

'We won't, Grey. All you have to do is pay. If you don't, we will take photographs of the children – as they die. Something for you to remember. I am sure their mother would enjoy the pictures too,' the man in front said.

'Where? How are we to find all the money you're asking for?'

'You sell everything. You borrow.'

'But we're not that rich! We can borrow only what we can repay! Don't you understand? Nobody will lend more than we can repay!'

From his knees, he tried to raise himself. Slowly, he succeeded. Swaying, he stood on the track again. Dazed, he tried to focus on the man in front, obviously the negotiator, the more important of the two.

'We asked for four thousand million. Two thousand for each child. You offer five hundred. Exactly twelve and a half per cent.' Monotonously, the negotiator stated the figures.

'I went to London. To raise the maximum. The children's mother did the same. The sum I mentioned is what I know we can pay. If we get more, we pay that too. You *know* it is a lot of money!'

'Not enough!'

'Not nearly enough! More or less – nothing!' the man behind mocked.

'I *can't* promise you more! You'd be even angrier if I did and then we couldn't pay! The children are innocent. Why won't you let them go?'

'Innocent? Not if they grow up to be like you. What are you? A passenger! It's time you moved on – one way or another – all of you.' For the first time, the negotiator's voice expressed a sentiment: distaste.

'I understand what you're saying! But none of us has ever taken anything from the people here, harmed anyone here – '

'Your existence, the way you exist, is harmful enough. And you're a liar, Grey! You can pay much more than you pretend. You have the house here, the apartment in London. The children's mother and her husband own two houses. We know! You have friends. Like the American banker. Aren't you sorry he got away? If he's a friend he'll help – '

'He *is* helping! Without him – '

'In that case his help is not enough! Listen, Grey! Listen carefully! You have one more week to raise two thousand million. Half of what we asked for. The day after tomorrow you pay one thousand million on account. If you don't, we will kill the boy. Think about it!'

Desperate, James wanted to plead at least for more time. A breathtaking jab to the side of his neck knocked him out.

Forty-four

THE SKY WAS beginning to fade with the first light when James regained consciousness. Birds called, here then there. The ground was cold against his face, his mouth full of sand.

He opened his eyes. The forest floor was grey. In the foreground, tree trunks reached upwards, straight and black. Beyond, the depth of the wood was in darkness.

He moved his legs, bent one knee and pushed himself on to his side. A sharp pain made him roll all the way over on to his back. Through the tree tops, he looked at the greying sky. He lifted one arm, then the other. He bent his knees. The sand in his mouth and throat choked him. The pain in his chest made him suppress the cough. He choked even more. In his pockets, he felt for a handkerchief. He found only the cameo of the Madonna.

He rolled back on his face. He pushed himself up. On his knees, palms still on the ground, he spat out the sand. The right corner of his mouth felt raw. It was cut. He sat back on his heels. He could see the track but not his car.

He stood up and turned. The Chevrolet was some fifty yards away. The parcel lay on the track.

He limped towards it. The wrapping was soaking wet. The smell told him that it had been urinated on.

He went on to the car. A dull ache pounded in his head at every step. He bent his knees more, to absorb the impact of his feet on the ground. A stabbing pain in the back of his knees reminded him of the kicks he had received there.

He started the engine. He drove to the parcel. He got out and opened the tailgate. With his fingertips he picked up the parcel. The money had not been touched. The damp urine stink revolted him. He dropped the parcel in the back of the car. He tried to wipe his hands with sand from the side of the track.

He turned the wagon some two or three hundred yards further on, where he found that the track forked a second time. He saw tyre marks in its soft surface. He tried to avoid rolling over them more than he had done already. Convinced that he would not be able to learn anything from them, he did not bother to stop.

In the early light, the drive to the road seemed shorter than it had in the night. At the junction, he tried to arrange himself more comfortably behind the steering wheel. He went on. He drove slowly, so that he would not have to brake. Behind him, the sun sent its first rays, level and slender, into the valley.

Suddenly a *carabinieri* Alfa Romeo was alongside him. Rossi gesticulated from the front passenger seat. He wanted to talk.

With his hands James lifted his right leg and foot off the accelerator. He steered the car to the side. Eventually, it came to a halt. He was rolling down the window when Rossi's face appeared in the opening.

'My God! What have they done to you?'

'Not enough money,' James slurred the words. 'Made them angry. Just pissed on what I offered. Thomas's ill. You mustn't – absolutely mustn't – tell his mother! No point frightening her yet more. Wouldn't do any good. Promise?'

Aghast, Rossi gave a nod. 'Did they say what's wrong?'

'No. Refused. Stinking bastards! Wouldn't hear of letting me arrange for a doctor.'

Pained, the officer observed the similarity between the Englishman and the pictures of the little boy he had in his file. A thought occurred to him. 'Maybe they made it up,' he suggested. 'To make you pay sooner.'

Surprised by the suggestion, James tried to recall the days before the abduction. The negotiator had insinuated that he, James, had known that Thomas was ill. But there had been nothing wrong with the boy. He had seemed livelier than ever.

'Shall I drive?' Rossi asked.

Grateful for the suggestion, James slipped over on to the passenger seat. Quickly, Rossi acquainted himself with the controls. Led by the Alfa Romeo, they set off. All the way, James thought of Rossi's idea. It seemed not improbable. Or maybe Thomas *was* ill. All children lived through a catalogue of afflictions as they grew up. Maybe his captors had exaggerated the severity of his condition.

They arrived at Terrarossa shortly before five. Rossi helped James

194

out of the car, up the stair and into the kitchen. Everyone – even Pasquale – had congregated there. The crew of the Alfa Romeo, too, came inside. In a halting mixture of English and Italian, James described his attempt to negotiate.

Confused by the bilingual account, Claire asked him to restate the new demand.

'One thousand million the day after tomorrow. The same again within the week – '

'A million pounds?'

'Right! Fifty per cent off.'

'And if we can't?'

He could not avoid the answer. 'They – they're threatening to kill Thomas.'

She collapsed. Anna caught her before she hit the floor. She helped her to a chair. Claire slumped over the table. Face down, she pounded the scrubbed wood with her fists.

Disconcerted, embarrassed, the others watched in the hushed room.

Claire's outburst subsided.

'What are we going to do, James?' she whispered.

'I don't know, Claire. Not yet.'

She sat up. Her face was white. 'I'm going to London! To raise the money!'

'It's too much, Claire! We're much too far short of what they're asking. There must be another answer.'

She turned to Pasquale. 'I want to go to Pisa. Now. Will you take me?'

Pasquale shot an uneasy glance at James.

'Take her, Pasquale. Please! Take my car.'

Forty-five

JAMES WAS IN his bath when he heard the helicopter. The hot water, painful at first, had begun to relax his body. He could breathe only shallowly. Bruises covered the sides of his rib cage, his hips and stomach, his arms and thighs. His neck and head hurt. But his face, except for the cut at the corner of his mouth, was unmarked.

He had noticed blood in his urine, a reddish tinge. To alleviate the headache – he could not tell whether it was inside his skull or outside or both – he had taken some aspirin, washed down with some black coffee.

'May I come in?' the Colonel asked from the open doorway.

James pointed to a cane chair, on which lay his clothes. 'Throw them on the floor.'

The Colonel put the clothes on the window ledge. He sat down. Concerned, he looked James up and down. 'Don't you want a doctor?'

'I'll live.'

'Rossi tells me they reduced their demand by half. At least that's a step in the right direction.'

'I didn't see it like that!' James gave a bitter laugh. Assuming that the Colonel knew most of what had happened, he kept his account very short. It occurred to him that he might not remember everything. But he was almost certain that his recollection was complete. When he had finished, he pulled himself up and let some more hot water into the tub.

'I didn't tell Claire about Thomas being ill.'

'Rossi told me. They may be bluffing. On the other hand – '

'What?'

'It may explain why there were no footprints.'

'I thought of that – '

'Still, they're probably exaggerating. It would suit them, would it

196

not? How is Mrs Rudd?'

'She's brave. She's going back to London to raise more money.'

'I heard. Is there any hope of that?'

'I don't think it'll make much difference. But at least it gives her something to put her mind to.'

They fell silent. With his hands, James made paddling, splashing noises.

'They're well informed,' he resumed the conversation. 'They know about what we own.'

The Colonel's eye seemed caught in the pattern of the tiles, behind James' head. 'It's frightening to see their connections spread. The enemy within, without, everywhere.'

James stepped from the tub. He moved carefully, as if concerned that he might slip on the marble floor. The Colonel handed him a bath towel. He began to dry himself, dabbing around the bruises. He went into the bedroom for a moment. He came back in the kimono.

'Let's have some coffee,' he suggested. 'If you go ahead on the terrace, I'll go and find Anna.'

'What do you want to do now?' the Colonel asked when he had returned.

'I've been thinking. To sit and wait is bad strategy. No strategy at all, in fact. It leaves the initiative entirely with them. I have more or less convinced myself: it's meaningless if we offer a few million more, we're too far apart. Could we get the television people to interview me? Today?'

'I can try. I'll call them straight away. What is it you want to say?'

'Something along the lines of – you have the children but we have the money.'

'So?'

'Despite their rejection of the down payment – they are still the ones selling. They should realise that we are the only buyers. Nobody is likely to outbid us.'

Anna came on the terrace with a steaming *napolitana* and two cups. She put them in front of the Colonel.

'I can pour!' James protested.

'You are not well,' she countered and was gone.

'A very commercial approach.' The Colonel began to pour. 'You must be aware of the dangers. I'm sure you are. It may put you in a position where no compromise is possible. They may bluff.'

'Are you advising a different approach?' James took the cup the

Colonel had slid towards him.

'Not at all! I'm persuaded that even they must understand that there is a limit to what you can pay. They rejected your down payment because they know full well that in the end there will be much more. It's standard tactics, I'm sure. Nevertheless, it'll be only too easy for them to frighten you even more. The boy's illness, the threat to kill him, it's all designed to make you comply. They may break you.'

'We'll find out. Is there anything else you can think of that I should say?'

'Time! We must win time! I believe there is still a chance that we can catch up with them. We nearly did.'

'What if you do?'

'If we have time to prepare, the chances could be good. It would depend on the circumstances, of course.'

James nodded. He looked across the valley. The air was beginning to turn hazy.

'I wonder what the Count is doing now?' he asked himself rather than the Colonel.

'Who knows? But you can be sure he does mean to help. Incidentally – we believe the woman was seen again yesterday. At Santa Anna.'

'Where is that?'

'To the east from here. In fact, not far from where we were – '

Forty-six

'WE'RE READY. Caroline is coming with me. Our bags are in the kitchen.'

Claire stood in the door to the study. Despite the heat, she had put on a headscarf. Her eyes hid behind the dark glasses.

At his writing table, James sat up. 'Caroline's going with you? Are you sure she should be travelling so soon?'

'She wants to.'

'What does the doctor say?'

'I don't know. She wants to come. That's all there's to it.'

He shrugged. He asked her to come in, to sit for a moment. She said she preferred to stand.

'I've been thinking, Claire. You mustn't ask Tony for more than he has given already. I know you have two houses – '

'I don't want to talk about Tony!' she said sharply. 'Have you thought about the newspapers again?'

He frowned. 'I've written a note for you to take to Richard.' He handed her an envelope. 'It's open. Please read it on the plane. I take it you agree we should sell the story.'

'Of course! We must! What are you doing?'

'The television people are coming to interview me. For transmission tonight, I hope. We are trying to win more time. I'm making myself some notes.'

She seemed about to say something. She hesitated.

'Yes?'

'Can you work out the difference? If I found another hundred thousand: what would it be?'

He took a fresh sheet of paper. He picked up a pencil. She moved to his side, to watch over his shoulder.

'Tony gave one hundred and fifty thousand. Counting the dollar loan, I have two hundred and ten thousand. The dollars should be here today. If you were to raise an additional hundred thousand, it would be – forty thousand short of half a million. The newspaper deal could bring the difference.'

He looked up at her. 'I really meant what I said about Tony. I have no doubt they will either accept what is already a very substantial amount of money – '

'Or?'

'Or nothing at all.' Abruptly, he stood up.

'How much is half a million pounds in Italian money, James? That's what I want to know.'

'Eight hundred and seventy five million *lire*. Approximately.'

'So if we could make it a thousand million – we'd be half way there! James, they must accept that!'

'You mustn't think like that, Claire. You're rounding up with huge amounts! They add up to far more than we can possibly get!'

He saw the change of expression round her mouth. Her eerie optimism – he suspected she had taken a tranquilliser or something similar – was about to break.

'All right, Claire!' he said hastily. 'Try! By all means, try! But please remember what I said!'

Forty-seven

James had been at the writing table for little over an hour since Claire and Caroline's departure when Anna knocked on the door.

'The television people are here,' she announced. 'The guards let them pass.'

Surprised by the earliness of the arrival, he asked her to show them in. Rapidly, he looked over what he had written and rewritten several times. He had intended to consult the Colonel over the radio. Now he would have to make do without the benefit of his advice.

The crew consisted of far more people than he cared to count. The study could not accommodate even half their number.

'Why don't we do it on the balcony?' he suggested to the journalist who was to conduct the interview. 'The light is better there.'

The director in charge of the programme was keen on the interior of the house. They were the first reporters setting foot inside it. 'We have brought our lights,' he said. 'The generator's outside.'

James baulked when a girl tried to put make-up on his face. 'What's wrong? I'm not that beaten up – or ugly – am I?' he asked, drawing some unsought giggles from the sound crew.

'All right! To work!' the interviewer cried when everyone was in position.

The lights, already tested several times, came on in earnest. The camera began to roll. Looking entirely serious, a young man dangled an old-fashioned microphone from a long pole not far from James' head. Half reading from a script, the interviewer spoke his introduction to the camera. Already it was hot in the study. The interviewer finished. He turned to James.

'Mr Grey, will you tell us, please, what happened last night?'

In simple words, speaking quietly, James gave an account of what had happened, beginning with the voice from across the ravine.

Several times, the interviewer interrupted and sought more detail, trying to pinpoint the location of the rendezvous and the actual times when the various stages of the encounter had been reached.

'Why do you think they beat you up? Because they are sadists or because they wanted to extract more money?' the interviewer asked.

'I imagine beating people up is part of their negotiating technique. In my case it's quite pointless. It cannot produce more than we have.'

'They asked you for two thousand million for each child. How much, in fact, did you offer?'

'I would rather not answer your question. As long as the negotiations are unresolved, it's better to be discreet.'

'Have they agreed to a reduction? Have they changed their conditions?'

'Again – I don't want to answer.'

'But your former wife, Mrs Rudd, is already on her way back to London. Presumably to raise more money?'

'Yes. She is trying to raise more money. But that is all I want to say on the subject – or about the conditions.'

Irritated by James' refusal to be drawn, the interviewer glanced at his script.

'Mr Grey, when you were finally alone again, in the dark forest, what did you think?'

'I wasn't thinking at all. They knocked me out before they left.'

'How long were you unconscious?'

'I can't tell. I don't think it was very long.'

'When you came round, what were your feelings?'

'I was cold. I had sand in my mouth. I was not sure whether they had broken any of my bones.'

'Did you not feel abused? Humiliated?'

'No. There is no humiliation when you're fighting for your children.'

'So what did you do?'

'I picked myself up from the ground.'

Somebody laughed, a short, nervous outburst. The interviewer frowned. Blinded by the lights, he tried to see the culprit.

'But when you were actually thinking coherently again,' the interviewer insisted, 'what were your feelings concerning your attackers? Have you been able to form personal impressions of them? Were you relieved they had gone?'

'I don't know who they are, of course, or what they are like. I feel there is no point in speculating here. It would not help to bring the children back. I did not feel relieved when I found myself alone. I felt they had broken off our conversation – if you can call it that – too soon.'

'Why?'

'First of all, because I wanted to plead with them to have more compassion, pity for the children. Also, I wanted to ask them why it is that they set themselves up as our judges – and scourges – without regard to what we are individually or can actually achieve with the help of those who choose to support us.'

'Is there anything you wish to say to them?'

'Yes, I do. I only hope they will hear what I have to say.'

James picked up the sheet of paper he had put beside him on the writing table. He put it down again. The microphone came down several inches in front of him. A hush had fallen over the room. Only the whir of the camera motor could be heard in the silence. One of the lights buzzed. He looked straight into the camera. He began to speak.

'What I offered you is – by any private individual's standard – a substantial sum. The children's mother returned to London today in order to raise more money. However, we depend entirely on other people. It is therefore not possible to say now what the additional sum may be. It may be nothing! We shall have to wait for Mrs Rudd's return. This must be clearly understood!'

He paused. Two sparrows angrily chirped on the balcony.

'When we are ready, I shall say so immediately. But we will meet you only if you accept that the money we bring with us will be the maximum – absolute and final – and that the children are released safely into our hands as we pay the money. This is an essential condition which I will not change!'

He paused again. The faces of those members of the crew not behind the lights seemed curiously without expression, blank, their eyes not quite fixed on him.

'Finally, I want to say this to you: we are the parents of two children. You hold both of them. To save one but not the other is unthinkable. None of us could live with that. If you want money – any money at all! – you must return *both* children – Thomas and Emma. If you don't – whatever you may try – you will get nothing! And then God help you!'

He had finished. The camera stopped. The lights cut. In the sudden half dark there was only silence. Hesitantly, one of the crew began to clap, then others. Head down, James sat on his chair. The heat in the room was unbearable.

'You have taken a very uncompromising position,' the interviewer half remarked, half asked James while his colleagues were shifting their equipment out of the house.

'I mean it!' James looked out over the hills. 'I only hope they get the message!'

Forty-eight

TONY RUDD UNLOCKED the front door and entered his house on Campden Hill. He was in the kitchen when something made him turn back. Claire's coat hung on the rack under the stairs.

He called her name.

She answered from the first floor.

'What brings you back unannounced like this?'

She had already unpacked her bag. Empty, flat, it lay on their bed.

She began to tell him of James' meeting with the kidnappers. She seemed restless. As she spoke, the urgency in her voice increased. A faint flush rose to her pallid cheeks.

'How much more do we need?' he interrupted.

'James says the money he offered is enough. They should accept it.'

'Did he offer all of it?'

'He offered five hundred million *lire*. He didn't get further.'

Tony sat down on the bed.

'They knocked him out. They pissed on the money he had taken with him. Literally!'

He shook his head. 'I warned him to be careful. I just hope he hasn't blown our chances.'

'They did come down by half!'

'That still leaves more than half a million to pay.'

'I know! But they may accept half that — one thousand million *lire*.

He only looked at her.

'James and I agreed to sell the story,' she said quickly.

'That's not getting us far. If I remember correctly, Claire, we had something like six hundred and fifty million. In total. That's between all of us. Including the interest-free loan from the Wright-Garrisons. Where's the additional three hundred and fifty million to come from? Where?'

'I thought – I was hoping – '

'What, Claire?'

'I was hoping – you'd help – '

'How? We sold Hansport! You know the overdraft!'

'Could we not sell – this house?'

For a moment, he thought he had misheard. He got to his feet.

'I don't think you understood what I said the other day, Claire.' His voice was firm, emphatic but low. He was aware that she was on the brink of breaking down. Yet an explanation was called for, was, in fact, absolutely vital, so he felt, if their relationship was to remain intact.

He took her hands.

Confused, she stood quite still.

'Look, Claire! You know there's a mortgage on this house. I'm aware it's now much less than the value of the house. But we'd have to pay one hell of a lot in capital gains tax if we sold both houses. So much, in fact, that in the end we'd be worse off, not better!'

She began to cry. Limply, her hands hung in his.

'I'm sorry, darling! That's the reality!'

'Couldn't the tax people make an exception under the circumstances?'

'How can they? They're bound by law. The laws are made by Parliament. Even the government can't help us. If it did, just think how many kidnappings there'd be!'

Forty-nine

FRIDAY MORNING. James ended a sleepless night by getting up at dawn. From the balcony, he looked at the new sky. Silent, an indifferent expanse of blues and greys, the hills lay before him. The day promised to bring the colours to life with its early heat before they quietened down again, bleached in its noontime blaze.

For a couple of hours or so, he worked in the study. Anna brought him some coffee. For a while he continued working. Then it was time to go to Siena to see Carlo Verga, the bank manager.

For a Friday, the market place was unusually quiet. Some of the shops in town were shut. Their owners, together with many other Sienese, had left for their summer vacation, to spend the hottest weeks of the year by the seaside. A hint of disuse – even decay – had entered the streets and squares of the old city.

Carlo Verga was an accommodating man by nature. Now he tried to be even more helpful, if that was possible. Tears glistened in his eyes when he pressed James' hand.

'I wish I knew what to say, *signor* Grey! I'll do everything I can to help! My wife and I, we thought you showed great courage last night on television. Every word you said! They will have to see the sense of it. If they can see sense at all.'

The balance of Tony's money and the dollars had arrived. Verga was not sure what the exact exchange rates would be. He had taken up the matter with head office. Since the amounts of sterling and dollars were unusually large for a private account, he hoped to be able to offer more favourable commercial rates.

James did not doubt that the bank would offer the best available terms. He thanked Verga for his concern. He had to promise to ask for help and to get in touch the very minute the money was required. The manager made him note down his home address and telephone number. Then he left.

He bought a newspaper at a kiosk. He did not bother to open it. Wondering how Claire was getting on in London, he trudged down Banchi di Sopra towards the Campo.

The heat in the concave square made him hold his breath. Fan-shaped and angled towards the south, it formed a sun trap of huge proportions. The street, which dropped steeply out of it to the market, offered no shade. He started the Chevrolet with the air conditioner at full blast. Few cars were still parked in the market place. His friendly parking attendant had gone to an early lunch.

Automatically, he took his usual way out of the city through Porta Roma. He turned east along the town walls. He crossed the railway line from Chiusi and joined the road to Montevarchi. Out in the country, its uncertain surface swam in the glittering hot air ahead. Soft and black, the asphalt was melting. There was no point in hurrying back to Terrarossa. He decided to cut through the hills.

On the dirt road he drove even more slowly at first. Gradually his speed built up. He was unaware of this. A trail of dust began to spread behind the vehicle. Rising, drifting back in the car's wake, it indicated the Chevrolet's cross-country progress.

The shrill sound of compressor horns made him jerk the steering wheel to one side. Instinctively, he looked in his mirror. Out of the dust he heard the metallic scream of an engine. A white saloon pushed alongside. It nearly touched the Chevrolet. It cut in.

Sharply, he stabbed at the brakes. He locked his wheels. In a straight line, he skidded along on the loose gravel.

The back of the saloon, an Alfetta, slewed around. Sideways, it now blocked the road. Swirling thick dust enwrapped the two cars.

For a split second, James wanted to ram the much lighter car. He floored the accelerator. Narrowly, he missed. Through the gap between two cypresses, he shot off the road, to his right.

Out in the flat field, he could turn back only towards the road and in the direction he had come from. Ahead, an olive grove, possibly concealing a ditch, barred the exit.

Wheels spinning furiously in the flying soil, the Chevrolet began a slow, wide circle some fifty or sixty yards around the Alfetta. James eased the pressure on the accelerator and the wheels began to grip. The wagon began to gather speed.

A submachine gun opened up. A volley of bullets ripped through the window behind him.

He ducked.

208

Desperate, he kept going. At the far side of the turn, the width of the wagon's body helped to shield him. But he knew he was an easy target.

He headed for the road.

Its engine roaring at full throttle, a *carabinieri* jeep arrived from the same direction he and his pursuers had come from. Skidding, it came to a halt.

A second and a third gun began to fire in rapid bursts.

Suddenly, the Alfetta's engine howled. Snaking wildly, the white car accelerated up the road.

Abruptly, the guns fell silent.

The dust settled slowly.

A body lay on the road.

'*Signor* Grey? Are you hurt?'

James lifted his head from the steering wheel.

Two *carabinieri* – he recalled one of their young faces from the gate – were looking through the window, their heads close together.

He killed the engine and opened the door. The two men stepped back, then came forward again to help him from the car. He shook his head. He jumped to the ground.

Flanking him, they walked back to the road.

Two *carabinieri* were with the body. His knee on the ground, one of them bent over the head.

'Is he dead?' James had meant to ask while they were still walking.

Face down, a slight body, long hair and clothes both dark, lay twisted on the white road. The back was a pulp of shredded flesh, riddled shirt and blood, ripped through from side to side, from the shoulder blades to the waist.

One hand and arm lay under the body. The other hand clawed the road. Shoulders and arms were covered by the remains of a brown shirt. The legs stuck in blue jeans. One lace-up leather boot had been blown off. The bare foot had been shot to a stump of bones and dripping tissue.

'Is it a man?' James asked.

'A man,' the *carabiniere* who had been on his knees confirmed. 'I can't wait to see his face.'

'We had better not turn him now,' one of the others warned.

In the grass by the road side, James saw what looked to him like a light machine gun.

'Did he shoot at me?' he asked.

'You were bloody lucky!' the men said. 'If you hadn't gone off the road and got so far away – '

A melodious horn used by the buses which provided local transport in the area sounded in the distance. James knew its nearest stop, a little further up the road, by an old shrine and next to a group of cypresses.

Presently the blue and grey vehicle appeared on the brow of the hill. Quickly, it came down the straight stretch of road. A thick cloud of dust trailed behind it, rising higher than it spread.

One of the *carabinieri* walked towards the bus. He raised his hand. Louder suddenly and deeper, the reverberating sound told that the driver had applied the motor brake. Taking up the entire width of the road, the bus stopped.

The *carabiniere* saluted.

Listening, the driver stuck his head from his window. The engine shuddered to a halt. He got out from behind the steering wheel and went into the back of the cabin.

One by one the passengers stepped from the bus, some nine or ten of them, mostly women in their visiting clothes. Slowly, they approached. They stopped a few feet from the body. None of them spoke. Shyly, they crossed themselves. Their eyes fixed on the corpse before them.

The blood on the back already showed signs of coagulation and had begun to turn black. Under the body it had not spread far. The dust had absorbed it. Flies increased in number all the time. Glistening, black and blue, they landed on the terrible wound. Busily, they ran around on it.

From a pocket in her wide and black skirts, one of the women pulled a rosary. She began to pray. Inaudibly, she moved her lips. Mechanically, the beads passed through her fingers.

Two of the *carabinieri* approached with a stained tarpaulin. They spread it out. In one movement, they brought it down over the corpse. In unison, with a loud buzz, the flies flew up and scattered.

James had gathered that the *carabinieri* were expecting assistance, and that nothing was to be moved before it arrived. He decided to have a look at his car. Alone, he walked across the field.

The Chevrolet's front, now facing the road, was unmarked. Its right side, which had been exposed to the gunfire for most of the attack, was damaged at the back. A trail of holes ran from the lower right hand corner of the tailgate. It rose across the rear body panel and on, into the window above. The bullets had pierced its glass. Through the opposite window and at a level slightly higher than that of their entry, they had exited.

James circled the car several times. He had no doubt: the *carabinieri* had saved his life at the last moment. Seconds later and the gunman would have shot him through the head.

The heat over the fallow field brought out the dry scent of the earth. Some late and solitary poppies interspersed the thin grass. The wagon's right side cast a narrow shadow. On its other side, to the south, the sun stood high, almost overhead.

He sat down.

He watched two tiny white Fiats line up behind the bus. Travelling together maybe, they each released two men and two women on to the road. A truck arrived from the left. The *carabinieri* stopped it some fifty feet from their jeep. The number of spectators grew, then stayed constant as some of them returned to their cars only to be replaced by new arrivals.

Still praying, the women stayed at their places in the original circle of onlookers. Out of the sparsely populated land, some of its inhabitants came together. Little by little the two lines of waiting cars grew longer. The corpse separated them. The cypresses marked the place.

The helicopter appeared over the hills in the east. It approached in a straight line, then circled and landed halfway between the road and the Chevrolet. Ducking, Rossi emerged from the dust. Under the rotor blades, still revolving fast, he began to run towards James.

'You escaped unhurt?' he asked, touching James' arm.

'Your men saved me. I suppose they didn't like what I said last night – '

Rossi ordered the men to clear the place of spectators. He had the corpse uncovered. Instantly, the flies were back. One of the men who had arrived in the helicopter began to take photographs.

The photographer said he had taken enough pictures of the corpse's position.

'Turn him over!' Rossi ordered.

A *carabiniere* took hold of the right arm. He pulled it up and to the side. The shoulder stretched. With a lolling movement, the head came round.

'It's Barea.' Flatly, Rossi announced the name.

The dead man's eyes and mouth gaped. Blood coloured his lips and teeth. On the chest, the bullet **wounds** were separate. They seemed less extensive than on the back.

'Could he have been one of the men you encountered before?' Rossi asked.

James was not sure. 'It's possible. Maybe. How do you know his name?'

'He's famous!' Rossi gave a bitter laugh. 'Infamous, I should say. He's graced one of the top spots on our most-wanted list for the last two years. You would have been his fifth or sixth kill. Who knows? We last heard he was in Turin.'

Numb, without feeling, James looked at the drained face. Maybe it had hidden behind the stocking mask of the man he had encountered first at Valcortese and then again at the rendezvous.

'How old was he?' he asked.

'Twenty-two,' Rossi replied without hesitation. 'Born in Rome. Father a doctor who became a conservative parliamentarian. Mother a teacher by training. He, too, thought he'd help the people! By killing them!'

The *carabinieri* wrapped the corpse in the tarpaulin. Lights flashing, a van edged past the long line of cars on the south side. Several times it stopped to wait for a parked vehicle to be moved out of its way. At last it arrived at the body.

Four men grabbed the tarpaulin by its corners. They lifted it easily. Once, twice, they swung it back and forward. A mocking laugh despatched the dead man into the back of the van. With a thud, the package hit the metal floor. The doors slammed shut. The van turned and began its journey back to Siena.

Rossi accompanied James to the Chevrolet. Behind them, the two lines of cars and trucks began to move. Melodiously, the bus sounded its horn.

As best he could, James described what had happened to him. The photographer took pictures of the damage to the wagon.

'Can you drive it?' Rossi asked.

'I think so. I'm curious – were your men behind me by accident?'

Rossi seemed embarrassed. 'Colonel Amorini ordered it. He was afraid they might have a go at you. On the other hand – '

Even more embarrassed, Rossi stopped. He looked over James' shoulder. By the cypresses a navy blue Alfa Romeo had come to a halt. Presently, the Colonel came walking towards them across the field. The lieutenant who had been with the Colonel at Camilliano

212

trotted close behind.

Rossi saluted. He stepped forward. Out of James' earshot, he began to report. Head bowed, the Colonel listened. He looked up. Rossi called one of the men who had been in the jeep. The man came running, stopped, saluted and stood to attention.

The Colonel was asking questions. The man answered. Rossi spoke once, a second time. The man saluted. He turned. Slowly, he walked back to his colleagues.

James shook hands with the Colonel. 'I'm sorry I caused so much trouble. Without your men I wouldn't have had a chance – '

'Even with them!' the Colonel interrupted. 'We almost lost you! We knew we might just catch someone if they tried to get at you. But not like this! Our men were too far behind!'

'You mean – you expected this?'

'We had to be prepared after what you said yesterday! Didn't you think of the likely consequences? I am assuming they are under the correct impression that it would be easier to extract money from Mrs Rudd than from you!'

'Maybe. But what went wrong?'

'My men say you went faster and faster. They found it difficult to keep the right distances – between you, your pursuers and themselves. Are they telling me the truth?'

James nodded. 'They are. They're good men. I like driving on these roads. I suppose I didn't realise. I drove the way I used to – '

Fifty

It was after four when, from a kitchen window, Anna saw an old-fashioned car stop at the gate. Expecting the guards to turn it away, like so many would-be visitors and sightseers before, she paid no further attention. Suddenly the open vehicle was outside the front door. A young woman parked it next to the Chevrolet.

Laura di Lando had driven from Montenano. The grey-haired man who had let James into the castle accompanied her. He pointed at the bullet holes in the wagon.

'The *signor* James is in the garden. I hope he is resting. He has not asked for his coffee,' Anna said.

'May I wait? Until he wakes?' Laura asked while her companion stayed with the car.

Anna showed the visitor downstairs and outside again, through the loggia. Max sat under a parasol, writing letters. From James' description he knew at once who it was he saw coming towards him. He put down his pen. He got to his feet.

'I am Laura di Lando. From Montenano. Mr Grey visited us the day before yesterday.'

'Of course!' Max bowed. 'He spoke of you. I'm Max Kleinschmied. A friend of the family.' He pointed at the olives at the far side of the garden. 'James is over there. Behind the trees.'

'Is he asleep?'

'He wasn't a few minutes ago. Have a look!'

Quietly, she walked over the soft grass.

She found James under one of the trees, in a deck chair. He wore a navy tee shirt and faded jeans which he had cut off above the knees. His eyes were shut. She thought he looked younger than she had remembered him. The tenseness he had displayed at Montenano was not visible. Completely still, he did not seem to be breathing. She noticed the cut at the corner of his mouth. She saw the bruises on

214

his arms and legs.

He opened his eyes. He saw her only when he turned his head. Silent, he looked at her as though he had not taken in her presence.

'News?' he asked.

She shook her head. 'Only a visit. We saw you on television. Last night.'

He sat up. 'Have you been here long?'

'Only a few minutes. I met your friend – '

'Max's an artist. This is his first visit to Italy.' He swung his legs over the side of the deck chair and put his bare feet on the grass. 'What's the time?'

'Half past four. Approximately. My watch's not very accurate. What happened to your car?'

He stood up. 'They tried to kill me – '

'When?'

'At noon. On my way back from Siena. The *carabinieri* got me out. They shot one of them dead. His name is Barea.'

'Barea?'

'Yes. Barea. Maybe it'll give the *carabinieri* a lead. I was just thinking. He was born in Rome. The woman, too, may be a Roman.'

Laura made no response to his statement. She seemed pensive.

'Is anything wrong?' he asked.

'No.' She shook her head. 'I was trying to think myself. It's nothing. I came to see how you were. My father sends his regards. He spent all day yesterday visiting people he knows. He says he feels very responsible that the message centres on him. If only he knew how to understand it!'

'I have told the man who gave it to me. I know he will do anything to get an explanation. There is no point asking him again.'

They fell silent. James looked at the sky. He began to walk towards the house. Laura was by his side.

Max looked up from his letters. 'Shall we have some tea? Or coffee?' he called.

James stopped. 'Will you have some?' he asked the visitor.

'A cup of tea. Then I must go back. Daniele came with me.'

'Daniele?'

'The man who opened the door for you.'

'Ah!' The flicker of a smile ran over his face. 'Won't he join us?'

'I don't think so. I imagine he'll be with the men at your gate.'

They went inside. James left Laura with Max on the balcony. He found Daniele in the kitchen, talking to Anna.

'I am pleased to see you!' James held out his hand. 'Is Anna looking after you?'

'Thank you.' Daniele pointed at the *napolitana*, which was on the table in front of him. 'I'm being very well cared for.'

James asked Anna to make some tea. He returned to the balcony.

'I hear, except for San Marco, your friend has still to see Florence!' Laura exclaimed.

'I know. I had promised Max to take him more than just once – '

'I'm perfectly happy exploring Siena!' Max protested. 'Florence is not going to run away! Reading about all the wars it caused I've come down in favour of Siena anyway. Goethe gave Florence no more than half a page! The other day I recalled reading his Italian diaries. When I was drawing the ruin above the village.'

James did not understand the connection.

Max told the story of how the German poet, at the beginning of his first journey to Italy, had stopped at Malcesine, on Lake Garda. He had attempted to draw its ruined fortifications. 'He very nearly got himself thrown in jail! As a spy. Despite the fact that the fortifications were ruins. Quite useless. It took all his powers of persuasion to talk the locals out of arresting him.'

Anna brought the tea.

'Why did he write only half a page about Florence?' James wanted to know while Max poured the tea.

'It's even less than that,' Laura replied. 'Many of the places he must have seen he never mentions at all. He came to find antiquity. He got far more excited by plaster casts – even fake ones – of Roman statues than by the country itself. I believe he never saw Italy – not as something belonging together, I mean. Of course, when he first came Italy was still nearly a century from its proper unification.'

Their conversation turned to translations of Goethe's work. Max had heard of an English edition of the Italian diaries. But he had never seen it.

Soon Laura wanted to leave. James walked her to the car.

'It was very kind of you to visit us.' He stepped out of the way so that Daniele could open the door for her. 'We needed a little diversion. Please come again!'

Laura started the old Lancia and began to turn it. Its heavy four-spoke steering wheel was considerably wider across than her shoulders. Stiffly, Daniele sat next to her. James had noticed, when the servant had opened the door, the butt of a shot gun which lay partly covered under his seat.

The *carabinieri* at the gate saluted. Slowly, the car gained speed on the road round the ravine. From the pool side, James waved as it reached the far side and was about to disappear round the bend. He was surprised to see Laura wave back.

Fifty-one

LAURA SAT WATCHING the evening news with her father.

On a split screen – one half a snapshot taken by his mother, the other a copy of the photograph in his driving licence – Sergio Barea looked harmless, even friendly. The dead terrorist's portraits contrasted oddly with the long list of assassinations and other attacks he had been wanted for.

A series of other portraits followed. Monotonously, a voice-over read out the names of Barea's confirmed or suspected associates – young men and women of the extreme left.

Perplexed, the Count jumped to his feet. 'But we know this man!'

'Montale, Gherardo,' the voice-over announced while yet another young face stared blankly from the screen. 'Twenty-three. Born in Rome. Height, one eighty-six. Last seen with a full beard.'

'He's one of the boys who came here with Enrico! Two, three years ago!'

'Four, Father,' Laura corrected. 'After Enrico's first year at university. He was the one he never invited again.'

'I think I'm beginning to understand – '

'The message?'

With his fist, the Count struck the flat palm of his other hand. 'Someone who remembers him must have seen him! But where?'

'They stayed here for some time,' Laura said. 'Then they went to Cerreto. I remember feeling sorry for them because it rained so much. I thought they must have been freezing so high up.'

Incredulous, the Count looked at his daughter. He stood quite still.

'How could I forget!' He let himself fall into a chair. 'Daniele gave them guns. If they're hiding up there – they may be at the lodge! Or Cerreto itself!'

Restless, he got to his feet again. He went to the door. He rang the bell pull which hung by it.

Presently, Paolo appeared.

'Is Daniele in tonight?' the Count asked.

'I think so, sir.'

'Ask him to come and see me, please. Immediately!'

Paolo bowed and was gone.

'You're going up there, Father?'

He gave a nod. 'We'll go at dawn.'

'You're not going – '

'Don't worry, darling! We're only going to look. We'll be back by noon. If we find something, Amorini will be able to go in before the day's out.'

Fifty-two

JAMES DREAMED HE was dreaming. But the voice was there. Booming, it came across the ravine again, waking him from a shallow and restless sleep.

'Grey! Do you hear us? Come out, Grey! We brought you a present! You may like it!'

He was pushing open the slatted shutters outside the French doors when a voice from below stopped him.

'Stay inside! Don't let them see you!' one of the guards hissed.

He stepped back. From the side, he pushed out one wing of the shutters. His cheek pressed against the window pane which, with its frame, was folded back inside the doorway. He peered into the night.

'Why don't you come out, Grey?' the voice echoed. 'Watch! Watch carefully!'

A thin, pale line indicated where the road rounded the ravine. It seemed deserted. The stone retention walls were a dull grey above and below it. The flat tops of the cedars cut a black silhouette in the starlit sky.

Scraping sounded from the bend by the trees.

For an instant, he saw the shadow of a figure. Bent low, it zigzagged backwards, dragging something on the ground.

A light flickered. A flame ran along the road. Roaring, it flared up, deep red and orange, blue and white on top.

A body lay in the flames. Its arms twisted. Its hands moved. Grotesquely, its back arched.

The body was small.

Petrified, he stared at the spectacle.

'The body's not small enough! It's too big!' his mind screamed.

His knees buckled. He gripped the door frame. He bowed his head. He could watch no longer.

'Remember Sachetti?' the voice called. 'He was a spy! He's entertaining you now!'

He closed his eyes.

'Your son is next, Grey! Tomorrow! Unless you pay!'

He looked up. The flames had begun to die down. He clenched his fists.

'I told you my conditions! I have not yet heard from the children's mother!' he called out.

His words were still echoing in the ravine when the *carabinieri* opened up. A barrage of automatic fire sprayed the far side.

Two shots rang out under the trees. A car engine howled into life.

'Hold your fire! They've gone!' a voice called across.

The guns fell silent.

A searchlight came on. White, it fingered the ravine.

Pasquale stepped into the beam, a shotgun stuck under his arm.

The jeep raced round to meet him. It slid to a halt in front of the body. Pasquale pointed down the road. Three *carabinieri* jumped from the jeep. They bent over the smouldering corpse. Pasquale continued on his way towards the house.

James was standing in the front door waiting for him when gunfire cracked in the distance. One, two, three bursts sounded from the direction of the bridge.

In the kitchen, James watched Pasquale break the gun, take out two spent cartridges and lean it against the wall behind the door.

'Did you get them?' James asked.

'I hit one of them. He was getting into the car. He fell half into it. The driver pulled him in.'

'Did you hit him? With your second shot?'

Pasquale shook his head. 'I saw his arm only. When he tried to pull the door. The body of the other one shielded him.'

'Was he dead?'

'I shot him in the face.'

James puffed his cheeks. 'That's two, then.'

'Maybe three. The *carabinieri* were waiting at the bridge.'

Rossi arrived half an hour later, at a quarter to four. In the faint light which fell from the kitchen window, he stood on the doorstep and asked for permission to come in. James got up. Max pulled out a chair from under the table for the visitor.

Frowning, the officer looked at Pasquale. 'You killed one of them! Why couldn't you have left the shooting to us?'

'You haven't done too well so far, have you?' Pasquale replied. 'I'll have to put it in my report – '

'I'd be dead if I hadn't had my gun.' Pasquale looked the officer straight in the face. 'What does it matter who kills them?'

Rossi shrugged.

'Did you get the other one at the bridge?' James asked.

'We did. Unfortunately, he too is dead. It's impossible to shoot accurately when things happen so quickly in the dark.'

'Exactly!' Pasquale said.

Irritatedly, Rossi eyed him. 'Look, Neri! Basically, I don't care how many of them you kill. I'll even cover up for you. But it would have been useful to take one of them alive. He might have talked! We would have made him talk! Don't you see?'

'Sachetti,' James pronounced the name hesitantly, 'was he an informer?'

Rossi was clearly uncomfortable with the question. 'I – I really can't say, Mr Grey. Maybe Colonel Amorini will tell you more.'

Silent, James nodded. He was not sure whether it would be wise to ask for an explanation. He recalled his encounter with Sachetti. It was difficult – impossible even – to imagine that the young man had been acting. Was it possible that he had been converted after the event? Several times, the Colonel had spoken of him in a way which had clearly indicated – at least seemed to do so – that he had known very little about him. But did that matter now? Sachetti had lost his life. The *carabinieri* had put his body in a lead-grey plastic sack. The whole – what was it? situation? affair? string of events? – the whole case had fragmented into separate scenes. Different groups of people controlled each of them. And, as always, there was chance. The scenes interacted. From his – James' – point of view they were both brutally simple in their effects and yet too complex, opaque, fragmented in their entwined ramifications to be grasped and understood.

He had no doubt that his uncompromising stance had helped to trigger the sudden acceleration of incidents. But then, what alternative in reality – a reality, it seemed, measured and tangibly expressed in sums of money – would he have had?

Fifty-three

THE DAY BROKE over the hills in the east.

At Montenano, Daniele laid a pair of shotguns on the floor behind the front seats of the old Lancia Lambda.

'Let's put down the top!' the Count suggested. 'Don't you think?'

Daniele looked at the sky. Despite the early hour it was low. Heavy, it promised a hot and close day. 'It's warm enough,' he replied. 'It's likely to break, though. In the evening. We had better take that into account if we find them.'

Standing on the running boards of the car on either side they folded the cabriolet top and fastened it back. They got in. The Count took the wheel. He started the engine. Clattering, it burst into life. Its sound was too soft to echo from the walls of the castle. In the grey light, the thin exhaust pipe emitted blue puffs of smoke. Soon it became transparent, without colour. The Count put the car in gear. They were ready to leave for Cerreto, high up in a forsaken valley of the Monti del Chianti, where the di Landos owned extensive forests, going back centuries.

They descended the steep drive between the inner and outer walls to the south gate. From the car, the Count activated the portcullis. Majestically, it lifted as they approached. They passed through the gate. Outside, they waited for the grating to come down again. It shut silently.

At the bottom of the hill they turned south. For a couple of miles they followed the asphalt road. Then they turned off it on to a dirt track going north. Deliberately, the Count had chosen a route which avoided all but one of the villages in the area. Unnoticed, they passed its shuttered houses and crossed its square. Behind the church, they took the road which led into the foot hills of the mountains.

They drove without speaking. They broke their silence only once,

223

when a pheasant flew up in front of them.

'They look a little better this year,' the Count remarked. 'I look forward to going out again.'

'It will not be long now,' was all Daniele replied.

They encountered a lonely *contadino*. A scythe over his shoulder, he came towards them. By the road side, the old man lifted his hat. With a friendly wave of his hand, the Count returned the silent greeting.

They made good progress, despite the car's age. Soon they were through the foothills and began their climb along the densely wooded valley. Desolate, dark, it lay under the first light, deep and narrow between the steepening slopes of the mountains. Even their peaks were still grey, not yet touched by the first rays of the rising sun.

About a mile before the Badia a Gerfalco – centuries ago a small monastery of the Franciscans, now only a ruin – the Count pulled the car on to a narrow side track. Presently, it opened into an old and no longer used marble quarry. On its far side where, because of the flatness of the slope above, the car was safe from falling stones, he stopped. He switched off the ignition.

They stepped down from the car. Daniele passed out the guns. From the back seat, he lifted a greenish canvas bag and a leather case, which contained a pair of field glasses. He handed the glasses to the Count. He pulled the strap of the bag over his shoulder. The Count gave him one of the guns. They were ready to begin the last part of their journey.

Daniele looked at the sky again. 'The light's still flat,' he said with a frown.

'We're not shooting today. At least, I hope not!' the Count retorted. 'It may even help us.'

Side by side, they climbed out of the quarry. In a straight line, they walked into the wood round its edge. Some three hundred yards on, they came to a path. It led to the far side of the mountains above Gerfalco.

The Count carried his gun broken, in the crook of his elbow. Behind him, Daniele did the same. In the faint light, the two men looked alike. Dressed in cord breeches, old-fashioned lace-up boots and canvas jackets, they could have been hunters. The fact that the season had yet to begin made it obvious that they were not out on a legitimate shoot, though.

224

They strode out with long and regular paces, like men who had grown up in the mountains. Less than half an hour since their arrival at the quarry, they passed above the Badia. At the edge of an old clearing, the Count stopped. Still under the trees, he took the field glasses from their case. The monastery lay several hundred feet below. He surveyed its remains.

'Nothing. Just as I expected.' He handed the glasses to Daniele.

'It'd be too obvious. Like the lodge,' Daniele said, holding the binoculars in front of his eyes.

They crossed the clearing and continued on the path. Straight for most of the way, it took them along the top of a densely wooded ridge on the south side of the valley.

A deer broke through the undergrowth ahead, unseen, only heard. The birds had begun their dawn chorus. Soon, the crescendo would reach its peak.

They came to a fork in the path.

'Cerreto?' the Count asked.

'Si! Cerreto!'

They went straight on. Faster still, they strode out on the slightly but steadily rising path. They got to the top of the valley. They crossed over the side of the mountain ahead of them. On its northwest flank they had to traverse a flat open slope. They ran, so they would be exposed for less time. Below them lay the trough of a deep and thickly wooded gorge. Black, it stretched due north.

'If we stay on this side, there's a point where we can look straight across,' Daniele panted over his shoulder. 'That's what I meant.'

'I understood that. You lead the way!'

As fast as the difficult terrain allowed, they made for the protection of the trees ahead. Thrashing, they disappeared into their thick undergrowth. Without a path, breaking their way through one behind the other, they made a lot of noise. But there was no wind, not even a breeze. They knew that the sound would not carry far.

Gradually, Daniele slowed their pace. Carefully, he began to choose where he stepped. Close behind, the Count did the same. To human ears they were barely audible now.

They disturbed another deer. For brief instants only, they saw it leap downhill. Then all seemed peaceful again. Only the birds were in full cry.

Daniele pointed at a huge rock. Mossy, it rose out of the forest floor, some fifty yards ahead to their right.

The Count nodded. He knew that the rock was at the very edge of the ridge they were on. Below it, the slope dropped almost vertically, five, maybe six hundred feet to the bottom of the gorge. Near-impenetrable trees and *macchia* made its depth uncertain.

They locked their guns.

Softly, they worked their way to the rock. At its edge, they got down on hands and knees. They crawled to the top.

An oak impaired their view across the gorge. With his hunting knife, Daniele cut a leafy branch. Inch by inch, he pulled it away.

The ruin of a tower stood on the other side. Thick layers of ivy had overgrown most of its remains. Stones and rubble which had fallen from the broken walls lay by its base. They were looking at Cerreto, the first stronghold documented in the history of the di Lando family.

The Count adjusted the field glasses from the setting Daniele had left them at. He focused on the ruin. A little lower than their own position, it was five hundred yards away at most. Methodically, he scanned the stump of the tower and the rubble around it.

He held the glasses very still. He readjusted them and looked through them again, obviously at one particular thing.

'I'm not sure,' he whispered. 'Look inside the door! On the right.'

Daniele took the binoculars. He adjusted them. He trained them on the only visible opening into the tower. A low doorway, it had been an internal connection with the house it had originally been built against.

Like the Count, Daniele stared at the opening until his eyes ached. Quickly, he scanned the rest of the ruin. He returned to the door.

'There may be something hanging,' he whispered. 'It could be a rug. To cover the inner door.'

'That's what I think! The damn light's on the wrong side!'

'We'll have to wait. It won't be — '

A man had appeared in the doorway.

Drowsily, he stepped to the side of the tower. Bare-chested, he undid the front of his jeans. In a long thin arc, his urine fell through the air and down into the gorge.

Eagerly, the Count took the glasses from Daniele.

The man was young. Barefoot, he stood quite still. His face — for a moment it looked up at the sky — was sallow. Unkempt dark hair hung to his shoulders.

'It's not Montale.' The Count handed the binoculars back to

226

Daniele.

'He's too short,' Daniele confirmed.

The man had finished. He zipped up his flies as he walked. He entered the doorway. He flapped back a grey rug. It served to cover the entrance to the only remaining room of the old castle.

'I had better run,' the Count whispered. 'I've seen what I wanted. I'll ask Amorini to relieve you as soon as possible.'

Daniele gave a nod. They had agreed in the evening that he would stay on the mountain if they found what they were looking for. He would keep watch while the Count rushed back to alert their friend the Colonel.

A woman appeared in the door. She went to a pile of rubble, opposite where the man had been. She undid her trousers. She pulled them to her knees. She squatted down.

'Now I've really seen enough!' the Count hissed.

He crept back from the edge.

'Don't lose them!' he whispered. 'I'll leave this here.'

He pulled the strap of the leather case in which he had carried the field glasses over his head. He put the case on the stone. He picked up his gun. Rapidly, he scrambled back up the ridge.

Fifty-four

THE POSTMAN HAD come and gone when James set off for Siena to telephone Claire. He had expected a cable from her. Apart from a note from Francesca there had been nothing of significance in his mail.

This early on a Saturday, the telephone office took only a few minutes to make the connection with London.

Tony's younger son answered the phone.

James asked for Claire.

'Hang on, I'll get Daddy.'

'Where's Claire?' James asked but the boy had already put down the telephone.

'Where's Claire?' Urgently, he repeated his question as soon as Tony picked up the handset.

'Claire's in hospital, James.'

'In hospital! When?'

'She was taken in last night. We got a garbled message. You'd been killed.'

'Who the hell – '

'The *Post*. The editor called saying he'd have to renege on the deal Richard had more or less concluded. She was already terribly worried because neither paper had improved on their original offer. The house here upset her too. She won't accept we can't sell it – '

'I told her not to think of it!'

'I know. Anyway. It was too late by the time I had established the news was wrong. I'm off to see her in a couple of hours. Last night we couldn't get through to her at all. I just hope – please pray! – that we get her back!'

Shattered, James tried to bring Tony up to date. He found it difficult to speak. Aware of his own incoherence, he struggled to

228

instil at least some hope in Tony, hope which he might pass on to Claire. But there was nothing to base it on!

Brooding, he drove back to Terrarossa. What was he going to say to the kidnappers now? He had the reserve – some one hundred and seventy-five million *lire* – which he had not mentioned at the rendezvous. There was no need to explain where the money had come from. Nevertheless, a suitable announcement had to be made. He hoped the Colonel would help him to formulate it.

A crowd of reporters greeted him at the gate. The burning of Sachetti's body had brought them out in force. To their surprise, he stopped the car.

'I would like to speak to Colonel Amorini, please,' James said to one of the guards. 'It's urgent. I'd be grateful if you could contact him on the radio for me.'

'Of course, sir. We'll call you directly we have him,' the guard replied, assuming James was driving on down to the house.

'Mr Grey! Mr Grey! I'm from the *Post*, Mr Grey!' An Englishman tried to push through the other journalists.

'So what?' With obvious distaste – hatred even – James looked down at the face he had not seen before.

'Our deal, sir. I arrived last night. I must remind you – '

'You must remind me? Of what?'

'The conditions. Our deal gives us the exclusive right to accompany you.'

The man put his hands possessively on the door of the wagon.

'After what you did to my wife? You'd better never let me see your face again! Get out of my way!'

Unaware of his slip of the tongue, James stepped on the accelerator.

The car leaped forward.

Frightened, the journalists scattered from its path.

Fifty-five

In its pink long case, which was decorated with a wealth of colourful little flowers and green foliage, the old Tuscan country clock struck one. Irritably, even more impatient than before, James eyed the cumbrous hands. Together, they pointed to the top of the yellowing dial. The half-light in the shuttered study softened their ornate outline.

Only a few minutes after his return, one of the guards had followed him into the house. Colonel Amorini was not available, the man had said, but an urgent message had been left for him to return the call. At eleven thirty, still waiting for the Colonel's call, James had gone back to the gate. If the Colonel was not available, would it be possible to speak to Captain Rossi?

He had waited at the jeep for the new call to be put through. The answer was instant. Rossi, too, was unavailable. He too would call back just as soon as possible.

On his way back, Anna had stopped him in the kitchen. She was concerned that her husband might be accused of manslaughter, even murder.

'He didn't mean to go out and kill anyone, *signor* James. When I woke up, he was already putting on his shoes, in the dark. He told me not to go out or switch on the light. He was afraid they might come down to the house. Then he took his shotgun and slipped out. I believe he had heard their car. Even before they called you.'

James had tried to put her mind at ease. He told her that Rossi had only been angry because none of the terrorists had survived, so there was no one they could interrogate about the children's hiding place. 'Rossi even mentioned he'd cover up for Pasquale,' he had said.

Back in his study, he had decided to write to Kazue. It would keep him busy. Besides, although barely five days had passed since her departure from Heathrow, so much had happened!

230

He had put a sheet of his letter paper into the typewriter. He had taken it out again. He had decided to write by hand.

Methodically, he had begun with their parting. He had completed his second sheet when Anna had brought him a cup of coffee. Now, at one o'clock, she would call him to lunch.

There was a knock on the door.

'I don't want to eat.'

She shut the door.

A few minutes later she returned. On a tray she brought him a bottle of mineral water, a glass and a white bowl. Ice cubes and water filled the bowl. A bunch of yellow muscat grapes and two purple figs swam in the water. A plate, a knife and an immaculately white napkin completed the offering.

He continued to write at the same slow pace. He found himself referring back to what he had touched on already, more and more often. Several times he stopped. He tore up some sheets. Inconclusive, his account – his story – led to an increasing number of unanswered questions, suppositions, guesses.

At last he arrived at the events of the past few hours. Claire's breakdown, his indecision at what to say to the kidnappers, his attempts to call the Colonel, the present act of writing.

Writing down what has happened since you left helps me to order my thoughts. But it has also made me even more aware how I dare not focus on the children even though there is not a moment when I am not aware of their absence. I dare not go beyond the anguish of having lost them to the even more acute pain of imagining, visualising, feeling for them in the place and situation they are in. Claire has broken down. If I were to do the same, the children would be without parents. I must not let that happen. Pray for us! James.

Outside, huge clouds had appeared in the sky. Billowing, they towered over the hills in the north. The heat was intense, the air close. The land lay silent.

Anna knocked on the door.

'Why won't you eat, *signor* James?' Reproachfully, she looked at the tray he had not touched. 'Colonel Amorini will be calling at four. He will be coming here. In person.'

'Thank God for that! Why didn't they call me to the radio?'

'I don't know, *signor* James. Will you have some coffee?'

With a nod, he accepted.

'Shall I take the fruit away?'

'No. Leave it. I'll have some later.'

At four there was another message. The Colonel would be delayed by an hour. Would James be absolutely sure he was there nevertheless.

A few minutes after six, a beige Lancia saloon stopped at the gate. Moments later it came rolling down the drive. It stopped next to the Chevrolet. A tall man in grey flannels and a white open-necked shirt got out of the car. In plain clothes, Enzo Amorini had finally arrived at Terrarossa.

James flew out of the front door and down the steps at the visitor. 'We need to make an announcement before the day's out! Claire's in hospital! She's been unable to raise more money. What kept you so long?'

'Let's go inside where we can talk,' the Colonel replied calmly, seemingly ignoring James' agitation.

In the study, the officer himself shut the door behind them.

'I'm sorry I did not get in touch. I didn't dare use the radio to speak to you. Di Lando found the hiding place.'

Speechless, James stared at the Colonel. He was not sure he could believe what he had just heard.

He swallowed. 'You have – you have found the children? Alive?'

'We have not seen the children. But there is no doubt in my mind that they are there. Alive.'

James still did not know how to accept the news. 'Can you – can you get them out?'

'That's what we've been working on. I would like you to come with me now. To Montenano. I'll explain to you on the way. Only a hand-picked group of my men know. You'll need a change of clothes for the morning. And a pair of walking boots with rubber soles.'

Dazed, James replied he had nothing of the kind. The Colonel asked what size shoe he took.

'Forty-three.'

'We can get you a pair by the morning. But bring some thick socks – as well as thin ones – in case they don't fit exactly.'

In his bedroom, James threw his overnight things and a change of clothes, including a pair of cords and a sweater, into a soft bag. He nearly forgot the socks. He remembered the Madonna.

'I'm ready. May I tell Max and Anna where we're going?' he

asked, back in the study.

The Colonel hesitated.

'All right! I'll say nothing – '

'You can tell them you're going to visit Montenano. You'll be back later tomorrow.'

'Is Max back?' James asked Anna on their way out.

'Not yet.'

'Will you tell him, please, I'm going to visit the di Landos. I'll be back tomorrow, in time for dinner.'

'I wish you luck,' Anna replied. She turned to the Colonel. 'Please look after him.'

The Colonel opened the boot of his car. On its carpeted floor, next to a bulky leather bag, lay a camouflage battle suit, similar to the ones James had seen at Camilliano.

'May I have your bag?' the Colonel asked James who seemed to have frozen at the sight of the unusual garment.

The Colonel stopped the car at the gate. He got out. 'Get me Captain Rossi on the radio!' he ordered the saluting guards.

For several minutes, James sat in the Lancia on his own. The air was even closer than it had been during the day. He wound down his window. He heard the Colonel's voice from the jeep. He could make out some occasional words, no more.

The Colonel returned and restarted the engine. Standing to attention, the guards saluted.

'You say you haven't seen the children,' James said while they were still rounding the ravine.

'That's right. At least – we had not seen them a little over an hour ago. That's when I received the last report from our lookout.'

'How can you be so sure then?'

'Because it's absolutely normal for hostages to be kept hidden. At all times! Only criminals are allowed the privilege of daily exercise when they're imprisoned!' The Colonel gave a sarcastic laugh. 'They need it. I know the place. I can see no other reason why the abductors should be there. Not if they had only themselves to hide.'

They drove over the spot where Sachetti's body had been burnt. A dull stain marked the pale road.

The Colonel put his car in second gear.

'What if only one of the children is there?'

'It's possible.' For a moment, the Colonel shifted into third. 'But I doubt it.' He stabbed at the brakes and shifted down again. 'For similar, entirely practical reasons. I don't believe they'd still maintain two places. Don't forget we have reduced their numbers!'

In the east, the evening sky was beginning to fade to blue-black. The clouds in the north did not seem to have moved.

'What are your plans?' James asked at last.

'I want to take them by surprise. At dawn.'

'Couldn't you – '

'Tonight?' The Colonel had guessed the question. 'The chances were not good enough. We considered them carefully. One of the lessons we learnt at Camilliano was that speed exposes one's weak sides all the more. We concentrated on a sitting target. Due to shortness of time we had poor plans for the possibility that it might move.'

'I was thinking of the deadline – '

'What deadline?' The Colonel looked across at James. 'It was your decision to call their bluff!'

Silent, they arrived at the bridge. A jeep was parked on the other side. Two *carabinieri* stood in front of the car. They were armed with submachine guns. Another two men stood by the junction.

The Colonel slowed down. He stopped. The first two officers saluted. Through the window the Colonel passed out his driving licence. One of the men pretended to examine it.

'All clear?' the Colonel asked.

'Yes, sir. All clear. Thank you, sir.' The man handed back the document. Both *carabinieri* gave a short salute, as they would have done to a passing motorist.

Waved on by the other two men, the Colonel turned on to the main road.

'At first only a man and a woman were there,' the Colonel said. 'Later another man joined them.'

'Do you know who they are?'

'We have an idea. Di Lando recognised one of them. Four years ago his nephew invited him to the castle. Laura remembered that they spent some time up in the mountains.'

'Is that where he saw him?'

'In the mountains? No. He saw him last night. On television. They showed a series of pictures we had lent them. Associates of Barea.'

'Is he as dangerous?'

'They're all dangerous. However, Montale – that's his name – is only wanted for kneecapping. At least, we don't know of any murders he may have committed.'

The Colonel continued their conversation with a description of Cerreto. 'Di Lando, Daniele and I occasionally camped up there when we were boys,' he said.

'What did your father do?' James asked.

'Ah! They told you!' The Colonel smiled. 'My father was head cooper. Daniele's was head game keeper. In those days many more people depended on the di Landos than one could hope to find now. Times have changed so much here! Thinking back, I often wonder whether I'm deceiving myself. Those days, too, were very hard. Violent. Far from romantic! And yet compared with what we do to each other today – they seem so soft now – I hesitate to say it – almost warm!'

A pair of jeeps stood at the junction where they had to turn south. Parked maybe thirty yards apart – on opposite sides and across the road – they formed a chicane. The joining road bisected it. Several *carabinieri* stood about. One of them stepped out from behind the first jeep. He held up a hand. The Colonel stopped his car in front of him.

The man touched his cap with two fingers and walked round to the Colonel's side.

From a pocket in the sun visor, the Colonel produced his driving licence for the second time. He handed it to the officer.

'The road is clear, sir,' the man said pretending to look over the licence.

'Thank you, Marullo. If someone tried your roadblock in earnest – from the side road – where would your gunner take cover?' For a second, the Colonel pointed at one of the men. A thick flak jacket covered the top of his uniform. He was armed with a big machine gun which looked considerably heavier than those carried by most of his colleagues.

Marullo blushed. 'We should have brought a second gun, sir.' He handed back the driving licence.

The Colonel smiled. 'Not necessarily. Remind me to show you a better way. For the time being, put him over there! Behind the tree. Out of sight.'

'Yes, sir! Thank you, sir!' Marullo saluted. Sheepishly, he waved the Lancia on.

On the minor road, the Colonel went a little faster. James thought he noticed that the officer enjoyed driving the car. The way he steered it through the corners was fluent and smooth. He could have gone faster still safely. The thought struck James that the Colonel was cautious probably by nature rather than by experience. How could he tell? The idea was based on intuition. If he asked the Colonel for an assessment of their chances this time, what would the answer be? He was tempted to risk the question.

'I wonder if we shall ever find out who sent the message to Pasquale?' he asked instead.

The Colonel seemed not to have heard.

James thought he had better not ask again.

'We may never know. Not now,' the Colonel replied finally.

Surprised, James wondered whether the 'not now' was meant to mean that the informer might become known in the future. Or did it mean that the way things had developed, the answer was redundant for all time? Again he decided not to persist with his questions, or at least, not to insist on probing into what was offered in terms of explanations. Here he was being taken to Montenano. He was a passenger in more than one sense. The negotiator at the rendezvous had called him a passenger too. A deep feeling of insecurity – total and absolute insecurity! – humbled him to the point where only his natural instinct to save his children gave him a resolve which, on the surface, passed for confidence.

'If the Count had not seen that man's picture on television – '

'Rossi would have shown it to him,' the Colonel completed James' tentative statement. 'He was on the track!'

The Colonel went on to explain how painstakingly Rossi had tried to interpret the message. Day after day, he had worked on the problem, deep into the night. One of his plans – only a couple of days old – had been to take the Count through their entire set of records. 'He intended to show him every single terrorist we have a picture of. Those of the right as well as those of the left.'

'He seems very competent,' James said. 'And kind – '

'He is competent! I'm proud of him.'

'He told me Barea was a member of the Red Brigades. Why did they kill Sachetti?'

'Barea was *Prima Linea*. As tough as they come.' The Colonel paused. 'Sachetti was our man. From the beginning.'

'When I caught him?' James was incredulous.

'Long before then. He was our spy. And bait.'

'Did he know?'

'That he was bait? Of course!'

'And the police?'

'They knew nothing. Still don't. They almost did too good a job on the poor man before we could get him out. Please forget what I said. One of the reasons we're starting out from Montenano is that even within our own organisations we can't be sure of everyone.'

James nodded. An unpleasant taste was in his mouth. 'I feel – I felt so outraged when I caught him. Indignant. I thought he was the perfect wretch to hate! Everything about him revolted me!' He gave a bitter laugh. 'It frightens me to think how wrong I was. How did they find out?'

'We don't know. Maybe he gave himself away. I doubt it, though. He was too good an actor. I'm afraid he was betrayed.'

For a while they drove in silence.

'I didn't tell you,' James suddenly said, 'Claire has had a nervous breakdown. Her husband told me this morning – '

'You did tell me. The moment I arrived.'

'Did I?'

'I meant to ask you about it immediately. Then there was so much else I had to tell you, I forgot. You said she was in hospital. Is she very ill?'

'I don't really know. Her husband was very concerned. He saw it coming.'

The Colonel shook his head. 'Another victim. Though I saw her – as the mother – as the worst afflicted from the beginning. Especially since there was so little she could do.'

They passed the stone gate on the north side of the castle.

James pointed up the drive. 'I still don't understand how Daniele saw me.'

'Didn't he tell you?'

'I didn't click at the time. He simply said he saw me – '

'You are a television man – '

'You mean – a closed circuit?'

'Of course! There are cameras right the way round. I guess someone even occasionally takes a look at the monitors.'

On the south side, the yellow grass shone in the dying sunlight. Golden, the dry blades reflected the sinking red rays. As if sculpted, each cypress along the drive looked greener than under the full sun of day. Softly, the trees' long shadows fell across the hillside.

237

In front of the gate, the Colonel stopped the car and got out. James watched him pull the bell handle once and return to the car. Presently, the portcullis began to lift. It slid silently into the cavity in the wall above. Displaying only the bottommost of its horizontal bars and a long row of sharp vertical ends, the black grating stopped at the top of its travel.

The Colonel drove slowly through the gate and up the drive. James turned. The portcullis was on its way back down. He wondered who had let them in. Daniele? He had meant to ask the Colonel whether his friend had been a partisan. It was too late now. Like so many of his questions it would have to remain unanswered. At least for the time being.

'My father is out. But he should be back very soon.' Laura held out her hand to James. 'Shall I call someone to help carry your things?'

'We've only got a couple of bags. We'll cope.' The Colonel kissed her hand. 'My God, you're growing beautiful! Still not engaged?'

'I stopped growing some time ago, flatterer! Are you proposing?' she countered with a smile.

'I wish I could!' The Colonel put his hand on his heart. 'I don't think your father'd be very pleased with me. Where is he?'

'He had to go to the *fattoria*. We had a delivery of vats this morning.'

Nodding, the Colonel opened the boot of his car. He took out James' bag and his own.

He held out the combat suit. 'This is for you, Mr Grey. Put it on in the morning. Over your underclothes.'

Silent, James accepted the suit. It felt much lighter than he had expected it to be. He picked up his bag.

Briskly, Laura led the way up the dual stairway in front of the house. Their steps reverberated as they crossed the hall. They lost their echo as they passed through the doorway on the right. Behind it, from the vestibule, James got a glimpse of the entrance to the library. Laura led on up the marble stair, which was symmetrically identical to the one on the other side of the hall.

They turned right again at the top, down a long stone-floored corridor.

Laura opened the second door from its end. 'Your rooms look out south. Will you take this one, Enzo?'

With a smile, the Colonel stepped inside. 'Rare are the days I enjoy such luxury!' He put down his bag. 'Where do we go from here?'

'The library. When you're ready.'

She went on and opened the next door, at the end of the corridor. 'Please!'

James stepped inside. The room was in the southwest corner of the house.

The tall windows looked out in both directions. The colours of the sunset shone in from the west. They reflected softly from the whitewashed walls. Red and golden, they tinged everything inside.

'May I open the windows?' he asked.

'Please do!'

Together, they opened the two windows facing west and fastened back their casements. Warm, more humid than the atmosphere in the house, the air flowed in from outside. A blackbird sang from the rooftop. In the distance, the flat disc of the sun was about to touch the horizon.

'There's my house!' James raised his hand to point it out.

'I was looking at it just as you arrived. It's more difficult to see today. The light's so red.'

Side by side, they waited for the sun to go down. Brooding, cold, it seemed to have come to a halt on its downward journey. Suddenly, its base dissolved. Flowing out to either side the red glowed. Blinding, it bled along the line it was about to sink below.

James broke the silence. 'It always surprises me how quickly it goes down finally. Thank you for giving me such a beautiful room.'

She smiled. 'I shall see you in the library.' She left him to unpack his bag.

Alone, he sat down on the bed. He looked at the bag and the battle suit. Was there any point in unpacking at all? He was staying for only a few hours. If they failed again in the morning to free the children, if again they were too late – but he could not allow any of that to obsess him. With a jerk of the head he chased the thought away.

He got up and opened the windows on the south side too. He stood in the centre of the room. In the garden, the leaves of the orange trees rustled gently. A breeze was rising. He heard the noise of windows being shut or fastened drifting up from the ground floor. The light was fading quickly. The earlier redness had vanished from the room. Blues and greys mixed with the browns and honey colours of the few pieces of furniture. A small four-poster flanked by a pair of low bedside tables, a desk, some chairs and armchairs, a massive wardrobe. Wild flowers had been arranged in an old *maiolica* vase and placed on a side table between the south windows. A pier glass hung over the table. Dimly, it reflected the back of the flower arrangement.

The horn of the old Lancia sounded outside.

James lifted his bag on to a chair and opened it. He took out his kimono and hung it on the inside of the bathroom door. He put his sponge bag on a table next to the hand basin. He returned to the bedroom.

There was little else that needed unpacking: his travelling clock, which he put on one of the bedside tables; a soft summer jacket which he slipped over his open-neck shirt. He shut the windows. He was ready to go downstairs.

Voices sounded from the library. James entered. The Colonel stood talking to Laura. They turned towards him. He was halfway into the room when he heard the Count behind him.

'I'm sorry I was not here to welcome you, gentlemen. This morning my schedule fell into slight disarray.'

'Don't apologise!' the Colonel exclaimed. 'Your daughter's far more charming – '

'That's not difficult!' the Count cut him short. 'Anyway! Don't listen to the rascal, Laura. All he's good at is putting up roadblocks – all over the place! What's the idea, Amorini? On my short journey I was stopped twice!'

'Show!' the Colonel replied drily, actually using the English word. 'I want to give the impression – to some of my own people too – that we're busy in an area quite distant from where we are actually going in the morning.'

'And around Cerreto itself? What happens if they decide to run again?' the Count demanded.

Alarmed, James waited for the reply.

'We'd either stop them or follow them. Depending on the circumstances,' the Colonel explained calmly. 'They've been surrounded since noon. Completely.'

'Good! I'm delighted to hear it!' Vigorously, the Count nodded his head. 'Will you take a drink, Mr Grey?'

James asked for a glass of wine.

'Red or white?' Laura asked.

'Why – red, since I'm here.'

'Ah! You don't know we've been experimenting, Mr Grey,' the Count interjected. 'I don't blame you for choosing the red. But you must try our white one day. We're still learning. I believe it's becoming quite light and pleasant now. Very different from the Vino Santo.'

Daniele appeared in the open door.

'Come in, Daniele,' the Count invited him in. 'I asked Daniele to join us. So we can talk.'

The man approached. He shook hands with the Colonel. He acknowledged James with a smile.

'When did you get back?' the Colonel asked.

'At four,' Daniele replied. 'Your chaps didn't have enough transport.'

'You didn't see the children?' Instantly, James had seized on Daniele.

He shook his head. 'I didn't. I believe they're there, though.'

'Why?'

Daniele looked uncomfortable.

'You must have some evidence!'

'I saw them bring out a can. Twice. They emptied it where the woman had gone – '

'I'm sure we understand, Daniele,' the Count interrupted. 'Don't you, Mr Grey?'

James shut his eyes. 'I suppose so. At least – at least one of them should be there.'

The young servant entered with a silver salver. On it, he carried a cut glass jug and several stem glasses. The jug was filled with red wine. He stopped in front of his master. He held the salver low, between them, while the Count took the decanter and filled three of the glasses. He offered one of them to James, another to Daniele. He kept the third one for himself.

'To the children, Mr Grey! To both of them!' The Count raised his glass. 'Like them, this wine is young and fresh. Still a little rough but full of promise!'

Against one of the lights in the room – Laura had gone round to switch them on – James looked at the brilliant, translucent, ruby red liquid. He put the glass to his nose. The scent of the young wine was strong, almost sweet. He drank.

'Well? Do you like it?' the Count asked.

'I like it. I wanted to grow wine like that – '

'You can learn! I'll teach you, if you like. The more people learn the art, the better for all of us. Paolo! Leave the wine on the table!'

With a bow the servant acknowledged the order. He put the salver on one of the library tables and left the room. Announcing that dinner would be ready soon, Laura followed him.

On their own, the four men drew closer together.

'Will you tell us, please, what you have in mind, Amorini?' the Count asked.

The Colonel looked round the room. The casement windows to the west terrace still stood open. Outside, the sky was dark. A faint grey line indicated where the sun had gone down. Gusts of wind had begun to break into the constant, still freshening breeze.

In a low voice, the Colonel began: 'A simple plan. We take up positions behind Cerreto by five o'clock. If at any time between then and six one of them comes outside, we shoot on sight. From the lookout. We take the others by surprise at the same time.'

'It sounds simple enough. I like that,' the Count said. 'What happens if nobody does come out? Why do you need a time limit?'

'Because I don't want my men to wait for longer than an hour. Even that's too long for maximum concentration. If no one shows by six, we'll storm inside and take the lot of them.'

'Can you do that?' James asked quickly. 'Even if they're aware of your impending attack?'

'That'd be difficult. We'd know, of course, if they became aware of us. They'd threaten us – maybe bargain with us. For such a case we have what we call siege tactics. But I'm quite confident we'll surprise them.'

'That room's very small,' Daniele said. 'The walls are hard stone. You can't just fire into it, Enzo! You'd end up with ricochets flying all over the place.'

'I know that, Daniele. There's no question of that, even if we assume that the children are right at the back.'

'So what are you proposing to do?' the Count demanded.

'The usual. Concussion grenades for openers. Then hands – or knives.'

Daniele nodded, obviously satisfied. 'The ceiling's absolutely solid. At least, I think it is. It shouldn't come down if you bang away in there. I like the idea of concussion grenades, if they're as good as I read. I suppose you'll have your best marksmen on the other side?'

242

'We've got two of them there already.'

Again, Daniele nodded. 'I should hate having to stab one of those miserable wretches!' he said with contempt. 'Far cleaner to shoot them!'

'What are we to do – while all that is going on?' Hesitant, James pointed at the Count and Daniele.

'I would like you to come with me, Mr Grey,' the Colonel replied. 'Just in case – if we have to make a decision – '

'And I'd like to watch. From the lookout,' the Count interrupted.

'So would I!' Daniele added.

'Agreed. But please leave your guns at home this time! We're embarrassed enough with Neri actually killing a man – '

The Colonel's eyes suddenly focused behind his listeners and he fell silent. They turned. Laura, now in a dark evening gown, had come back into the room. It was time for dinner.

The Colonel offered her his arm.

With an amused curtsey, she accepted the gallant gesture.

'We had better close these doors before we go in,' the Count said. 'I can hear thunder.'

They stopped by the casement windows. The night had turned black. The wind was growing in strength. Thunder rolled in the distance.

'Let me do it!' Daniele stepped forward. 'I'll catch up with you.'

With the Colonel, Laura led the way. James followed close behind. He tried to visualise what he had just learnt. He would have liked to ask the Colonel about the grenades he had heard him mention. Daniele had sounded as though he knew what they did. The battle plan seemed plausible enough, provided circumstances did not change. It was going to rain! Suddenly, the thought alarmed him. Laura laughed. He looked up. They had arrived in the candlelit dining room.

'Mr Grey, will you sit here, please!' Laura invited him to the single place which had been set halfway down the long side of the table.

'Enzo, you're opposite. On Father's side.'

'Can't I sit with you?' the Colonel protested.

'I don't mind! In fact, I prefer Daniele's conversation, Amorini!' the Count exclaimed, trying to sound gruff. 'Please sit, Mr Grey.'

The Colonel held Laura's chair, which faced her father's at the other end. They sat down as Daniele entered and took the remaining place, on the Count's left.

243

Presently Paolo and a second servant began to serve the first course. Both of them wore white jackets and gloves.

'Do you like our local dishes, Mr Grey?' the Count asked.

'Yes, I do.' Distractedly, James tried to see what it was that Paolo was offering to serve from a deep bowl held by the other man. 'So far, I have been very unlucky finding wild mushrooms in the woods.'

'Really?' The Colonel was obviously surprised. 'There must be lots near your house! Especially after rain. Tomorrow, for instance.'

James looked up. He wanted to see whether the rain had started. Solid shutters concealed the windows. Their tall panels were painted with the colours and patterns typical of the early Mannerists.

Paolo lifted a small amount of *tagliatelle* on to James' plate. He covered them with several spoonfuls of wild mushrooms which had been cooked in a reddish sauce.

'Is it true that in England you don't eat wild mushrooms at all?' the Count asked.

'Almost,' James confirmed. 'We never see this kind at all. Most people are convinced that all of them are poisonous. Very dangerous.'

'Some of them are,' Daniele said. 'I'll never forget those children from Radda. Five of them died!'

'That's a long time ago! Before the war, Daniele. Let's talk of something more pleasant!' the Count suggested.

Paolo circled the table, filling the wine glasses from a decanter.

'I like this even more than what you offered earlier, di Lando.' The Colonel raised his glass.

'I thought I saw you drinking scotch,' the Count objected.

'That's right. But I took a sniff. This is superior.'

'So it should be! It's nineteen seventy-five. One of our best recent years.'

For a while, the conversation turned to recent vintages and their relative merits.

'When do we have to get up?' James asked during a suitable pause.

'We must get going by three,' the Colonel replied. 'I'm afraid you will not get much sleep here.'

James was about to reply that he would not be able to sleep anyway when the servants brought the second course. On a huge oval platter, Paolo carried a number of massive steaks. The scent of charcoal entered the room with them. The other man brought a bowl of salad. Quickly, they served the food.

James stared at his plate. His lack of appetite was about to turn into actual nausea. Afraid that he might already have given offence, he searched for something to say. 'I remember,' he looked up, 'I remember my first Florentine Steak. I couldn't believe its size! Even American T-bones seemed small in comparison.'

'And tasteless,' the Count added. 'They don't let their beef mature, they just freeze it. And they don't have our wood for the charcoal either.'

'What is it you use?' the Colonel asked. 'My father used to swear oak was best. Of course, as a cooper he was biased.'

'I think olive wood gives the best flavour to meat,' Daniele ventured.

'So do I,' the Count agreed. 'This is olive – '

'Holm oak, Father,' Laura cut him short.

'What?' Incredulous, the Count cut a fresh piece from his steak. He stabbed it with his fork. He held it under his nose. He sniffed it noisily.

'I can't smell oak! And I'm supposed to have a good nose!'

'We won't tell, di Lando!' the Colonel teased. 'After all, it isn't wine! Only a bit of smoke and masses of hot air!'

Everyone laughed. Even James had to join in. He forced himself to eat. Methodically, he cut the meat from the bone and carved it into small pieces. He chewed slowly. He knew that he would not be able to eat even one quarter of what he had been given.

A loud clap of thunder made him sit up suddenly.

'It's close,' Daniele said. 'It'll last a while.'

'How do you know?' James put down his knife and fork.

'It was long in coming. It'll be more than just a short cloudburst, I'm sure of that.'

'Will that – will it make your plans more difficult?' Anxiously, James turned to the Colonel.

The officer shook his head. 'Please don't worry. In some ways it may even help. Think of it that way!'

'You mean the rain conceals,' the Count stated rather than asked.

'Exactly! And it may help to make them less attentive,' the Colonel confirmed.

The Count and Daniele finished eating at last. Paolo served fruit and cheese. A little later, the other servant cleared the table.

'Shall we have our coffee here?' Laura asked.

'Let's stay!' the Count said. 'Mr Grey, will you have some of our special *grappa*?'

'I'm fine. I'll just finish my glass – '

'Leave it! In that case I'd like you to try something a little older.' The Count rose from his chair. 'I'll be back presently.'

Laura watched her father leave the room. She smiled. 'I think he likes you, Mr Grey. I believe we may be treated to his reserve.'

'You're very kind. I must apologise for being so unappreciative. I don't normally – '

'Please, don't apologise – '

The telephone began to ring. It sounded far away.

'Answer it, please, Paolo,' Laura said.

The servant bowed.

The ringing sounded louder, more insistent, as he opened the door.

'I hope – '

James bit his lip. He looked at the Colonel. Impassive, the officer sat quite still.

'It's a bit late for a telephone call,' Daniele said.

Rapid footsteps approached in the corridor.

Paolo appeared in the door.

'It's for you, Contessa,' he announced a little out of breath.

'Who is it?' she asked coolly.

'The Principe Ortini. He's calling from New York.'

'Tell him I am entertaining, Paolo. He can call tomorrow. No. The day after. I may be here. Don't promise!'

A bow and Paolo was gone again.

'Ortini?' the Colonel exclaimed. 'You're not – '

'Definitely not! In fact, I don't even like him,' Laura cut him short. 'Every time he alights from an aeroplane he tries to impress me by calling long distance. When you see him in person he's got nothing to say. He's an imbecile!'

'It's raining!' Daniele pointed to his ears.

They listened. Single drops tapped on the window panes behind the shutters. The continuous rushing of the rain was about to set in. More frequently than before, the rolling growl of the thunder was punctuated by the noise of single claps.

'I wonder if anyone can guess the age of this wine?' From the doorway, the Count asked the question. He put a plain glass decanter on the table.

246

From the sideboard, Paolo brought five glasses. He lined them up by the decanter.

The Count began to pour. His hand and arm moved steadily from left to right. The others watched silently as he filled each glass to a third, maybe a little more, of its volume.

He finished. He raised one of the glasses. The candlelight made the wine glow. A warm red, it shone softly.

The Colonel stood up. He pulled back Laura's chair. James and Daniele got to their feet.

Paolo served Laura first, then James and the Colonel.

He turned with Daniele's glass.

It shattered on the floor.

Black in the subdued light, the wine spread across the pale marble.

Paolo turned to the Count. He opened his mouth. He could not speak. He fell to his knees. Frantically, he tried to gather up the fragments.

'Leave it, Paolo!' Calmly, the Count gave the order. 'Glass often breaks. Give him another one.'

The servant got up. His face was white. He took a fresh glass from the sideboard. The Count filled it.

'I am sorry!' Paolo offered the glass to Daniele.

'It was my fault,' Daniele said. 'I dropped it. I'm the one who must apologise.'

The Count raised his glass for the second time. He smiled. 'My grandfather made this wine. In the year nineteen hundred and one.'

He drank. The others followed his example. Perturbed, James tried to concentrate on the wine.

'It's still strong!' Gently, the Colonel swirled the glass under his moustache.

'I have never seen such an old wine,' James said. 'Did you decant it just then?'

'I did,' the Count confirmed. 'Being so old it can only take a little air. If you leave it too long, its nose is prone to fade quite quickly. It gets to a point and – puff! – it's gone! Vanished!'

'I might have been able to tell it's Chianti,' James said. 'But little else. Where did it grow?'

'I guess most of the grapes must have come from the two main vineyards. On the south side,' the Count replied and distributed the last drops.

'Is this one of your bottles without label?' the Colonel asked.

247

'Ah! One of them!' Daniele laughed.

The Count turned to James. 'Some of our bottles – like this one – are without labels. Age has destroyed the paper. But we still have our cellar books. From them and from the position of the bottles on the racks, we can tell the years.'

'Can't you also tell – '

A shattering blast cut the Colonel short. Deafeningly, the thunderclap shook the house and made the windows rattle.

'That hit the tower!' The Count dropped his hands from his ears.

'It's right overhead,' Daniele said. 'It's time for me to go to bed. It's been a long day.'

'I agree,' the Count said. 'I'll see you a little before three, then.'

'Yes, sir. And thank you for dinner,' Daniele said. He smiled at the others. Paolo opened the door for him. He was gone.

James put down his glass. 'Would you mind if I, too, went to my room?' he asked.

The Count excused him. 'Please, Mr Grey! Of course not! You only have four hours and you'll be on your way again. I hope you will be able to rest.'

'Thank you!' James bowed. He faced the Colonel and Laura. 'Thank you all! Thank you for everything!'

In his room, the shutters had been closed. A reading light shone softly over the bedside table on which he had put his clock. The bedspread had gone. The blanket was turned.

He undressed and put on the kimono. He remembered the Madonna. He put her by the clock. He set the alarm for half past two.

He opened the shutters and windows to the south. Cold, the scent of the rain fell into the room. The wind had stopped. Visible only in the light from the window, the rain fell through the black night. The noise of its splashing was constant and loud. Lightning and thunder were slowly moving south.

He turned out the light. He lay down on top of the bed. He did not expect to sleep. He was going to wait until it was time to leave for the mountains. He thought of the children. Was this their last night in captivity? Thomas was frightened of thunderstorms. If he was ill –

He stopped himself. Deliberately, he turned his thoughts to Claire. What did it mean to suffer a nervous breakdown? Was it an illness? Or was it simply a condition which the return of the children

248

would switch back to normal? He remembered what Kazue had said about time. Time heals. Did it heal because we forget? Or because we accept? Maybe both, he thought: we accept because we forget the circumstances. Some of them, anyway.

Fifty-six

His travelling clock woke James at half past two.

At the first sound of its alarm he jumped from the bed.

He staggered. In the dark room, he knocked over a chair. He steadied himself on a piece of furniture he did not recognise. Disconcerted – guilty because he had fallen asleep – he dimly distinguished the windows he had left open.

He listened for the rain.

It was falling constantly through the night.

His eyes had adapted to the dark. He was leaning over the desk.

He went to one of the windows to look out at the rain. Its fresh, cold scent, the rushing sound, the splashing in the gutters above him, the noise of dripping trees below, they were all the same as they had been when he had turned out the light.

He shivered. He pulled the kimono more closely around him. His chest felt tight.

He drew a bath while he shaved. He sat in the old-fashioned tub for a minute at the most. He got out and dried himself. He was ready to get dressed.

The material of the battle suit, which he had left over a chair, felt damp. Overprinted with a brown and olive camouflage pattern, the texture reminded him of a raincoat. The trousers were baggy. Cuffed at the ankles, they seemed to have pockets everywhere. He tightened the belt. He had to go to the innermost eyehole. He left the cuffs of the trouser legs undone. He slipped on the tee-shirt he had brought and put on the jacket over it.

He stuffed the thick socks the Colonel had told him to bring into one of the many trouser pockets. He put on the thin pair and over them his shoes.

He folded up the clothes he had arrived in and put them into his bag. He collected his things from the bathroom and packed them, together with the clock. He put the Madonna into the right-hand pocket of the battle jacket. At ten minutes to three he began his way downstairs.

A dim light lit the corridor. The door to the Colonel's room was shut. Halfway down the stair, he heard footsteps.

He encountered Daniele in the vestibule. In shooting clothes, he was on his way out.

'There's some coffee in the library,' Daniele said. 'We must be leaving soon.'

The Count and the Colonel were bent over a large map which they had spread on one of the library tables. They looked up.

'Did you sleep?' The Colonel asked.

'I did,' James replied. 'I didn't expect to.'

The Count handed him a large cup of black coffee. 'Do you take milk?'

James shook his head.

'You can't go in those shoes!' the Count exclaimed.

'I arranged for a pair of boots for him to be brought to Gerfalco,' the Colonel said.

'In this weather he'll be much more comfortable if he starts off the right way from here,' the Count said. 'You must be about my size.'

'Forty-three,' James said.

'Do you have socks? Thick ones?'

James pointed at the bulge on his right trouser leg.

'I'll be back presently.' Quickly, the Count left the room.

'What were you looking at?' James asked.

'I was just showing di Lando where we meet up,' the Colonel explained. 'We drive as far as Gerfalco. Here!' He pointed at a place on the map.

'I don't know it. How long will it take to get there?'

'Forty-five minutes. Some of my men are waiting for us there. The rest of the way we walk.' With a pencil the Colonel followed a path which had been drawn on the map. 'Here, on top of this ridge, we make contact with the men who have been surrounding the place since yesterday.' The tip of the pencil stabbed at the approximate point where the Count and Daniele had begun their descent to the rock which was now the lookout.

The Count returned with a pair of lace-up boots, similar to the ones he was wearing. 'Try these, Mr Grey. They should fit. I brought an extra pair of socks. In case they're too big.'

251

James sat down. He took off his shoes and socks. He put on his thick socks. He loosened the laces and pulled the boots on to his feet. He stood up.

'Well? Do they fit? the Count asked.

James bent his knees. He rocked on the balls of his feet. 'Perfectly!' he announced and sat down again.

'You can do the laces up in the car,' the Colonel said. 'We must go!'

James wanted to put his shoes into his bag.

'You can leave your things here,' the Count said.

'We're coming back,' the Colonel explained.

'I shall not see you. Until afterwards,' the Count said. 'I wish you luck, Mr Grey. I'm convinced Amorini has the best possible plan.'

They shook hands. They were on their way out when Daniele – now in a green loden coat and a soft felt hat – came back into the house to see what was holding them up.

They went through the front door. The rain was falling as steadily and heavily as before.

A jeep waited at the bottom of the stairs. Its engine was running. The young lieutenant James had first seen with the Colonel at Camilliano and then again after the ambush sat inside its open door. He got out and saluted.

'I thought we'd take your car,' James said.

The Colonel was already too far down the steps to hear him.

The lieutenant held the door of the jeep open. He waited for James to climb into the back. Then he followed and sat next to him.

'I'm Croce,' the officer said and held out his hand. Raindrops rolled off his sleeve. His hair smelled damp. Outside, the driver walked round the back of the car. He shut the passenger door after the Colonel, who had taken the seat in front of James.

The old Lancia pulled up alongside. Daniele sat upright behind the steering wheel. Its long thin column pointed straight at his throat. The Count, too, now wore a coat and hat entirely similar in appearance to Daniele's. The car's black cabriolet top protected the two men from the rain overhead. But there were neither screens nor windows to shelter them from the wind or rain which might blow in from the sides.

'It must be difficult for them to drive in this weather,' James remarked. 'Will they be able to keep up with us?'

'They're taking a different route,' Croce said. 'They have more time than we do.'

Daniele switched on the headlights. Their white beams penetrated the strings of falling raindrops. The Lancia began to roll. It turned in a wide circle and disappeared down the drive.

'Let's go!' the Colonel ordered.'We're nearly five minutes late.'

The driver put the jeep in gear. He caught up with the Lancia as the portcullis was being raised, already higher than halfway up.

'I'm convinced this is the only modern gadget di Lando actually likes,' the Colonel remarked as they sat waiting behind the old car. 'It seems to amuse him to operate his gate the way lesser mortals open and shut garage doors.'

'Is it radio-controlled?' Croce asked.

'That's right,' the Colonel replied. 'His nephew installed it.' He turned to James. 'Together with the closed-circuit television.'

The portcullis had reached the top of its ascent.

The Lancia passed through the gate. It stopped. The Count emerged. He waved the jeep on.

The driver switched on the headlights. Slowly, he advanced through the narrow gap. The Count called out to direct him.

The jeep was through. The Count waved. They were on their way.

'I want you to make up for the five minutes,' James heard the Colonel say to the driver.

'Yes, sir!'

In front of the first hairpin in the zigzagging drive, the *carabiniere* floored the accelerator. He stabbed at the brakes. With armfuls of lock he negotiated the corner. Accelerating, he brought the jeep out of the bend and gunned hard down the next straight.

James braced himself as best he could. Bumping up and down, thrown against Croce and back, he remembered the Colonel's estimate for the duration of the journey. Forty-five minutes. To clip five minutes off that – given the rain – seemed a tall order indeed.

They turned south at the foot of the hill. They began to follow the route the Count had chosen the previous morning. The driver switched the windscreen wipers to their top speed. In addition to the headlights, he put on a pair of powerful driving lights. A motley of washed greys and blacks, the wet road unwound out of the dark landscape in front of them. Milky, the rain flooded across the flat windscreen. It fell solidly through the beams of the lights and bounced on the waterlogged asphalt ahead.

'It's not going to stop,' James said.

The Colonel did not react.

James caught Croce's eye.

'It makes no difference,' the officer said. 'It's uncomfortable. But it may help us.'

Grateful for the answer, James nodded. He looked ahead again.

They approached a junction, slowed, turned on to a dirt road and regained their previous speed.

The Colonel picked up the handset of the radio telephone. He bent forward to adjust the controls. He began to speak. James could not hear what he said. He tried to lean back. He closed his eyes.

The thrashing sound of the engine and the whining howl of its gearboxes testified to the jeep's rapid progress on the tortuous road. Even on the shortest straight, the driver accelerated as hard as he could. Setting up the car for the corner he was about to enter, he braked harder still. He dropped gears. On the throttle he steered the car through the bend and accelerated hard again. Changing every second, the noise inside the jeep was deafening. James wondered how far they could be heard through the night.

The noise diminished. They were slowing down. James opened his eyes.

He saw a house. Then another one. A square. A small church. He did not know the village. Behind the church they turned on to another road, left then right. A few more houses and they were out in open country again. The road began to climb. The driver accelerated to regain his previous speed.

'How much longer?' James shouted much louder than he had intended.

The Colonel started. He turned.

'Twenty minutes. Less if he keeps going like this. Are you feeling sick?'

James shook his head. 'It's better than the helicopter. I'm cold.'

'You'll soon warm up! When we're walking.' The Colonel turned to face forward.

James leaned back into his corner and closed his eyes again. His teeth chattered. He clamped his jaws shut. His body began to shake. He opened his mouth. His teeth chattered again. His body continued to shake. Annoyed with himself, he concluded that the cold had combined with fear to cause the unpleasant sensation.

From the downward gear changes and the laboured sound of the engine, he could tell that they were climbing steeply. He heard the

254

Colonel speak. The ride softened. The fierce sound of water, which had been hitting the wheel arches and the floor pan of the car, died down.

He opened his eyes, He felt for his boot laces. Working upwards, he pulled them tight. He knotted them. As best he could, he fixed the cuffs of his trousers over the tops of the boots.

The Colonel slid back his window. The sound of the motor bounced back from the overgrown bank along the forest road. Raindrops came flying into the car. The air was cold. It smelt of pines.

Finished with his boots, James sat up. The wipers were sweeping across the windscreen only slowly. The driver had dipped the headlights. The trees began to recede from either side of the road. Ahead, a torch flashed twice and twice again. The night was no longer black. Day was about to break.

'Gerfalco,' Croce announced and looked at his watch. 'We're on time.'

Behind the ruin, their backs close to one of its few remaining walls, a couple of jeeps had been parked. Next to them, forming a neat row of three, the driver stopped his vehicle. He switched off the lights. He killed the engine.

A *carabiniere* saluted by the Colonel's door. He was in battle dress. His face was blackened and he wore a helmet. In one hand he held a pair of boots. It was Rossi.

The Colonel stepped from the jeep. He looked at the sky, which was beginning to lighten to a dull and solid grey. Holding a hand over his head, he turned right round.

'We don't need the boots,' he said to Rossi. 'Di Lando gave him a pair of his. This isn't likely to stop, is it?'

Rossi glanced at James. 'I don't think so, sir. It's a little less wet in there.' He pointed at the forest ahead. Black, it rose on the steep slopes on either side of the valley. Rainclouds hung over their tops.

'Let's go! Quickly!' the Colonel ordered. 'Who's going to lead?'

'Pacelli,' Rossi replied. 'And Gabino. They had a good look around yesterday.'

Rossi handed the boots to the driver who was back in the jeep. 'I'm sure the Count's boots are more comfortable than ours,' he said. 'There's a helmet for you.'

James followed him to one of the other jeeps. From its back, the officer produced a grey helmet. James tried it on. It was too small.

'Let me see.' Rossi took the helmet back. He adjusted the headband of its lining. 'Try it now!'

James put the helmet on again. It felt strange. Nevertheless, it seemed to fit. Its rim came down to his eyebrows. He tilted his head. He felt the rim touch his shoulders. He wondered whether he really needed it. At least it protected him from the rain which had already soaked his hair.

The Colonel called his men to order. Helmeted, their faces blackened, they appeared different only in height. Kitted out with an arsenal of weapons, field glasses, knapsacks, radios and other equipment, they looked like soldiers. James counted. Including the Colonel, Rossi and Croce, who looked no different, they were eight, plus the three drivers, who were to stay with the cars. It was probable that he had seen some of the men before. But in the grey twilight they all seemed strange, forming a body of trained men he did not belong to although he wore their clothes.

They set off. In single file and at a quick trot, they made for the edge of the forest, east of the monastery. A steep path led from there to the top of the ridge from which the Count and Daniele had surveyed Gerfalco the previous morning. Glad to escape the direct impact of the rain, the men entered the dripping darkness of the trees. At a fast pace, they began their climb. Pacelli and Gabino led the way. Croce and the three men, whose names had not been mentioned, followed. Rossi, James and the Colonel brought up the rear.

Rossi's prediction that it would be less wet in the forest proved correct only in part. Weighed down by the water which over the hours had accumulated in their foliage the trees had begun to unload it again. Gallons suddenly crashed through the branches. The water hit the ground with splashing thuds. Twice James escaped. The third time he was not so lucky. Irritated by the flapping of the chinstrap on his helmet, he had taken off the unaccustomed piece of headgear. Cold, the water hit his face. It ran down his neck and on down his back. Angrily, he turned. He looked up at the offending tree. Promptly, a second torrent almost blinded him. Muttering, he shook himself. He tried to wipe the water from his hair. He put on the helmet. Behind him, the Colonel bit his lip, pretending not to have noticed the incident.

Out of step, the column made little noise. Gradually, Pacelli and Gabino increased the pace. At a quarter past four, the nine men had skirted the lower edge of the clearing above Gerfalco and disappeared into the forest again. Along the top of the ridge, they advanced rapidly and to the point where they were to make contact with the *carabinieri* who had spent the night on the mountain.

Pacelli raised his arm.

He ducked.

He dived into the undergrowth.

'Hide, Grey!' the Colonel hissed. 'Don't move!'

James fell to his knees. He crept under a bush on his right.

The Colonel crouched next to him.

They listened with bated breath.

Footsteps came pounding down the path. They approached at high speed.

'Friends!' Croce called out further up.

The Colonel scrambled on to the path. He ran on ahead.

On his own, James pushed the dripping branches out of his face and emerged from the hiding place.

Ahead, the *carabinieri* had gone into a huddle. On the path and its edges they crouched round the Colonel and a man whose helmet was covered with twigs and leaves.

Apprehensive, James approached. Suddenly his heart was in his throat.

The men stood up. They looked at him.

He tried to swallow. He knew something had gone wrong. Had the kidnappers carried out their threat? Was Thomas dead?

The Colonel stepped forward. In front of James, he stopped.

'They heard – they think they heard – your daughter scream. It was very short. They're not sure they understood. Possibly something about the boy. They may be about to leave. The rain ruined our radio batteries. We must run!'

James held out his hands. He steadied himself on the Colonel's shoulders. He moaned.

'Let's go, Grey!' The Colonel shook him by the arms. 'Let's run!'

Already, the *carabiniere* with the camouflaged helmet had set off, back in the direction he had come from. One by one, the others broke into a fast long-distance trot, leaving gaps of some fifteen yards between each other. It was James' turn to start running. There was nothing he could do but follow the man in front, no longer Rossi but one of the men whose names he did not know.

Softened by the rain, muddy in places, the ground absorbed the dull, irregular impact of the men's pounding feet. Soon it was the sharp whistle of their breath which could be heard above the noise of the rain. His eyes fixed on the back of the man in front, James hardly saw where he was running.

Terrible pictures formed in his mind. A shoot-out. Desperate, the bandits used the children to shield themselves. Thomas. His throat. A red line cut it from side to side. Dead – yet full of untold terror – the eyes stared from the small face.

James shook himself. He pressed his eyes shut, trying to chase the images away.

Headlong, he fell on his face, a foot caught in a root which grew across the path.

The Colonel pulled him up. 'Can you go on?'

'Only slipped,' James gasped. 'What are we going to do?'

'Move in!' The Colonel breathed heavily. 'Let's go!'

They ran on. James could no longer see nor hear the man in front. How far had they fallen back? He pushed himself to run faster. His lungs felt raw. His thighs hurt. There was no question of increasing his pace. Just maintaining it was a problem. Behind him, the Colonel exhaled with sharp puffs.

The path led straight into grey sky. They were about to go over the top of the ridge. Grey-green, an open slope lay before them. At its far end, where the path led into the forest again, the last two of the men in front were about to disappear from sight. They ran steadily. Their guns were in their hands. On their backs, their knapsacks bobbed up and down.

From his memory of the map the Colonel had shown him, James knew they could not be far. He looked for the gorge. Black, it lay to his left. In vain, he tried to spot the ruin. He pointed downhill.

'Yes!' the Colonel hissed behind his back.

They re-entered the forest.

Gabino appeared from behind a tree.

'Down there!' He pointed away from the path.

'How far?' James wanted to know.

'Five – six hundred metres,' the Colonel panted. 'From now on – follow me! Gabino – lead the way!'

Gabino turned. With his hands he parted the undergrowth by his side and stepped into it. He held the branches aside for the Colonel

'Go on!' the Colonel urged.

Gabino let the branches go. Impatient, the Colonel overtook him.

258

'They can't possibly hear us here!' the Colonel hissed. 'Let's move!'

In a straight line – except where trees forced him to turn to the side – the Colonel leaped downhill. With fast, sharp steps he stamped down the undergrowth. He ran where the ground allowed it. He waded into soaking fern.

He pushed aside whatever appeared to offer least resistance, threading his way through the gaps. On his heels, Gabino and James followed, whipped by the branches the man in front had pulled with him, soaked by their foliage which brushed their sides.

The undergrowth thinned. The forest floor flattened. Less soft under foot, it began to rise.

James spotted two of the men in front. They darted forward from tree to tree.

'Faster!' the Colonel hissed. 'What do you think this is? Red Indians?'

They caught up with Croce. Then with another man. Tall pines stood about.

The Colonel slowed down. He began to choose where he placed his step. He motioned Gabino and James to come with him. He directed the others to follow Croce.

The Colonel stopped. He ducked in front of a thick pine. He took his pistol from the holster on his belt.

'We take the right!' he whispered. 'Stay close to me, Grey! Watch where I go!'

James gave a nod. Shyly, he glanced at the weapon in the Colonel's hand.

The Colonel got up. He looked out from behind the trunk. He dashed forward. He took cover behind another pine.

He waved James on as he set off again.

On tiptoe, ducking, James followed. His eyes were trained on the ground. Behind him, Gabino took up the place he had just left.

Twice they repeated the action.

James looked out again.

The Colonel beckoned. He appeared to be pressing against a flat and densely overgrown wall with his back.

James followed.

'Here,' he read from the Colonel's lips. 'The tower. Inside. You agree we go in?'

James gave a nod. He closed his eyes.

259

Gabino joined them.

The Colonel peeped round the corner of the wall. Rossi and the others were in position.

James pressed into the wall between the Colonel and Gabino. His heart pounded. Its throbbing constricted his throat. He tried to swallow. His mouth was dry. The Colonel changed the gun to his other hand. For an instant, he pressed James' elbow.

James looked at the officer.

The Colonel gave an encouraging nod. 'We're in time.'

A blackbird landed at their feet. Sideways, it hopped up and down. Its black eye showed no sign of even seeing them.

Faint footsteps.

Tall, bearded, Gherardo Montale – Barba – appeared in the doorway of the tower. He carried a submachine gun. A rucksack hung on his back. He looked up. He turned.

'Come on! Let's go now! It isn't going to stop. I'll carry her for the second half if she won't walk.'

He turned from the door.

He threw up his hands. The gun dropped. He fell forward. A salvo of shots cracked and echoed across the gorge.

Shot through the chest, Barba lay on his face.

Croce leapt from behind the rubble.

He flew at a figure he saw in the doorway. He knocked the woman to the ground.

Over them, Rossi went in. He saw Emma, kneeling by a bundle by the wall. He jumped. He covered her and the bundle.

Pacelli was immediately behind.

The third terrorist raised his gun.

Pacelli hurled a concussion grenade at his chest. With a crash it exploded, blinding the terrorist and himself, taking away their equilibrium.

With a jubilant battle cry the rest of the men stormed Cerreto. They disarmed and took prisoner the two surviving terrorists. Neither of them was seriously hurt.

Crying and very frightened, Emma sat on the floor. Rossi removed her gag. Emaciated, feverish, Thomas lay by her side. The kidnappers had decided to leave him behind. Although Barba had promised Emma that he would let James know where her brother was, once they were safely out of the way, she had refused to move.

At first, the children did not seem to recognise James. He took off his helmet. Dirty, shocked, they looked at him in disbelief.

Hiding his face in his hands, he began to sob, violently, uncontrollably.

Thomas sat up. He prodded James. Emma patted him on the shoulder.

'Why were you so long?' she asked.

Silent, he shook his head.

'You mustn't cry, Daddy,' Thomas whispered hoarsely. 'I knew you would come.'